SURF FU

THE LOST TRAVELER

John C. Nippolt

ReadersMagnet, LLC

Surf Fu: The Lost Traveler
Copyright © 2022 by John C. Nippolt

Published in the United States of America
ISBN Paperback: 978-1-955603-48-5
ISBN Hardback: 978-1-956780-55-0
ISBN eBook: 978-1-955603-47-8

All rights reserved. No part of this publication may be reproduced, stored in a retrieval system or transmitted in any way by any means, electronic, mechanical, photocopy, recording or otherwise without the prior permission of the author except as provided by USA copyright law.

The opinions expressed by the author are not necessarily those of ReadersMagnet, LLC.

ReadersMagnet, LLC
10620 Treena Street, Suite 230 | San Diego, California, 92131 USA
1.619.354.2643 | www.readersmagnet.com

Book design copyright © 2022 by ReadersMagnet, LLC. All rights reserved.
Cover design by Kent Gabutin
Interior design by Renalie Malinao

This book is dedicated to all surfers: past, present, and future. We come from the sea and the sea is within us. We must be committed to the preservation of our common place of birth, the cradle of origin for all life-forms on the planet Earth. We must strive to keep our oceans clean and alive.

INTRODUCTION

There are times when the interaction between fantasy and real-life blur, and the end result is a delightful juxtaposition of a bit of both. Such is the case with Surf Fu, a fantasy tale written by master storyteller John Nippolt. Nippolt is a lifelong advocate of the surfing lifestyle and has demonstrated his love for the sport in various forms of expression, including sculpture, paintings, and this latest incarnation, the written word. Combining a bit of Star Wars and Big Wednesday, he has come up with a tale that is both for the young and the young at heart. Drawing upon his life experiences as a surfer, artist, and Renaissance man, Nippolt has captured the spirit of the sport mixed with the philosophical teachings that come with a free-spirited lifestyle. As you submerge into the mysterious water world of the Shallow Temple you will meet Travelers, surf boards that are alive, created by the Master Shaper himself. You will be introduced to the monks of Shallow Temple, who ride the Travelers and transcend time and space by the art of surf fu. A variety of characters carry out this classic tale of good overcoming evil in such a way that will pique your interest, while at the same time immersing you in a lifetime of wisdom. There has never been such a tale written before, and you will revel in it as it unfolds before your eyes and imagination! John Nippolt has spent his entire life pursuing the goal of unlimited pleasure and presentation, drawing on his life experiences. His sculptures have been commissioned by shipbuilders and private collectors. He also carved the Triple Crown of Surfing Championship trophies for twenty-seven years. He is a talented artist, with paintings owned by and hung in galleries from Honolulu to Hong Kong, and an accomplished surfer with more than fifty years of experience riding waves. Father, husband, teacher, he is a unique individual who inspires those who know or interact with him to come away with enriched lives!

—Randy Rarick, Legendary surfer, shaper, and former director of the Van's Triple Crown of Surfing

"A delightful takeoff on kung fu, except the monks from the Shallow Temple surf. This is a tale to be enjoyed by surfers and non-surfers alike. Although John is a good friend and fellow surfer, I can honestly say Surf Fu is a great read for all."

—*Tom "TT" Biondi, Surfer, former owner of TT's Surf Shop, Laie, Hawaii*

"I read John's book and loved it, so I went surfing in front of Mom's house, got barreled, and came out in the sixties with long hair and illumination."

—*Jock Sutherland, Legendary surfer, Hawaii State Surfing Champion, 1967, 1968, 1969*

"We are all creator beings at heart. Some gifted spirits like John Nippolt seem to know how to unravel the mysteries of things held tight by less nimble minds. His imagery and imagination in this wonderful story reflect someone who knows the ocean has flowed through his being. The fabric of this tale is a journey tightly woven to delight young and old. With heartfelt understanding and curving intuition, this is a moving picture into another realm."

—*Bill Hamilton, Legendary shaper and surfer.*

"Only an island artist could write with this much olioli."

—*Bernie Baker, Legendary surf photographer*

"It is within the ordinary we observe the complexion of the extraordinary. The same can be said of that which is natural. Life-forms inherently share nature as both participants and spectators. Fuse these traits as one and reveal the essence of supernatural. The magnificent oceans of the water planets contain the origins of all life. Cultivate your entire being to become one with the life vibration to honor and acknowledge the natural. Prepare to join the waves where the portals of travel through time and space occur." From the sacred teaching Compositae Nautical, perfecting mind power in the observance, understanding and recognition of water system environmental equilibrium.

~ Book of Surf-Fu

"Earthlings think they see clearly because their vision convinces them they have all the information they need. They are wrong. Based on their powers of observation more often than not the obvious will remain unseen"

~ Master Cylinder

"Never lose your Traveler"

~ Master Shaper

"Bitchen!"

~ Sid Bitchen

ACKNOWLEDGMENT

First and foremost, I wish to acknowledge my wife, Candace, who has worked with me from the start as an editor and writing mentor. She honed my writing skills making this work a reality. My thanks go out to Randy, Jock, Bill, Bernie, and TT for their positive outlook and endorsements. I am grateful for the insights from Phil Gallagher who opened my eyes to a possible story based on the adventures of surfing monks. Thank you, Nicky Black for bringing my book to life with your brilliant illustrations. My thanks to all the surfers and friends who read the first words and encouraged me to keep at it. Finally, here's to Sow, Skinny Wally, Preacher, and Lester, who are all alive and still surfing.

NALU: THE SEA OF MISTS

The whisper of a vibration flowed through the water into a deep cave and the monster awoke with a start, her antennae sensing the motion. It was the end of her hibernation; the timing couldn't have been better. She was ready to give birth and the baby would be ravenous. Sea dragons grew at an alarming rate and had to be fed continuously. Soon enough, the young beast would be lord of this ancient underwater cavern and the surrounding stretch of ocean above it.

The excited movement of the beings in the water caused her lateral triangular fins to stiffen. Now she was in attack mode and instinctively began to slither out past the entrance of her lair. Not even an eagle has better eyesight than a sea dragon and she was no exception. She came spiraling up from the deep, surfacing beyond the farthest outside reef.

She spotted a couple of beings playing in the surf close to the shore. That they were young was unfortunate. Normally she would not devour young or strong living organisms of any group; sea dragons took only the old, weak, or dying. Although this was not a good decision, her newborn came first. She could not afford to pass up fresh meat offered her baby. She was vulnerable now, her skin penetrable these three days before delivery and up to five days afterwards. She could not risk going ashore in search for food during this period.

Prince Gnarles was lying on his blanket near the water, in the shade of an umbrella, daydreaming. He shut his left eye, blotting out the sky and horizon line of the ocean while keeping his right eye open to see up close: The edge of the blanket, the heat waves shimmering up off the sand, the white foam of the crashing waves. He would switch eyes, closing his right eye to eclipse sand and foam, opening his left eye again for a distant view of the ocean's edge and the cloudless blue sky. Blink, the nearby sand and shore break; blink, the sky meets the ocean. He played this game of alternating each eye until he began to understand how his vision worked.

Every so often his parents would come into view, emerging out of the foam that rushed toward the shore. They rolled playfully with the recessing water and together they would disappear into the shallows. They were members of the Shoal clan and both were of royal lineage. Shoals were beautiful beings, whose physical features were similar to those ancient Polynesian groups on planet Earth. They were born with gills and raised in and about the ocean. Shoals possessed photographic memories which made them formidable sea people and the finest navigators on the planet Nalu.

While he watched them at play in the surf, the little boy wondered why they didn't take him into the water that day? He could swim like a fish. He dozed off and when he opened his eyes, he was staring at something he instinctively felt was a cause for alarm. Breaking the surface of the water, a very long single row of triangular fins, swirling in swift moving semi-circles, approached his parents silently, faster and faster, closing in on them. They were too far away to hear his high-pitched screams lost in the sound of the pounding surf. Lifting his little form up off the blanket, he stood erect. He was going to break his parent's rule for going to the water's edge without permission.

In a sudden burst, the sea dragon's immense ugly head exploded out of the water directly behind his mother and father, now running for their lives. She roared so loud that it shocked all of them into a moment of disbelief. Paralyzed with fear, the young parents could not force themselves to keep moving, they knew it was of no use. They stood there frozen, until terrible razor-sharp teeth bit them into halves and the enormous mouth gulped them down.

The beast smelled the child before she turned her gaze on him. His look was not one of fear, but that of determination. The little warrior was coming for her. *"How brave he is,"* she thought. She decided she could not take him. Her only resort was to hypnotize him; she was aware of the memories of these amphibians: They could not forget. Although it was too late to wipe away that sequence recorded in his mind's eye, the dragon knew of a place to deliver the child where she knew he would be discovered and taken in. The little prince would not remember how he got there.

NALU: THE SHALLOW TEMPLE

The monks of the Shallow Temple on Nalu, were the first to recognize that something was amiss in their quadrant. Data delivered from an annual surveillance monitor recorded numerous missile launchings from planet Mars. A mass exodus of Martian transport cruisers was annihilated trying to leave the planet; none survived.

Judging the reports of the locations from where the missiles were fired and where they intercepted the transports, it was presumed those Martians in the doomed spacecraft were headed in the direction of a larger, near-by water planet the Martians attempted to colonize long before their planet's problems arose. The planet was named Earth. Most authorities on the subject of star distribution agreed water planets close to one another in the same solar system were believed to be a galactic rarity.

The trouble demanded a closer review of other data pertinent to current problems on Mars. All recent information and reports were collected and relayed to the monks on Nalu, from other Shallow observation outposts. To their great horror, the monks of the Shallow Temple found a wasteland. The oceans of Mars were gone, entirely drained! There was no visible vegetation on the planet; the great Martian forests had been decimated. There was no water or plant life to be seen on the surface of Mars!

The Martians disdain and contempt for one another was no secret from the inhabitants of the other water planets. It was believed the Martians were fools, so the thinking was that the small colony of Martians left, now called Earthlings, would behave in the same manner. Their propensity for violence among themselves and others kept most civilizations throughout the galaxy away from Mars. Constant warfare led to the ruin of the Martian environment to the point where the planet could not recover. The monks of Shallow had to organize quickly. The thought of allowing such a mindset to rise again on Earth was unthinkable.

There were rumors the Martian population suffered a terrible fate at the hands of its infamous premier, Ontez Neuron. Pitting one nation against another eventually gave Neuron control of Mars, but in so doing, he also destroyed that planet. Were all his foul deeds on record, he would easily be regarded as the most sinister, evil and corrupt being known to any civilization, let alone Mars. The handful of survivors left after his first purge would be the only known successful escapees from their planet. Neuron doubled his efforts to track them down and eliminate them and their knowledge of his great betrayal. He would stop at nothing to get those exiles. His relentless pursuit of these Martians brought terror into many lives on many planets. A horrible death was reserved for those he knew conspired against him. He had plans in motion to capture all of them. There would be no pity for those who stood in his way.

In all the solar systems and billions and billions of stars in this universal quadrant there were only twelve known water planets: Aquaria, Cycloid, Earth, Fluidon, Jam-bo, Nalu, Nemi,

Nautilina, Ola, Pelagos, Rollon, and Mars, which was now just a remnant of its former self and for all purposes, extinct.

A mood of seriousness uncommon to the monks of the Shallow Temple fell over them. With all the information they had accumulated about Mars, they could only wonder how the death of Mars would affect civilizations living on other water planets.

Preparations were being made to send monks from other Shallow Temples to build a new temple on Earth. One look at Mars was reason enough. They had to find Neuron before he destroyed another water planet. The masters of Shallow thought that he would be on Earth searching for Martian exiles. He would be there all right, but for a very different reason. The first deployment of monks had already departed Nalu and would arrive on Earth soon.

Z SERIES THRUSTER

One by one they emerged from the saline tanks in their unfinished new forms; their bodies taking shape. Without a word, they filed through the immunization rinse. Their anxiety was obvious and the excitement of what lay ahead was contagious within the group. This was the best part of the job and they were happy. They laughed at the sound of their new voices and they pointed at each other making jokes about each other's body parts. These bodies were great.

In this solar system they would be known as human beings. The long journey that had brought them here was at an end. They wondered at the mysterious sounding name of the water planet that would be their new home: "Earth."

Sent out from the various Shallow Temples, these caretakers would go into unchartered territories to establish protective systems to preserve any water eco-system planet in their quadrant of the known universe. There had been times when they arrived late, or, as in the case of Mars, they would have no knowledge of an impending disaster until after it occurred. This, of course, was a great blow to the Protectorate. The loss of a water planet and its many life forms caused immense sadness.

They dressed themselves in the style and manner of the inhabitants on the beautiful green and blue planet in the distance. Flight assignments from the Shallow Temple on Nalu proved their calculations to be exact. All instruments indicated they had arrived in this solar system within the correct time estimations. The civilizations on their new home had not yet gained the capability to see them coming.

The interior of the command bridge was spacious and afforded a spectacular view of the star system through which they were traveling. Animated conversations between the older star traveling monks were not lost on the young novitiates aboard ship, especially the youngest member of the expeditionary group, Gnarles a.k.a. "The Gnar."

No one knew how he got there, who brought him, or even why he was left on the steps of the Shallow Temple. Master Cylinder discovered the comatose, male baby amphibian, under the portico of the North facing study hall named, "Teeth of Winter." He was wrapped in a hand-woven blanket still textured with patches of fresh sand from some nearby beach. He looked to be almost 18 months old. Master Cylinder immediately recognized the boy was from a nearby tribe, the Shoal Clan. His gill slits, hidden by the hair immediately behind his ears, offered proof of his birthplace. Master Cylinder knew the chief of the Shoal clan through the chief's brother, Master Ed-Eye, Lord of the Niele, a notorious sect of forensic scientists. The Niele were the temple's experts in the art of investigation. Master Cylinder was shocked to learn the boy was the chief's grandson. He would have to visit their village to meet with the chief personally.

He knew full well he would find the chief grieving. Upon hearing news that his grandson was alive, the chief brightened and regained some of his composure, yet he asked the inevitable question, "What of my son and his wife? Where are they?"

Master Cylinder shook his head slowly, having no answer for him.

The chief, in his sadness, felt he would be unable to face his grandson, who would always remind him of his greatest loss. No, it would be best that the child lived at the temple. He requested Master Cylinder to take charge of Prince Gnarles. He was not to be told he was royal until he became a master of the temple. He would be educated in the art of Surf Fu by the monks.

Of all the indigenous civilizations on planet Nalu, the Shoals were the only ones with the ability to change body dimensions. It was a physically draining procedure, difficult and painful, demanding considerable energy and focus. As a rule, this special function was used by members of the Shoal clan only in life-threatening situations.

Gnarles was curious and extremely intelligent. He was able to do things with his body and mind leaving his peers two steps behind. His abilities seemed to bring trouble more often than not. He managed to get into predicaments where he had to be disciplined for causing embarrassment. He was mischievous as were those who hung with him. He always took the blame even if he hadn't done the deed himself. He was never upset at those who opposed him. He would listen to others opinions before he took action. He was protective for those he felt were at a disadvantage; he did not bully. All agreed he was a natural leader, he had charisma. It was in his lineage.

Outgoing and optimistic, Gnarles behaved much like any other youngster on a long trip. He had questions, so he headed straight for the flight commander, Daylong Terrain. Story had it that Daylong's ancestor was the famous Martian explorer, Manly Terrain. He organized the group of pioneers for the one and only

Martian colony on planet Earth. Daylong was the first Martian Gnarles ever met and his crush on her was obvious. An attractive woman, she looked to be in her early 40's, had an athletic build and was a figure of authority. She was busy checking the guidance monitors when she felt the small hands tugging on her robe. It was the Gnar asking the age-old question, "Are we there yet?"

She smiled as she looked down at the lad, recalling that she had asked that very same question in a different time. She and her brother were forced to separate and leave their parents and the planet she had loved so dearly. She stored that thought for further reflection later.

"Well, Gnarles, just about. I think we are just about there."

Gnarles whirled around and ran over to a monk who was making his way toward the Navigation Telecine. In his rush, he tripped and fell into the aqua colored robes of Master Flow, the only Shallow Master who rarely grew impatient with his endless stream of questions. A muffled voice rose from the folds of Master Flow's garment, "Areweeareet?" It squeaked.

The monk eyed the boy untangling himself.

"I said, are we there yet?"

Gnarles yanked on his sleeve; Master Flow rolled his eyes.

"Are we there yet, can we see it?"

"Yes, Gnarles, my boy, we are almost there, and yes, I think we can see it. Let's go into the Navigation Telecine."

Master Flow's name came from his renowned surfing ability. He looked to be in his late 30's, had the physique of a body builder and his moves were actions that could only be described as *"In the flow."* The Gnar could barely keep up with his enormous strides. Following as close as he could, he thought *"I'm going as fast as I can and Master Flow is just walking, I wish I was bigger."*

Gnarles would have to learn to fight such urges or not even think of them because his body would start to respond before he knew it. The Shoals of Nalu were changelings. Master Flow always seemed to be aware when Gnarles had unintentionally set that chemistry off and would remind him to be careful. He never said anything though. He just gave Gnarles, *'that look.'*

"How did you know I was about to…?"

Master Flow didn't give him an answer, only a smile.

The Navigation Telecine, provided a spectacular view of the solar system around them. Smaller screens inside the larger panels presented different aspects of the thruster's direction, with trajectory charts plotting various navigational data, relay systems, thermal dynamics and other flight information. The planet Earth was coming into view and Gnarles persisted with his question for the umpteenth time, "Can we see it?"

Master Flow looked at the youngster with affection, lifted him up and sat him on an observation mount. "Yes, now we can see it."

"Which one is it?"

As was his custom, Master Flow arched his tremendous eyebrows, emphatically waved his arms across the vast panoramic view in front of them to answer the boy's question with one of his own. "You know why we have come; which one do you think it is?"

Gnar was being asked a serious question. Earlier on the voyage, he noticed everyone's concern over the planet they were going to make their new home. He summoned details he had studied about this water planet and in an instant, he knew what he was looking for. Staring straight ahead he lifted his hand and pointed, "If I were navigator, I would steer us toward the green and blue one over there."

Master Flow looked at the Gnar with a hint of admiration, thinking to himself that indeed, this boy had done his homework.

"A good choice Gnarles, a good choice. That is where we will find him and put an end to his madness once and for all."

Gnarles was sure he knew the answer to his next question, one that had been on the minds of every person aboard this ship, one that had not been asked. He looked around at the monks who were present in the Navigation Telecine and then back at the screen that zoomed in on planet Earth. Gazing thoughtfully at the aquamarine jewel that lay out there in the distance, he solemnly asked his last question of the voyage. "Are you sure there are waves on it?"

EARTH: WAVE CALLERS

Water rushed over a pair of feet. A young monk in ceremonial robes was waiting in the water at the shore. Two older monks, also wearing ceremonial robes, walked into the water and removed the young monk's robes. Master Flow handed the recent graduate his water tight travel pack filled with the proper gear he needed to fit in with the people and time of his destination. Master Cylinder then presented the newly ordained monk with his Traveler. Travelers looked much like modern-day surfboards but they were alive! Born and raised in the ancient forests and waves of Nemi, the tree planet, Travelers were trained to surf and transcend time and space through wave portals.

The departing monk returned from Nemi with a group of graduates who completed initiation rites. They were monks of the order of the "Brotherhood of the Trees." Some initiates, in addition to establishing sufficiency in the art of Surf-Fu, completed dual rites of passage that put them into the elite group of Shallow monks known as 'Wave Callers.' They could summon waves with their drums.

Initiates were chosen by the very trees they had to use to create their Travelers and drums. Only after a unanimous vote of approval from the surrounding forest could any tree be harvested.

Master Drummer was the spiritual leader of those who summoned waves. He personally supervised the creation of every drum that would be made on Nemi. It was the same for the Travelers. Master Shaper, the spiritual guide for all the surfing monks of the Shallow Temple, would personally oversee the harvesting and sculpting of every new-born Traveler.

The new troupe of drummers set up on the outer edge of the lagoon. Everyone in the temple could hear the voices of their drums. There was an aura of power emanating from within this circle. They were calling waves for a transcendence.

The bright morning sky was clear, the air crisp, and under the direction of Master Drummer, the troupe played all night. Interwoven rhythms were developed, evolving into a driving crescendo, making wave conditions perfect for the send-off. The drummers had produced the desired effect, and everyone in the temple gathered down at the lagoon.

Before the drummers began, the surf was flat. Now, the sets were arriving in ten-minute intervals with seven waves to a set. The six-to-eight-foot surf was peeling off the point and the sound of the cascading water exploding over the reef was in perfect sync with the drums. The beat finally subsided. Everyone gathered around the departing monk. Farewells and good luck wishes were said, the surfer lay down on his magnificent new Traveler and paddled out to the point. He moved easily through the water, directing his Traveler to the perfect wave. His mind buzzed from the bond of communication with his Traveler and the excitement welled up inside him, stroking over the first wave. The small crowd on the beach could not take their eyes off him. A lone figure slipped from the group and walked back toward the temple.

It was Master Shaper. Master Cylinder noticed him leaving and leaned into Master Flow, nodding towards the direction where the monk was headed.

"Did he put something in the water?" Master Flow thought to himself, he knew no one else had a clue to what happened right before their eyes.

The wave he wanted was rapidly approaching and the surfer monk moved into position. In the ancient manner, he chanted his destination coordinates softly to his Traveler and spoke the mantra, *"Water above, water below, water within."* The water lifted him into a no paddle take off. He stood easily, dropping in underneath the hook and in that instant thought, *"What is that?"* Something was flashing toward him from within the barrel he was entering! He lost his focus and his balance!

"Oh no! No!"

He splashed down into the wave, clawing awkwardly for the Traveler. The last thing he saw was an explosion of brilliant neon light as it disappeared into the blue portal.

EARTH: ENGLAND, 18TH CENTURY

The sun peeked over the rim of the horizon, casting golden morning rays down the empty coastline along the southwest tip of England. Two young boys were running side by side on the edge of the tide line. Jumping and stomping on each other's shadows, they laughed and squealed while trying to avoid the incoming surf breaking on the shore. Even though it was summer, whenever the cold north Atlantic water wrapped around their ankles they would yelp at the frigid grasp of the sea. Then they raced with the waves that poured onto the sand.

Saturday morning runs on this stretch of beach began early in their childhood, usually during the summer months. It was a way for them to rinse off at least once a week. Over time they learned that this little ritual of theirs was a good way to get their bodies used to the cold water. They spent most of the morning enjoying each other's companionship carousing in the water and by mid-morning they would be completely soaked. After, they would lie down on the warm sand, spreading and flattening their bodies out to hasten the drying time of their wet clothes.

Stretching out on a nearby dune, they warmed themselves, basking in the midday sunshine. They sat up, faced the water and continued their most recent topic of conversation: the future. They became quite animated, discussing what might lie ahead for them.

A wiry young boy, John Thomas Moore, spoke to his best-friend, Philip Carder.

"As sure as I sit here, Carder, I tell you the sea calls out to me."

He spoke while pointing at the surf and then waved his hand expansively across the ocean.

"I know what you mean. I feel the same about it as you, but in a different way. As you know, I'm going to make the sea…"

Carder was cut off in mid-sentence. Moore was jabbing his finger at a bright neon flash in a wave where the missing Traveler suddenly appeared.

"Look at that will you! There is some type of plank cutting across the surface of that comber. What do you make of it? What could it be?"

Carder knitted his fingers over the top of his eyebrows, searching the water to find what his friend was talking about.

"I don't see anything. Where are you looking? Wait, I see it too!"

Carder turned and found he was talking to himself; his friend was already running down to the water to meet the dart shaped object gliding perfectly along the wave, making its way toward shore.

Moore turned and shouted to his friend.

"It's not a piece of timber and it's coming in!"

He wheeled around to face the ocean.

"It's coming straight to me!"

Carder joined his friend.

"Grab it, Moore, it's aiming for you!"

Moore leaped on the Traveler as if it were a toy of some sort, immediately flipping backwards as it skimmed away; he was not expecting such buoyancy. The Traveler shot out from under his weight and he fell headlong into the ocean. He jumped up out of the water, laughing and coughing and both boys played around the new found treasure all the way up to the beach, where the incoming tide deposited it safely on the shore. Catching up to it, they dropped to their knees in the sand, fascinated.

"What could it possibly be? Where did it come from? Who made it?"

These questions were asked over and over for they had never seen anything like it.

Moore searched his friend's eyes.

"When I jumped on it in the water, I felt some type of shock. Even as I hold it; it feels alive."

"I didn't want to say anything," his friend replied. "But I knew you must have felt something. I felt it too!"

"It's bloody gorgeous isn't it, Carder?"

His friend smiled at him.

"Yes, it is. What are you going to do with it?"

"I haven't figured that out yet, but I do know this. It has come to us as an omen, a sign of the future and it concerns our destiny."

John Moore had no idea how close he was to the truth.

"Let's turn it over then and have a look."

The boys rolled the board over gently, sharing a knowing look as they felt the tingles of life from the Traveler. It had to be almost three meters long and not quite two thirds of a meter at its greatest width. The front of the board narrowed to an uplifted point at the center and near the rear of it there were two fins not quite a third of a meter apart, standing parallel to each other. There was an inscription between the two fins and the boys quickly brushed the sand aside to see what it said. It was a circular crest of some sort. Peering down at it for a closer look, they saw an outside band that said: *Water Above, Water Below, Water Within.* On a band inside of that inscription were more words: *Shallow Temple.* Both boys read the inscription out loud at the same time. In the very center of the design there were four crescent shapes placed in such a manner that it might be described as the profile view of a cascading wave. The smallest crescent descended to the center forming the lip of the overall image. The next three crescents lined up behind the first one, increasing in width and height as they rounded downward to complete the overall motif.

Moore could feel the intensity of his friend's stare.

"You have that look, Moore."

"I think this board here…I think this board is for riding those combers out there. I am certain of it, Carder! It was created for riding those waves."

"Wave riders! I like that!

EARTH: THE SHALLOW TEMPLE

The young monk who wiped out and sent his Traveler to the 18th century without him, was swimming toward shore. His heart heavy, his mind was full of dread, he would have to face Master Shaper. He looked at the lone monk waiting for him on the beach. The drums were now quiet, heightening the ominous mood, forever marking his first attempt to travel through time and space. His fellow initiates, along with all the others, had returned to the temple. He knew this was done as a sign of respect for him. There had been other failures before this one and more would follow. They would give him time to be alone because they knew how he must be feeling. Every member of the Shallow Temple understood his need for privacy to gather his thoughts and work things out.

He reached the shore and walked towards Master Flow, who was waiting for him with some fabric to dry He took it gratefully and used it to wipe the tears that mingled with sea water dripping from his hair and down his face.

"I'm so sorry, Master Flow. I don't know what happened." He said softly, "Everything was perfect and then something appeared directly in front of my line ... it came from out of the portal in front of me. I simply lost focus and the next thing I knew..."

The young surfing monk broke into a hushed sob.

Master Flow had already decided to intervene in this situation. He knew Master Shaper created some type of divergence strong enough to cause the ride to fail. He would approach the matter by suggesting a strategy for the young surfer to use when he met with Master Shaper. Something that would surely give the old master pause to think about later. He told the anxious monk.

"Remember what I'm about to say! Be confident when you tell Master Shaper, *intrigue connects those things that are not always as they seem.*"

"Intrigue, Master Flow? My Traveler went on without me and Master Shaper is going to be furious. Even you respect and obey his rule. Never lose your Traveler!"

"Master Shaper may be rough edged ... then again perhaps not. Don't forget what I said."

The young monk repeated, "Intrigue connects those things that are not always as they seem."

"Very good." Master Flow thought back before the young monk's departure, *"Master Shaper was doing something suspicious by the water."*

"Reflect on this before you face Master Shaper. Don't make any excuses for the lost Traveler; it is not lost. Keep your Traveler mentally and spiritually alive. This duality insight is offered as a meditation. It will illustrate for you how you didn't lose it. Hold on to the thought it will return."

Master Flow turned away and commanded, "Speak of this to no one. I know you had nothing to do with losing the Traveler!"

Master Flow smiled inwardly with satisfaction. His job was done; he put things right. He and Master Cylinder were the only ones who saw Master Shaper place something in the water.

EARTH: SOUTH AMERICA 16TH CENTURY

The ability of men to adjust to extreme weather conditions equaled the difficulty they had navigating ships safely around the southern tip of South America, through the straits of Tierra Del Fuego. Sir Francis Drake, captain of the *Golden Hind*, was on a mission for his queen; plunder Spanish ships and cities to gain riches for England. He was under order to sail up the western coast of South America with his companion ship, the *Elizabeth*, but lost her attempting to round the horn. Unknown to Drake, the captain of the *Elizabeth* had decided his ship should forego any more battles and return to England for repairs.

Drake was seated at the small desk in his quarters talking to two members of his crew, Peter Carder and William Pritcher. These trusted and able seamen would lead the search for their missing companion ship. The captain was finishing with his instructions. He told them four other men had been picked to join them and maintain a watch for the *Elizabeth*. The five-ton shallop Drake had in tow to store booty, would be used for this mission.

"Remember gentlemen, there are cannibals. Do not head for the shore. Observe for fowl and possible water sources from a distance."

"Aye-aye captain," replied both men.

Carder and Pritcher turned to take their leave and Drake followed them with his eyes as they exited his quarters, hoping for the best, but knowing the reality of what those men faced.

The four men were waiting in the shallop and Carder noted the small vessel was rigged for sail. He and Pritcher scrambled down the rope ladder, making their way to join the others. They pushed off the *Golden Hind*, not knowing it would be the last time they saw her.

On the second day out, the men learned how totally unpredictable the weather was at Tierra Del Fuego. Moments ago, they could still see their ship, the land was close and the sea was calm. In a rush, an unusual breeze started up, pushing the surface of the water into a froth of whitecaps. The first gust alerted the men to the storm coming upon them quickly and seemingly out of nowhere. Carder looked over at Pritcher, eyed him warily and gave him a nod.

"Get ready boys, she's gonna blow!"

No sooner were the words out of his mouth, the breeze transformed into a hard driving wind. The surface of the ocean broke up and a freak storm hit the small boat and crew. The men pulled their oars in and lashed themselves to a line they attached to the bulkhead oar screws. They secured a canvas sail over their heads and held on. The storm tossed the little vessel about. By the end of the day, the storm finally passed, leaving the sailors a bit shaken but without incident. It was dark, the winds had subsided and the men would wait until daybreak to get their bearings and head back to the *Golden Hind*. They awoke the next morning and their ship was nowhere to be seen. The shallop had drifted farther away from the mainland.

Carder could see fear and desperation beginning to show on the faces of the men. He would have none of that and as their leader he voiced their mutual thoughts aloud.

"Well lads, now we're in for it. I know the captain won't leave us for a day or two. We haven't a day's rations and our water will need replenishing soon. We can't stay out here much longer. We must make a decision to stay and keep watch for the *Elizabeth* or take our chances and go ashore."

Carder was talking to the men when William Pritcher sighted a small off-shore island in the near distance. He leaned over and whispered into Carder's ear. Carder pointed it out to the rest of the men.

"We could head for that island, set up camp and have a signal fire at the ready!"

He suggested they take a vote, "What do you say? Make our way to the island?

They all responded together, "Aye-aye, Mr. Carder."

"So be it." Carder declared. For lack of wind that morning, the men dipped their oars into the sea and put their backs into their heading. They made land before nightfall, and immediately began to search for food, water and shelter. They gathered dry wood and stored it at the campsite they established under a stone outcrop not too far from the water's edge. That evening after they finished a meal made from the last of their stores, they sat together by the fire and discussed their alternatives.

They knew Drake would be forced to move on without them because of the uncertain weather conditions. Backed by Pritcher, Carder explained that the captain had warned them about going ashore and they must keep the *Golden Hind* in sight. They were not marooned purposely. They could not risk dissention in the group so they agreed they would not talk on that subject again. Their discussion turned to options available to them to make their way back to England. William Pritcher hated the Spanish and warned everyone, "We know that the Spaniards and their filthy Jesuits are all about this place." He spat in the fire to emphasize his disgust.

"Aye," said Paschie who was the youngest member of the group, "And there are cannibals."

It was Peter Carder who spoke next.

"The captain warned us about them. He told me and Mr. Pritcher here, to stay off the mainland."

"It's true," agreed Pritcher. "We must also take into account that the Portuguese are here and they stand with Spain."

Carder had sailed along the eastern coast of South America only once before and being the most skilled sailor among these men he said, "It may be best for us to make our way north along this coast, staying on the windward side of the off-shore islands. We have to avoid contact with native tribes and the Spaniards at all costs."

Pritcher stood in support of Carder. "I am certain that Mr. Carder is correct, so if we are in agreement, we should be getting on with it."

None of the men could come up with a better alternative and all agreed with the decision to work their way up to the Caribbean where their chances of finding a ship sailing back to England would be more likely. They set off, making their way north along the east coast of South America, moving from island to island to avoid enemies and the native tribes. They made good time and fortunately for them when they had to make mainland explorations, they encountered only a few natives who did not wish to stay and fight men with superior weapons.

The voyage had been smooth and the men, having seen no enemies, were feeling bold. In need of fresh water and stores, they wanted to go ashore again.

Mr. Pritcher had arranged some twigs in his closed hand.

"We shall pull long and short for duty assignments. The four long will go ashore to forage; the two short will stand by at the ready and guard the shallop."

The men pulled the sticks from Pritcher's hand. Carder was the last to pull and all knew it would be long because Paschie had pulled the second short stick and his turn was right before Carder. "It appears I have pulled long."

Pritcher studied the men, "It's decided then. Tomorrow morning. Paschie and Arthur pulled short, so they will guard the boat. The rest of us will go into the jungle."

They were up before dawn making preparations. They were only a couple of miles from the mainland and decided to row instead of raising a sail. Keeping a low profile was always best. It took them less than an hour to reach the shore and within minutes the four men who had pulled long had dispersed into the thick green jungle.

Paschie turned to say something to Arthur when a bloodcurdling scream startled both men into action. They began pulling the shallop out into deeper water, climbing into the boat to man the oars. They heard gunfire and more screams. In the mixture of shouts from their mates and the wild yells from a tribe of headhunters, the two guards watched in horror as a couple of bloodied men staggered out of the dense green overgrowth. Two others burst out of the jungle at full speed, leaving those who were screaming in agony behind them. They reached the boat flinging their bodies inside to help Paschie and Arthur row to safety.

"For God's sake men, row hard!" Carder yelled. "The others have been slaughtered, let's not join them!"

Their efforts put them out of reach of the warriors' weapons. Secrecy no longer mattered and Carder and Pritcher put the sail up, gaining momentum and lengthening the distance between them and certain death.

Paschie had an arrow in his shoulder and Arthur's dead eyes looked over the two darts in his belly. Poor young Paschie cried out, "Look at my arm! I'm going all numb!"

Carder could only try to console the young man and Pritcher looked the other way. "There, there, Paschie. Lie still."

Paschie was really frightened now; he knew this was bad, he wasn't going to make it. "Looka Arthur over there. He's already gone!"

"Do as Mr. Carder says, Paschie, lie still." Pritcher told him. "You must try to stay calm."

"Can't catch me breath," moaned Paschie as he lay there shaking and dying.

Carder stayed by his side. "Just lie easy now."

Pritcher and Carder made it back to their base camp, dropped the fore and aft anchors and pulled their dead shipmates from the shallop.

"The savages must have poison on the tips of their arrows." Pritcher lamented.

"You are right Mr. Pritcher. This island will be their resting place then. We will have to move on after we bury them."

"Aye, those natives watched us until we were out of sight, so they know our heading. We know they have been out here because of those."

Pritcher was pointing towards some recently used fire pits that were in all likelihood constructed by the tribe who had attacked them.

"It may be just as well we should place these poor devils in the bush and cover them with leaves and have done with it. I mean no disrespect for the men; I want to leave this place as soon as possible."

"Right you are, Mr. Carder. I know these sailors will make no complaint."

The men carried the lifeless bodies of their mates into the nearby foliage to cover them with large leaves cut from the dense vegetation. They took only a moment to recite a prayer they knew, gathered up the few belongings and weapons that were left and climbed back into the shallop. They set sail keeping a sharp watch for any sign of the natives who may have followed after them.

After many days passed Pritcher and Carder were faced with another very serious problem. They were sitting at the water's edge of a tiny island. They had landed on this barren rock a few nights before during a storm and their boat had been utterly destroyed by getting dashed against the rocks, leaving them with only their weapons and two oars. Both men were burned, blistered, and parched. It was the beginning of another day and each one had a large leaf on his head for protection from the sun. Another terribly long day enduring the intolerable heat and the insufferable glare. Feeble from lack of water and desperate to get to the mainland, the men had been drinking their own urine, now running red, in order to survive. The marooned men could only sit there in the sand by the water and stare out at sea.

"I think we may be saved, Pritcher!"

Pritcher let out a grunt trying to open his swollen eyes. A large log amid other debris was floating by the two sailors only a few feet away. Unable to gather their weapons or the salvaged oars, the men clambered onto the log and hung on for dear life. They were drifting away from the island rapidly and the current began pulling them toward the mainland.

Miraculously, the swift current delivered the men to the shore of the mainland near a stream that emptied into the sea. Pritcher was delirious with thirst. He saw the stream and fell into the ocean. He reached the shore first in his mad effort to get to the fresh water. Crawling into the stream on hands and knees, he began to drink.

Carder's eyes got big when he watched his shipmate gulping from the streambed. He tried to warn him. "Hold, Pritcher. Go easy with your intake, you will make yourself sick."

Although only a simple chemical mixture that consists of two parts hydrogen bonded to one of oxygen, water is essential to all forms of life. It accounts for 99 percent of the molecules in a human body which amount to 60 percent of a man's weight. Water content must be kept within fairly narrow limits for healthy functioning cells and tissues.

If a person is in a severe state of dehydration and drinks too much water at one time, he is in danger of water intoxication. Medically defined as hyponatremia, sodium levels in the blood become very low and the intake of too much water causes further dilution of the already low sodium content level. Because excess water can only be excreted in the urine, sweat, or breath, rehydration has to go slow. Excess disturbs the water balance in the brain causing epileptic seizures and even death. Peter Carder knew nothing of water intoxication, but he had seen men who had been without food and water before. He reached the stream and bent his head down to take a sip of the cool refreshing liquid.

He called over to William Pritcher, remembering how terrible it was to witness men drink themselves to death.

"Go easy, Mr. Pritcher, take your time."

He was physically unable to stop the sailor from drinking too much too fast, so he continued to try and persuade him.

"Pritcher! Stop! For God's sake man! Pritcher! You will kill yourself if you don't quit drinking so much water!"

William Pritcher had gone mad. He looked up at Carder with a crazed grin on his face and then returned to gulping down as much water as he could.

"Come now, Mr. Pritcher, there is plenty of time for that. Hold man! Stop drinking!"

Pritcher started to speak, "I think…aagghhh!"

He stood up holding his skull and ran onto the sand where he collapsed, writhing in pain. He agonized for some time turning about until he rolled over and died. Carder's last shipmate was gone and now he was alone. He buried his mate in a shallow grave and stared up the beach ahead of him. One more look at his mate's gravesite and he headed north to continue his long journey home.

Easing his way along the shoreline, Peter Carder hadn't been paying attention to what lay ahead of him. He was lost in thought about the things that happened since they were separated from the ship, starting out with five companions who were all dead now. His head was so full of images from what had occurred; he began to imagine that he could hear some type of beat that accompanied his thoughts. He stopped to look up and was startled to see a group of natives; men, women, and children. He realized they must have been watching him approach for some time. *"How odd,"* Carder thought to himself. He stopped in his tracks to assess the situation, *"They are dancing and making music."*

EARTH: SOUTHERN CALIFORNIA

The head was barely visible in the lifting fog, appearing, disappearing. There, not there. The bobbing head peered out from the pickle weed and bushes on the cliff side, looking like one of those little figurines people place near their rear windows, behind the backseat of a car. Whoever is driving behind such a car gets to see how the head bobs up and down, to and fro, to the beat of the bumps in the road. To an ordinary onlooker, the sight of the person in the bushes may have appeared comical, but the situation was deadly serious. The surfer hiding in the shrubs, focusing on his next move, was the Gnar. Older, tattooed and muscular, he was uncertain of who or what was chasing him and the stress of staying one jump ahead was visible on his face. He was anxious to leave and his instincts told him there was trouble closing in on him. *"If only a drummer was around, I know something is getting close, I can feel it. All I need is a decent swell and I'm out of here."*

He focused on the horizon and saw the escape he'd been hoping for! *"It's about time you've come for me, now I can leave."* He could get back to the temple with his news; the monks of Shallow were waiting.

Gnarles moved swiftly down the trail in front of him. His concern was someone might be watching for him, but there was no time to lose. He was a blur, racing across the ridgeline. In less than a minute, he was above the point, on a steep but negotiable cliff. The path forked here, one direction doubled back along the ridge and the other way, went down to the ocean. Half way down, the Gnar reached into one of the many little caves that dotted the side of the cliff and extracted his gear. He made a quick inspection, making sure he had everything. He pulled out his beautiful Traveler. Feeling the board's power surge through his body, the Traveler glowed; coming alive to his touch. They were ready! He repeated the sacred mantra as his eyes passed over the design etched on the Traveler, *Water Above, Water below, Water Within*.

Moments later they were in the water making their way toward the outside reef. The sound of the breaking waves told Gnarles the ride he was waiting for was on its way. He paddled faster. Once outside, he moved closer to the impact zone getting ready for the right set. The water was glassy and the early morning stillness made for perfect conditions, yet this offered him little comfort.

It didn't bother him that he was alone in the water. He wasn't really, he was with his Traveler. Yet, he sensed a different danger nearby and he couldn't shake it; an unseen presence moving in on him. No other surfers were in the water but he kept looking over his shoulder. Turning back to face the horizon, he prayed for the ocean to bring that wave to him.

A few meters underneath him, the huge fish was watching, savoring the smell of its prey. It felt the surfer enter the water, knew where he was headed, and where he would stop paddling. It relished those moments anticipating the prey's approach. Pleased with itself because it knew the surfer had no idea how close it was, the beast shuddered with delight as it felt each determined stroke coming right to where it waited. The water giant knew this was indeed his quarry and without a sound, moved closer to the surface.

The monster accelerated and broke the water so ferociously it scared the wits right out of Gnarles, who fell off his Traveler. He had an instant to look into the eye of that terrible fish as it breached directly in front of him. Gnarles thanked his luck that it wasn't a serpent, but this giant tarpon from the planet Aquaria was an equally formidable adversary. He pulled himself up out of the water to get back on top of his Traveler, eyeing the fish warily, wondering who brought this hunter-killer to these waters. He didn't have much time. He recalled his "History of Water Beasts" class at the Temple. The voice of Master Cylinder came into his head. *"The tarpon on a tracking mission…"*

INTERLUDE: THE SHALLOW TEMPLE

Viewed from the water, the mirage like quality of the temple rose up out of the sea majestically. One might compare the image of the Shallow Temple to the famous chaitya halls and natural stone carvings throughout India and Southeast Asia, although the temples of Shallow were much older. The intricately carved sandstone cliffs depicted the Shallow Temple as a place of wonder; standing above a lagoon that separated and protected this part of the island from the relentless pounding ocean.

There were four major theaters in the temple and one could reach them by going up the carved stairwells at each corner portico in the outer courts, or climb an ornate stairway in the rear of the great hall behind the inner court to gain access to these rooms. The stairway through the great hall separated at the first-floor landing and climbed to the upper balconies where the library study halls were located. Each library had an allegorical name associated with seasonal ocean swells. The halls were referenced to the four major points on a compass rose. The east library was the

Breath of Spring, the south library was the *Lips of Summer,* the west library, *Mouth of Autumn,* and the north library, *Teeth of Winter.*

Teeth of Winter, was standing room only for students. All were waiting in anticipation for this special morning lecture. None other than the great surfing monk, Master Cylinder himself, would be the guest keynote speaker at the workshop's seminar for students of the 'History of Water Beasts' class.

Master Cylinder entered the room. Those who had never seen him in person before lowered their heads in awe of his presence. It was said that he was a founding father of the Brotherhood of The Trees, those who have passed all rites of initiation to become a monk of the Shallow Temple, but he did not look old enough to have done that. He was huge and powerful. It was known by one and all that he was from the tree planet, Nemi. This fact alone made him famous and mysterious. No one else could claim Nemi as their rightful birthplace for it was thought that only trees were known to live on that planet.

Master Cylinder projected a hologram of the giant tarpon from Aquaria in the air above his captive audience. It was known he could make one pay attention to what he said by altering decibels in his voice; a sound only comparable to the description given the voices of sirens and sea nymphs from Greek and Roman mythology. It mesmerized and commanded anyone within hearing distance to listen. This was why the room was packed. Everyone there hoped the great master would speak the ancient sound.

His lecture highlighted the different areas of habitation and locations where the giant tarpon could satisfy its voracious appetite. Everyone's head visibly jerked to face Master Cylinder's special voice!

"*The tarpon on a tracking mission is a very serious predator. A wrong move may mean death even if this insipid water beast is supposed to bring you back alive. They can forget easily in the excitement of the hunt. They might bite and chew instead of engulf and swallow. There is but one way to throw the tarpon off balance. You must surprise the monster fish when it begins its initial verbal probe. You have to keep your wits and use your ability to conjure up a meaningful question to ask the tarpon within the first moments of confrontation. Catching the tarpon off guard is key! The beast has a habit of reorganizing itself, analyzing and adjusting by way of comparing and contrasting past and present data, especially when it deals with concerns or information about water. Doing this diverts its attention span which can alter the mission sequence imprint. The fish will stop whatever it is doing immediately and submerge itself just under the surface of the water to consider the question and try to resolve the closest option or solution.*

Because of the tarpon's genetic structure and evolution, it carries a physiological code that will focus on problem solving. It demands itself to shut down all other internal and external functions completely. Use this knowledge to your advantage, it will give you time to move away unnoticed. This is a secret, share it wisely. Remember, the tarpon is quick to adjust! This may be the only chink in its armor and your only chance for survival and escape!"

EARTH: SOUTHERN CALIFORNIA

Gnarles was sitting upright on his Traveler, the impact of knowing why Master Cylinder used his special voice in that lecture flowing through his mind. It wasn't to get you to listen; it was so you could never forget what he told you! Gnarles looked the deadly tarpon square in its magnificent crimson-orange, catfish ugly face. The fish began its initial verbal probe sequence.

"What do you know of the Shallow…?"

Despite its fierce reputation, the comic effect the tarpon's melodious voice had on Gnarles made him snicker. He didn't know about its voice. He heard part of the question but the snicker changed to laughter; the monster had not expected it. Stopping the prepared verbal probe sequence, it asked menacingly.

"Why does a creature who is about to be swallowed whole laugh at me?"

The question told Gnarles how unprepared the tarpon was for his plan of action. Gnarles surprised the fish even further. He posed a simple but demanding question.

"So, how does the water here on Earth compare with that of Aquaria?"

The tarpon stiffened, its great lower flat lip jutted out and its rigid facial spikes now hung limp. Its jaw dropped, its flared gills slackened and its eyes changed color as it repeated the name of its home, "Aquaria?"

"He took the bait," Gnarles thought.

The giant tarpon, true to form, needed time to consider this question, and abruptly disappeared into the ocean. No sooner had the mammoth fish sunk below the surface of the water, a set poured through to rescue the young monk from the Shallow Temple. Composing himself, he repeated the sacred mantra, 'Water above, water below, water within."

As if on command the Traveler turned and he paddled over the first wave of the set. It was tempting but he was focused on the third wave, the one behind the sparkling wall approaching him. He didn't hurry or waste any movement. The Traveler ducked through, resurfacing in plenty of time to position them for the oncoming third wave. He began to relax. Stroking into the moving mass of liquid released his tension. He gained momentum, stood while dropping into the face of the wave. A sparkling take-off! He leaned into the wave shifting his weight forward, holding his body inches above the water with his hands that planed the surface of the wave for support. Cranking a seamless bottom turn, his Traveler exploded with acceleration along the blue wall that was jacking up in front of him.

Under the surface, the reef worked its magic and the Traveler picked up speed, in synch with its rider, raging down the line. The surfer punched his trailing hand into the mirror-like skin of the wave, the Traveler stalled for transcendence and they pulled into a righteous barrel.

"Yeeaaahhh!" Gnarles yelled, his voice ringing out in that hollow, moving, marine, slow-motion chamber. The lip of the wave threw out in front of the surfer and his companion, completely covering them up. The young monk smiled, as only one who has performed this ritual could.

Had anyone been on shore to see the surfer riding this wave, they would have wondered, "Did he disappear?" They would have been right.

Bright green and blue neon like flashes permeated the inside of the wave, surrounding and absorbing both Traveler and rider into the tunnel. Their entrance turned into their exit as they came flying out of the tube, the spray of the closing portal blowing out behind them.

EARTH: SOUTH AMERICA, 16TH CENTURY

The Gnar was not prepared for what he saw. Forgetting to share coordinates with the Traveler; he blamed the monster. *"That stupid fish caused this,"* he told himself. He knew perfectly well; Master Carver would have been angry at this feeble excuse for such a blunder. Or was it a mistake?

Gnarles thought about his encounter with the giant tarpon. *"It wanted to know if I was from the Shallow Temple!"* He was upset, mumbling to himself. *"How did a creature like that recognize me, or even know such a place existed?"*

He took a long look towards shore. He didn't see the temple or the date palms that lined the nearby lagoon. He was nowhere near the headland jutting out and away from the temple cliffs, the projection under the surface of the water which produced perfect waves for the temple. *"Where am I?"*

He couldn't imagine who or what would come after him next and he didn't care to guess. How that giant tarpon from Aquaria was transported to the Earth to track him was something to think about. One thing for sure, greed was the motivating factor for whoever was tracking him. They want the ancient secrets; time and space interface, command of the elements. The temple would be utilized to achieve universal dominance for personal gain. They would do whatever it takes and use any means to get to it ... and him!

There was nothing more amazing for him to see than the dramatic changes that replaced the landscape from his original take-off location. He was no longer looking at the cliffs and the oil wells that pumped night and day along the southern California coast. Gone was his view of the paved over backwater area that would turn into tooth by jowl sub-divisions.

What he saw in front of him was lush tropical vegetation and a long stretch of immaculate white sand. "It's almost like home," he said to his Traveler.

He started paddling towards the shore, and stopped, to make sure what he saw was real. It looked like a large group of indigenous people who were observing a lone figure, standing about 20 or 30 yards away from them. The Gnar didn't know he was about to meet the marooned sailor, Peter Carter, great-great grandfather of John Moore's friend, Phillip Carder.

Peter Carder was experiencing his first encounter with the Tuppan Basse, a tribe of moon worshippers who practiced ritualistic cannibalism. Carder would spend the next eight years of his life with them.

The group of natives seemed to be dancing and the Gnar could hear the distant sounds of their rattles shaking in sync with the beat of their tabors. Gnarles wondered if they were putting a spell on the white man, who appeared to be alone. He thought this because every time Carder moved toward the group, they would move away, always keeping the exact same distance between themselves and the man. During this whole time the tribe danced and played music.

Carder had already figured out why the natives kept the exact distance between him and them. They had surely encountered foreigners before, ones who had weapons. They remained just out of range of a musket.

The Gnar was intrigued with what he saw and remained next to his Traveler in order not to be seen. He knew that he would have to contact the white man sometime soon, but not now. He continued to watch.

The natives stopped again, this time to attach what appeared to be cloth to the end of a spear. They stuck the sharp end of the weapon into the sand and moved away from the pole. They kept the same distance from the man as before. Carder approached the spear.

He reasoned this was a test of some kind meant for him. He untied the cloth to inspect it. When Carder finished, he tied it back onto the pole, leaving it as he found it. The Indians now waited for him to join them. Carder would come to find out the idea of the cloth on the stick was meant to be a gesture of friendship. His instincts to be courteous and wait, proved to be correct. He made the right choices determining his fate; his years with the tribe would show him how others would not be so lucky. He was welcomed with the respect afforded a family member and the whole troupe continued their journey in the same direction Carder was headed.

Gnarles paddled parallel to the group walking along the beach. He remained unseen except for the surprised looks he was receiving from Peter Carder.

When it was almost dusk, the tribe stopped and made camp. They shared food and drink with Carder, who began to realize he was now a member of the tribe. After the meal the natives stretched their netted hammocks so they hung about two feet off the ground. They gathered wood until each member of the group had enough to light two small fires, one on each side of their hammock. Carder was given a hammock and did not need to be told to follow suit. He saw that this ingenuous method would keep most ground predators, mosquitoes, and other insects away.

While the group set up camp, the Gnar decided to paddle in. "We can't make any noise," he said softly to his Traveler.

Gnarles saw Carder check on him from time to time during the afternoon. This helped him decide to let Carder take the initiative to find a way to come to him. Silently reaching the shore, he brought his Traveler up the beach but not far up enough to where the sand leveled off and receded into the foliage. He could not be seen unless someone walked down to the water. He took his waterproof backpack off and removed a T-shirt from it and put it on. Crawling up the sandy incline, he peeked over the ridge to see what was happening. A chance to speak to the Englishman came when Carder left the camp to relieve himself.

The natives started to rise instinctively but Carder just grabbed his crotch with one hand and pantomimed holding himself as though he was urinating. The natives chuckled, nodded their heads and lay back down in their hammocks. Carder reached the beach and started looking around immediately.

The Gnar whistled out softly and the man turned to find who was signaling him. Carder turned apprehensive. Gnarles had his finger placed to his lips warning the man not to cry out. Carder nodded his head in mute understanding and waved the Gnar to come closer. When he was close enough, Carder saw that the Gnar was not white and started to speak broken passages that sounded like a language similar to Spanish. Gnarles interrupted him and asked, "Do you speak English?"

"Bloody Hell!" came the reply. "You're English? What ship are you from?" Carder realized that Gnarles was not only not a priest or Spanish or Portuguese, he wasn't English. In his excitement to get information, Gnarles was raising his voice and Carder pulled his blade, flashing it under the Gnar's chin. "Your tongue, fool… if the savages hear us, we're in the pot."

Carder motioned his head towards the Traveler and both men went to sit near the board. Peter Carder was fascinated yet confused as looked at the stranger. Gnarles was the person he imagined he saw in the water. "You are the one I saw this afternoon."

"I knew you saw me, thanks for not…"

Carder glanced back at the Traveler and interrupted the Gnar. "God man, you expect us to make it back to England on that?"

"I'm sorry mister, but you have it backwards, I'm not here to rescue you. The fact is, you have to rescue me. I need to know where we are and find out what year this is."

Carder took a long look at the Gnar. It dawned on him that he had never heard English spoken like this. That was when he noticed how the man was dressed. He'd never seen anything remotely like those clothes. He pulled lightly on the sleeve of Gnarles T-shirt appraising the fabric. He stared at the bold black letters that said, 'NO FEAR'.

"You don't know where you are or the year?"

Carder's interest returned to the Traveler. "What is that crest?"

He bent down to get a better look at the crest design of the Shallow Temple and run his fingers over what he at first thought was engraved lettering.

"Water above, water below, water within? I make no sense of this."

This was taking too much time, Gnarles was getting nervous. He wanted to leave.

"Listen friend, I can't … there is no time for me to explain this, it's too complicated. I need the year."

Carder pulled his blade out again and used it to etch a copy of the crest of the Shallow Temple and the mantra on the back of a piece of bark he picked up off the sand. Gnar's impatience was getting the best of him, "the year mister, what's the date?"

Carder finished his rendering. "The year of our Lord, 1577, in the reign of her Majesty, Queen Elizabeth …"

This time it was Gnarles who cut Peter Carder off.

"1577? 1577? Rising tide! More than one hundred years off!"

The Gnar jumped to his feet! "Where are we? What country is this?"

Peter Carder was thinking hard and he stood up.

"I will be having an answer from you before another word. From where do you come?"

The Gnar scratched his head, having a tough time trying to understand what Carder just asked him.

"I come from the ocean and I have to return. It is impossible for me to go back in until I know the name of the country of where I am."

"Darkness and devils' boy, do you take me for a fool?"

"If you tell me where we are, I will personally show you how the sea takes me back."

Carder still had his blade in his hand and pointed it at Gnarles' heart.

"You will never set a live foot on this shore again, lad, if the sea will not have you."

Gnarles took off his shirt, folded it carefully and placed it in his backpack.

"Why would I lie to you? Please, tell me where we are and I'll show you something you will never forget."

Peter Carder was staring at the tattoos on the Gnar's muscular frame. He saw a copy of the crest on the Traveler that had been branded somehow or cut into the back side of his shoulder. It appeared to glow under his skin. Carder was looking at the backpack Gnarles was putting his shirt in, and the Gnar caught his glance, pulled the shirt back out and handed it to Carder. Carder looked at the shirt and then at the Gnar who was grinning at him. Peter Carder had never been in the presence of anyone like Gnarles in his life. He couldn't help but grin back at the charismatic young man.

"You are standing in the Southern Americas."

"South America? No way! I'm out of here!"

Gnarles slipped his backpack on, lifted his Traveler off the sand and ran to the water. He turned to look back at Carder and waved farewell.

"This will blow your mind!"

Carder didn't understand what the young man said and it didn't matter because he couldn't take his eyes off the Gnar. He watched the surfer paddle the board out to where the waves were breaking. He could see him silhouetted against the silver-blue, moonlit surface of the water. He walked down to the water's edge, staring in disbelief at the surfer who was paddling into a wave. To his astonishment, the surfer stood up on the thing he had called a Traveler, his silhouette gliding across and in front of the glistening wall of water. He positioned himself for the wave to cover him, which it did. The wave exploded, collapsed into foam after it broke and the Gnar was gone.

Utterly amazed, Carder stood and watched for Gnarles to pop up out of the water, almost hoping that he wouldn't. Carder would not be disappointed, for the fellow never resurfaced. This man was from the sea. Now a believer, Peter Carder looked down at the shirt with the No Fear logo.

EARTH: ENGLAND: 18TH CENTURY

The year was 1768. Ten years had passed since that Saturday morning when John Moore and Philip Carder saw the Traveler appear out of the blue, sliding across a wave that seemed to come from nowhere.

At the time, the boys were in their early teens, now they were sturdy young men. Their mutual interest in the ocean developed through their choice of careers, each going his own way to learn more about the sea and exploring possibilities for the future. They kept their friendship intact and continued to share ideas and knowledge.

Soon after finding the Traveler, Philip Carder became a midshipman in Her Majesty's Royal Navy and began his training on the *Endeavor*, moored at the Isle of Wight. Carder's family was not well off. Normally, patronage was important, if one wished to be an officer. On the other hand, his grandfather, who helped raise Carder after the untimely deaths of his brother, father, and mother was a clergyman with connections to very prestigious people in London.

While a midshipman, Carder learned about the sea and every detail of the ship, the duties of each member of the crew and every function of the officers aboard a ship of the line. He also prepared for his lieutenant's examination and review by a panel of naval officers in order to advance. Carder excelled in his studies; he was first on the list in his navigation courses and he developed an expertise in the art of map making and drafting charts. When the time came, his confidence served him well and he presented himself to the reviewing board ready for promotion. He passed his examination, a rarity for one's first review.

After receiving his commission, his orders required him to remain on board *Endeavor*. This assignment was a great stroke of luck for Carder. His many abilities, in addition to his pleasant manner, gained him recognition from Capt. James Cook. The captain personally saw to it that Carder would be on the list of officers readying for England's first "Voyage of Discovery" on the very ship he'd been assigned. He had mentioned the possibility of being a part of this mission to Moore and couldn't wait to send word to him. There would be personal matters and business necessities put in order in case of any unforeseen emergencies.

Meanwhile, John Moore had gained a solid standing in Cornwall as a master shipwright. He had finished his apprenticeship at almost the same time Carder became an officer. The boat yard his father had built below his cottage at Land's End had been busy and profitable since Moore took over as proprietor. His reputation had spread throughout all of Land's End. He was known as honest, hardworking, and a fine craftsman. This was the best advertisement a man could wish for.

Gathering clouds darkened the late afternoon sky and Carder quickened his pace, walking full stride up the weathered path leading to his friend's home on a small knoll overlooking the ocean. He could see the boat yard down below, filled with a variety of vessels and so many different masts pointing up to the clouds overhead, acknowledging John's expertise.

Carder felt happy for Moore, seeing there was plenty of work for him. Moore inherited everything when the disease that had taken Carder's family, returned to take Moore's. The land and business had belonged to Moore's family for as long as Carder could remember.

Carder's thoughts returned to why he came here to see Moore in the first place and he knew his story was going to rock Moore's world. Carder had uncovered some papers written by his ancestor, Peter Carder, who sailed with none other than the infamous Sir Francis Drake. Unbelievably, the tale included information about a Traveler and the man who owned it. Carder thought that must be a name used for the board he and Moore found when they were boys. He also uncovered four gold necklaces that he couldn't wait to show his friend. He only read parts of the diary because he wanted to share this discovery with Moore. By the time this evening would end, both men would have more questions than they had the first day they found the mysterious board.

"At last." Carder arrived at Moore's cottage. Out of habit, he started banging wildly on the door.

"You in there, open the door! I say, come open this bloody door before I break the bugger down!"

Carder raised his fist to pound on the door again, but before he could do it, the door opened wide and there stood Moore with a storm lantern in his hand.

"You might break wind, old sod, but never this door. Come on in now and let's have a look at the lord admiral."

"Go easy with the flattery young fellow, the tales you have heard about men at sea are true."

The men broke into laughter and hugged each other. Carder knew this cottage as well as his own home and both men headed straight to the kitchen table and sat down. It is not unusual for good friends, after not seeing one another for some time, to pick up their conversation as if they had not been apart and it was true for these two. They carried on as though they had been together all day.

Moore made his way to the hearth between the kitchen and the parlor.

"Would you care for some tea, Carder?"

Carder rose, grabbed a couple of mugs off the shelf over the hearth and set them on the table.

"I have a special brand of tea I brought with me for this occasion. Perhaps you would prefer to have a sip of this?"

Carder brandished a bottle of rum fresh from Jamaica and as Moore stoked the fire, the sound of the rum spilling into the mugs was all the enticement he needed to rejoin his friend at the table. "Here's to the Jamaican rum that helps keep our Royal Navy afloat!" Carder clanked his mug against Moore's and both men took a hearty drink.

"I'm really quite happy to see you, Carder, yet, how did you manage to get away? You put to sea in five days, don't you? I am rather surprised that His Majesty's Royal Navy set you free."

"Emergency leave. There were personal matters to be taken care of here and loose ends to be tied at me digs. You understand old boy, sweep it up a bit and replace locks on the old storage bin. By the way," he said slyly, "when I changed those locks, I decided to scrounge about. I discovered something that may interest you."

"A treasure, I suppose?"

It was Carder's nonchalance that made Moore pay closer attention. From the beginning of their friendship, when there were pressing situations, matters of urgency, or something that

Carder was excited about, he would become noticeably calm. Showing signs of that trait, Moore was alerted.

"It's funny though, Moore, this has to do with a special day, back when we were boys."

Moore's patience was wearing thin. He thought Carder tormented him on purpose.

"What are you saying; tell it!"

"I found my great-great grandfather's dunnage."

"Confound it Carder, will you never change? Just tell me what you uncovered."

"I found a connection, Moore."

"Come again? You re-connected to your great-great grandfather?"

"I've suspected you never had one, but regular gents like me get two. This man was my dear brother's namesake, Peter Carder. He sailed with Drake, who, you surely know, served Elizabeth as her chief privateer, intercepting Spanish ships for profit and plundering Spanish cities in the new world. It was on that voyage Peter Carder became marooned with five others in the South Americas. He was the only survivor. He lived with savages in the jungle, cannibals they were, and he lived to talk about it. After ten years he managed his way home to England."

"How is it that I never knew about this?"

"Good God, man! I just found out myself! I came straight away. Why do you think I'm here?"

"I thought you were so lonesome on that great ship of yours, you were here to press me."

They laughed at that remark and took another taste of rum.

"Your life with the sea is different from mine, mate. The choice to enter the service of the king would have to be yours. Now then, you may need another health, Moore. I couldn't believe me own eyes when I came upon these."

Carder reached into his waistcoat pocket and removed a small leather pouch. He found the ends of the thin leather cord, untied the cord, loosened it and turned the pouch upside down, spilling its contents out onto the table.

"What make you of this, my friend?"

Moore leaned over the table to get a closer look at the sparkling gold necklaces with tiny gold medallions attached to each one. His eyes widened and a huge grin replaced the frown of concern on his face when Carder first brought out the pouch. It was hard for Moore to keep his emotions in check while he stared at the beautiful jewelry.

"Well, you almost had me there for a moment. Where in England did you have these made? And how did you come by so much gold? I just can't believe you thought this up yourself!"

Moore picked up one of the necklaces to hold it closer to his face. He was fascinated by the detail of the crest. It was an exact replica of the design on the board they found.

"They are beautiful; water above, water below, water within."

Carder looked at Moore with amusement. It was obvious to him that his friend didn't really understand what was being shown to him.

"You are not following me. Remember the clues? Great-great grandfather, Drake, marooned, sea-chest?"

"You are joking of course!"

"This is no joke, Moore."

Carder picked up a necklace and ran the chain through his fingers until he reached the medallion.

"Companion to these necklaces is a tale of intrigue and murder. It seems that this great-great grandfather of mine was summoned by a lord rear admiral for an audience with Queen Elizabeth."

"Bleeding hearts, Elizabeth, herself?"

"Great-great grandfather was honored for living among the cannibal savages for eight long years and returning to the homeland. He was granted an interview by Her Majesty so that she could get a first–hand account of all the gory details."

"That is the Queen's job, isn't it?"

"Afterwards she gave him twenty-two angels as a gift for his story and sent him on his way."

"Swear 'tis true! Twenty-two angels is a handsome lot of gold, Carder."

Carder continued as if he had not heard his friend.

"Listen. He found a goldsmith and commissioned the man to fabricate the necklaces and create the four golden medallions."

Carder stopped talking so his story would sink in and take hold. An awkward silence fell on the room as the two friends sat there, thinking their thoughts. Carder poured two more drinks and both men stared at the glittering pile of gold on the table in front of them. Moore had questions, lots of them and he didn't really know where to begin.

"That's it then?" You mentioned murder."

"Hold, Moore, the story will unfold. The night after great-great grandfather collected the necklaces, the goldsmith was seen staggering about Drury Lane."

"By the looks of these, he was probably well paid. So, he celebrated, going on about his artistic skills and bragging up and down the street of his grand commission, I'll wager."

"Right you are, Moore. Before the evening star appeared that night, he found himself in the company of some very dangerous men. The story allows that these villains were not there to rob the goldsmith."

"I'll bet those gents were want to know the name of the bloke who…"

"Just so! They had more than fellowship in mind once they got their hands on the man who ordered those necklaces."

Moore got up to stoke the fire and then went outside to relieve himself. When he returned, he asked Carder, "And what became of your great-great grandfather?"

"There's the rub, Moore. The cunning and wily Peter Carder was a survivor. He commissioned the goldsmith to do the work under the name of a mate of his that he sailed with. A man by the name of William Pritcher."

"Why did he create a ruse for the goldsmith? Hmm, what became of Carder's mate, William Pritcher?"

"I'm getting to it!" Carder rose from the table, making his way outside to do as Moore had a moment earlier. Moore sat at the table, thinking over his friend's news. He started to construct a timeline from the probable date of Philip's great–great grandfather's return to England up to the morning he and Philip found the Traveler. Philip came back into the cottage and Moore could see by the look on Carder's face, he was trying to remember where he left off before nature called.

"Where was I?"

"The cunning and wily…"

Their game made Carder smile. He sometimes pretended to forget, a ploy he often used to make sure his friend was paying attention.

"My great-great grandfather probably wanted to keep this business private, as it was common practice with people like him to not attract attention; he was being careful. Rightly so, I might add. He used William Pritcher's name, who was the last man to die, save Peter Carder, himself, after being marooned from the *Golden Hind*. When the blackhearts caught up with the goldsmith, they offered him a choice: The name or die!"

"The goldsmith sent death after a dead man."

"That he did. The road to hell is paved with good intentions. Three days had passed since his meeting with those scoundrels and I suppose the goldsmith thought that would be the last of it. Our unfortunate chicken in question was found in the kennels of St. Giles that evening with the initials W.P. carved in his cheeks and a dagger through his heart."

Both men fell silent again; this time there was a different kind of quiet permeating the room. The men looked about the cottage and then at each other. Their eyes signaled a mutual acknowledgement that the night might be listening. As if on cue, they started to speak at the same time. They stopped, hesitated, and then they both started up again. Moore was saying that he had one more question to ask, while Carder spoke out about having one more detail to add. This made them laugh, relieving the tension and breaking the spell of uneasiness that they unwittingly conjured up.

"When I was going about my business cleaning up and finding the sea-chest…"

Carder paused a moment to reflect on what Moore asked him earlier, about how he never knew about the chest and his great-great grandfather.

"I began to wonder why nobody ever spoke of my great-great grandfather. After my brother died, mum sort of died a little along with him. It was bad enough when pa died."

He stood up and walked over to the window in the kitchen and looked out into the darkness. He wasn't really looking at anything in particular, it was just that he needed to move around when he talked about the deaths of his brother and father.

"I was lucky to have you as a friend, Moore. I think mum must've known all about the murder and decided to take that terrible tale to the grave. I also believe something had to have happened to keep her from speaking out."

"The poor woman probably received the amulets in good faith knowing they were handed down from your ancestor and that they came to your family as a remembrance of a great honor."

"I fancy that she found out all the terrible details that came along with the necklaces. My great-great grandfather noted that word of the entire incident reached him by way of a shipmate who witnessed the goldsmith's unfortunate run in with the three strangers and saw the results of his sad end. When my mum heard the story, she realized how dangerous the situation might be for me and my brother. She would have none of it. Not a word to us in order for the story to remain a secret and die with her."

"As it were."

"That's why had I known anything about it, you would have known too."

"I understand that now, Carder. I never set eyes on that sea-chest lying about your place, although I don't understand why she didn't just burn the whole lot?"

"Devil if I know, Moore. Unseen, it was probably forgotten, hidden away in the storage bin. I suppose when the sickness came, she had more important matters on her mind."

Moore stretched, stood up, and walked over to the wood pile. He selected a few dry pieces of kindling plus two fair sized logs, the bark already stripped from them. The fire that almost died while the men talked was restored. The heat and light brought some needed life into the room and Carder poured more rum into their cups. Moore sat back down at the table and smiled.

'Well then, show it to me."

Carder didn't understand the question at first, and he looked at Moore, wondering about the weird smile on his face.

"I have shown you."

When Moore's smile turned into a grin, his amusement further disrupted Carder's concentration causing him a moment of confusion. Moore had to bring Carder back to the present.

"On my word, Carder! Show me the diary that told you the story that explains the meaning of it all."

"The diary that tells the story? Oh, right you are! I have always liked that about you, Moore, you are there to remind me. I almost left out the most important part!"

Carder was the one smiling now; he knew his friend needed to see the journal.

"Out with it, Carder, or I will go bloody daft! Why I put up with this I cannot understand. You have been doing this to me since we were lads!"

"Prepare yourself for this."

Carder moved into the parlor, retrieving the small sea bag he placed there at the time he arrived. He rummaged through it for only a moment. He returned, placing a worn, leather bound sheaf of papers in front of Moore and sat down. He was holding something else, some material or garment in his other hand. He unfolded it and held it up in front of himself for Moore to see. It was the 'NO FEAR' t-shirt Gnarles left with Peter Carder.

"Let me see that! Who made this? Not the savages? I have never seen anything like this!"

Moore marveled at the shirt, paying no attention to Carder, who had undone the leather binding and began to read from the diary of Peter Carder.

"He spoke a strange English. He said he was from the sea and he wanted to know where we were and he demanded the date."

Carder continued to read his great-great grandfather's story, revealing Peter Carder's understandable fascination with the beautiful Traveler.

"So, he had seen one! I knew it!"

"Yes. Moore, he had. He also met the owner of one."

The two friends stopped and looked at each other, sharing this thought without words. Carder was reading again and Moore was satisfied to listen, entranced by what he heard.

"He left me standing on that shore under a full moon, holding my gift, his garment. He maneuvered himself into the approaching combers in such a way that he could stand on the plank he called his Traveler and ride them! Then, he was gone."

"I have a Traveler!"

"Yes, Moore, you do."

Once again, quiet descended on the two friends sitting there in the cottage, both reflecting about that day when they were children, running along the beach. The men were tired, the fire was low and the bottle empty.

"There is a great deal to consider, Carder, the hour is late. I propose we get some sleep and read over the diary again tomorrow with clear heads."

The men stood and Carder made his way into the parlor where Moore had arranged a palette for him during his stay.

"It is incredible isn't it, Moore? Fate and destiny?"

"Aye, that it is. Tomorrow, fate and destiny will provide you with more to think about."

He readied his make-shift bed and blew out the lantern. The darkness brought a sense of calm to the cottage and with it, rest. It invited them to take comfort in it, which they both did by falling asleep immediately.

Carder thought that he was the first one awake; he hadn't heard Moore moving about in the cottage earlier. He rose and pulled on his trousers. He was heading for the water closet when he saw the note and leaned forward to read it: *'Carder, hot water is in the kettle. Help yourself to a cup of tea and then come join me down at the beach.'*

Still groggy from the night before, he wasn't clear what day of the week it was. He wondered if their meeting this morning had anything to do with those days spent with Moore on that beach during their childhood. He figured he would be down there waiting to reminisce about old times and the thought made him laugh aloud. Memories of their youth flooded into his head. He looked at the teapot on the table already steeping. He located his mug sitting next to John's above the hearth.

Carder sat down, poured his tea and looked toward the kitchen. Something seemed out of place in there. It smacked him in the eyes! A doorway had been cut into the kitchen wall that faced the ocean. *"Funny,"* he thought, as he got up, *"I've never seen that door before and he made no mention of it."* Carder reckoned he was too excited yesterday to even notice it was there. He forgot about his tea and pushed the door open.

The ocean breeze met him full in the face with its wonderful, natural aroma of saltwater mixed into air. He sucked in his breath when he saw that Moore had constructed a platform, what you would call a deck in modern times. There were wooden walkways connected to this main platform, leading around each corner of the cottage. He built additional overhead roof protection from the weather that extended from the cottage to cover the walkways and the deck. Carder was delighted by his friend's common-sense approach in creating a comfortable vantage point to observe the ocean. It occurred to him to look out at the vast expanse of sea in front of him. As he did so, shock and amazement registered in his eyes as they zoomed in on the figure sitting out in the water waving frantically at him. He could not take his eyes off Moore, who was lying in a prone position, using his arms as paddles to gain momentum. Comprehension sunk in when Carder watched him glide into a comber and stand up on the board, directing it all the way into the beach. A yell emerged from Carder's gut, flying out of his mouth to the figure down on the beach below. "Wave Rider!"

Carder saw the new trail leading to the beach. He ran down the slope to congratulate his friend on his new athletic prowess. *"Waverider! Bravo, Moore,"* he thought, *'Bravo!"*

INTERLUDE: THE SHALLOW TEMPLE

Master Shaper finished his lecture to the class on *'Care and Respect for the Traveler.'* These students had not yet been inducted into the Brotherhood of the Trees and would attend a multitude more such classes before their final rites of initiation, becoming ordained monks of the Shallow Temple.

Master Shaper was not in robes because he gave this particular lecture at the lagoon in front of the temple. He wore a pair of surf shorts called, 'quitas' as did all the members of Shallow. Master Shaper was 'cut.' His muscles had muscles. He was aged but not aged and it was this character trait, an undefinable youthful quality of all the older monks, that kept the young students of the temple wondering about them.

Master Shaper abruptly stopped talking and looked out toward the eastern horizon. A student heard him say: "He is riding the Traveler again." Master Shaper turned back to the class and dismissed them. As they were leaving, he called one student over and asked him to find Master Drummer, Master

Cylinder, and Master Flow. The student nodded and ran to the temple to fetch them. They came down to the lagoon in a group to approach Master Shaper.

"You felt it?" he asked. The monks all nodded in unison.

"Only moments ago," Master Drummer replied.

"I think it is time we get everything ready. The man is riding the Traveler and it wants to return to us. Also, Ontez is going to be near once again. I'm not sure when it will be, with Ontez one never knows. Please see to it that Gnarles is alerted. He will start training for the superhuman effort it will take to accomplish his mission. If he has questions, extend my invitation for him to come and see me at any time. Perhaps a trip to Nemi would help him."

The other monks traded knowing glances and acknowledged their agreement. The plan would be set in motion by Master Shaper when it was time.

EARTH: ENGLAND, 18TH CENTURY

"I wouldn't have believed it if I hadn't seen it with my own eyes. That was a tremendous display, Moore, congratulations!" Carder looked upon his friend in admiration. "That was spectacular."

"Please, don't bother me with compliments, I'm only a novice."

"Oh no, you have learned to ride the Traveler and that is remarkable!"

Moore decided he should explain something to his friend about the surfboard.

"It took me a great length of time to do it, Carder, and there is something that I must tell you. Remember how we felt some sort of tingling that came from this 'Traveler' as your great-great grandfather called it, when we first touched it? Or for that matter, we thought somehow it might be alive when we found it?"

"By all means, I most certainly do recall the feeling."

"Feel the Traveler now, Carder."

Carder reached out, to lay his hand on the board. He jumped back so fast he almost fell down. What he felt made him automatically jerk his hand away in recognition!

"By the sun and moon, Moore! How long have you known about this?"

Carder had felt something that was warm and alive, but that wasn't all. The Traveler actually responded and vibrated to his touch this time.

"The Traveler seems to have a life of its own. I found that if I just think about which direction I want to ride the wave, the Traveler responds and guides me in that direction. Something else occurs that I couldn't explain before. Until we read Peter Carder's account of his meeting with the person who rode his Traveler into a comber, only to disappear, I would have said nothing about this."

"Does the Traveler try to take you under its own power, Moore?"

"Not quite like that, Carder, no. But you are spot on how the Traveler does try to lead me into that tunnel created by a breaking wave. It takes every ounce of my own willpower to make the Traveler straighten out and return me safely to shore."

Right then and there the men made a pact, an agreement to discuss this matter with no one else. They had stepped further into the realm of the unknown and until they found out more about the mysterious Shallow Temple, they alone would share this secret.

"Now then, where's my tea?"

Carder had left the pot of steeping tea on the table.

"It's quite ready by now, wave rider."

The young men did not want to negotiate the steep incline up to the new kitchen entrance and decided to walk to the cottage by way of the gentle slope near the boatyard. They reached the door where Moore entered a small side chamber and set the Traveler in a special rack he built. He returned to the kitchen; Carder was sitting at the table looking into his cup of tea.

"You know, Moore, I haven't any idea when I shall return, so I believe you will have to take care of this."

Carder handed him the bag and Moore looked inside to check the contents. There was the T-shirt, the leather-bound diary and the pouch that held the necklaces. Moore sat down and pulled out the pouch. He started to untie it in order to select one of the amulets. Carder realized what his friend's intentions were; he shook his head "no."

"I think it best that everything stays with you, Moore. I have no idea what encounters lie ahead on the voyage and I would prefer the lot be kept whole until my safe return."

"You are right. It was just a sentimental notion, you understand."

"Don't worry wave rider," Carder said good-naturedly, "One of those belongs to you, although it may not be a good idea to wear it for the time being."

Moore understood the warning and put everything back in the sea bag. He tightened the drawstring and took the bag into the chamber where he stored the Traveler to hide it away. When he returned to the table a fresh cup of tea was waiting for him.

"That package has been put in a secure place. Until your return, Carder, there it shall stay."

"I know it will be safe."

Moore noticed Carder had placed his gear by the door and he knew what he was about to say.

"I am very poor at goodbyes, my friend, but I believe that it is time for me to take my leave. I've made allowance for a couple who will stay on to mind things during my absence. I hope it won't inconvenience you, but I have told them you will be stopping by to check and make sure that everything is in order."

"By all means, Carder, I will be happy to keep an eye on things while you are away."

The sun was almost directly overhead and they had to squint in order to see, walking out into the bright light.

"I have arranged for travel on the postal carriage, so there is no need for you to feel obligated to accompany me any further. As always, it was a joy to see you again."

The friends shook hands and hugged each other in a warm farewell. Carder turned and started off down the path leading to the main road. Before he was out of earshot, he made an about face toward Moore, who was still standing in front of the cottage looking at him. He shouted, "Until I return then, wave rider!"

His friend shouted back, "Until your return, lieutenant!"

Carder saluted, turned back smartly and marched away toward the road to await the carriage that would take him back to London.

EARTH: CORNWALL

It is often said that time moves at a snail's pace when one is young, but speeds up as you age. The days pass swiftly, much like the turned pages of an enjoyable read. This is how it was for Carder and Moore. Their lives were filled with so many responsibilities there never seemed enough time in the day to get everything done. After Philip spent almost four years at sea on *'Endeavor'* he returned to John's cottage and John could not have been more surprised. There was also a surprise waiting at the cottage for Philip that day.

He raced up to the door of the cottage so he could bang on it loudly as he always did and the door swung wide open. Carder halted in his tracks when he saw two small children staring up at him. They stopped looking at him to trade knowing glances with each other and then turned back to Carder. Bright smiles began to stretch across their faces. They ran back inside shouting in unison.

"It's Lt. Carder, it's Lt. Carder! He's here! He's arrived! Lt. Carder is here!"

Carder was dumbfounded. He didn't know who those children were; he'd never seen them before in his life. They acted as if they knew him. His mind was reeling with mixed thoughts as he followed the children into the cottage.

"Moore, old friend, where are you?"

Moore burst into the room through the kitchen door and the little girl and boy ran to him, almost pulling his trousers down as they tried to hang on to his legs.

"Carder! By God man, look at you! How good it is to see you! Sit down, sit down! I say, how are you?"

Carder could only beam at Moore standing there with two children hanging about his legs.

"The question is my lad, how are you? It is quite difficult for me to imagine that you married! Where is the poor wretch, out fetching…?"

Moore shot a warning look at him, stopping him in mid-sentence.

"Oh my, so sorry, I saw the children and I assumed…"

"It's quite all right. I shall explain in good time. Perhaps we should acquaint ourselves with each other, shall we? Lt. Philip Carder, allow me to introduce you to the charming, Eleanore Jane Moore, who we know and love as Jane."

Carder did his best bow, extending his right foot forward and holding his hat at his side as he gently took hold of the girl's tiny hand.

"It is with great pleasure I make your acquaintance."

'Thank you. I knew that you were coming and I told my brother Sidney."

"That's right! She told me you were coming, Jane did."

"I see. And, who are you?" Carder gave Moore a questioning look.

"Lt. Philip Carder, allow me to introduce you to the one and only Sidney Alexander Moore, who we know and love as Sid."

Philip again performed his best bow.

"Sir, this is indeed an honor."

Sid shouted with glee.

"Yes! Jane knew you were coming, Jane did! She told me and I'm her brother, I am!"

The children turned to run outside and play where they could do their little kid thing out of earshot of the adults. Sid took the lead and bolted out the front door. They would run down to play in the boatyard where they could shriek and laugh while performing all sorts of crazy antics, making silly faces at each other with some rolling on the ground for good measure. These things were just not done in front of adults. Jane started after him and then decided to spin back to Carder, crooked the pointing finger of her right hand and motioned for him to lean closer, as if she were going to tell him a secret. He leaned downward close enough to hear her whisper a question that would knock him a step back.

"Are you going to tell my uncle about the island, Lt. Carder?"

Carder could not believe his ears. What was going on here?

"Come now. How in heaven's name do you know about that?"

Jane smiled, shrugged her shoulders and scurried outside to play with her brother.

Moore took hold of Carder's arm and led him outside to show him a bench he finished building, on the walkway that headed toward the beach trail. He suggested they sit to test it out.

"Let's sit somewhere comfortable, Carder, and enjoy this good weather out here in front of the kitchen. Now then, you old sea dog, tell me all about your travels and fill me in on the events taking place in the new world."

"Wait a minute, Moore. You can tell me a few things first. How did that little girl know who I was before she ever met me? How did she know I was coming? She opened the door before I knocked! You couldn't have told her because you had no idea of my whereabouts, let alone the knowledge that I had returned to England and who are they anyway?"

"They are, … were, my cousin Gwyneth's children. She and her husband went the way of your brother and father."

"That bloody damned consumption?"

"Yes, it was that filthy disease. It cares not, that one, taking young and old alike and quickly at that. As for Jane, she has 'the second sight' as did her mother. It is supposed to be a family trait but none of it came my way."

Moore explained the children were twins, who had been living with him for a year and a half. They were five years old when Jane gave instructions to her father's barrister on how to find Moore's cottage, with the three of them traveling from Wales together. Neither Jane nor Sid had ever set foot in Cornwall.

"They have been a blessing for me, Carder."

"On my word! She hasn't let the cat out of the bag then, has she?"

"I take it you have a bagged cat?"

"Not now. I saw it, Moore."

"Remarkable, old friend. Did you have to take it out of the bag to get a proper look at it?"

He expected a laugh from Carder with that remark until he spied his demeanor, his calm. His thoughts about what Carder was about to tell him stifled his impulse to say another word.

"I saw the island where the Travelers come from."

Moore was electrified, the hair on his arms and neck stood straight out.

"Impossible! Bloody hell! When? I mean where? Good God, Carder, how do you know? Why didn't you tell me?

"I am telling you! I haven't seen you for almost four years."

"Then, blast it all, let's have the whole tale."

"It was on our return, somewhere in the middle of the South Pacific, the island just appeared."

Moore's mind flipped as he repeated that ocean's name, "The South Pacific."

Carder studied him, staring out into space, probably daydreaming about the South Seas.

He wasn't about to let him wander off the subject.

"You had better listen carefully."

"On the king's word, I am listening. That ocean's name, it sets my mind to wandering."

"Believe me Moore, I understand. Now then, where was I?"

Both men laughed at their old habit of banter and the familiar question he always posed before telling Moore a story. Carder didn't wait for his answer.

"It was daybreak, I was about to be relieved from my watch. I was entering notes on my charts and in a sudden; I felt an urge to look up. There before me was a speck of land. I pulled my glass and saw our crest carved into the face of a cliff just above what looked to be some sort of temple. The whole place carved right out of the cliffside."

Moore whistled, "The Shallow Temple." He couldn't wait and had to ask, "What of the Travelers? Did you see any Travelers about?"

"There were men, women and children, all in the water, all on their Travelers, riding the waves."

"Wave riding! Now I like the sound of that, Carder."

"Yes, friend, I knew you would. But there is more to tell and I don't think you are going to like the sound of it. I thought how peculiar no one shouting out the sight of land, not even from the fore topmast lookout. I was bent over marking the location on my chart and checked again to make certain of what I'd seen. I looked up and It was gone."

"No one else saw it?" He wanted to be certain about this and he could tell Carder was holding something back. "How can you be so sure?"

"I'm not sure about anything since that day. To a man, no one made mention of it and because of what we know, I spoke to no one about it, not even the captain."

Moore stood and started to pace up and down the walkway, "Do you have the chart?"

The color drained from Carder's face. A look of surprise doused with great concern told Moore he had struck a nerve. The mere mention of a chart shocked Carder enough for him to start looking about the area surrounding the cottage to search out any eavesdropper, although no one except Carder lived within miles of Moore's place.

He wanted to go inside but tried not to show his sudden anxiety to do so.

"I wonder what the children are doing? The wind has stiffened a bit, if those two are still playing outside, they may get a chill. Perhaps we should gather them up, go inside and have some tea."

Carder motioned toward the kitchen door and the two men went inside. They heard the children knocking about in the parlor. Moore checked to see if Jane and Sid were alright and everything was in its place. He needed Jane to fetch water from the catch barrel for her and Sid to wash for dinner. He asked Sid to go to the well and bring a bucket for drinking water. The children were happy to do small chores and ran off, challenging each other who would return with the water first. Moore went back into the kitchen joining his friend at the table.

"Now tell me, what is wrong," he demanded.

"Taking a navigator's chart is a serious offense, Moore. One could be swinging from the wrong end of a rope if proven guilty of such a charge."

"I know you didn't pilfer a map. I think perhaps you may have a copy of a chart, but that is not the question I put to you, old boy. Tell me what happened?"

"I copied the chart I was working on when I saw the island. I noted the approximate position by degrees of latitude, date and time of day."

Carder retrieved the chart from his bag, unrolled it and gestured for Moore to sit beside him while they looked at it.

"I gather no one saw you with this?"

"I think not. The captain noticed that a sheet for drafting charts was missing. I immediately brought his attention to my error and explained that I had made a serious blunder, spilling ink on the chart. In my embarrassment, I confessed my hasty decision to burn it."

Moore was worried for his friend and admitted as much. "That was a terrible risk, Carder."

"I expected him to notice. I showed him the ink stain left on the table from my clumsiness."

"Clever fellow, did he believe you?"

"Don't forget Moore, this sighting and the notes I made only matter to us."

Carder explained how he made notations as evidence of his actions in case someone might ask questions about the missing sheet.

"I showed the captain a copy of the missing chart which was really the original, with a signed statement on the back of the chart noting the time of the accident including how I destroyed the original draft."

"I dare say your foresight probably saved you from the gallows."

"The good captain said he would make no mention of it in his log and I would save face. He did not hesitate to warn me that in the future, should anything like this occur again, l must alert him immediately and take no action without his direct authority."

Moore had to start a fire and feed the children. He stood up and gathered food to prepare the evening meal. He looked over at his friend who was resting his head in his cradled arms on the table top. He had forgotten the long trip Carder made from London. He walked over and shook him gently.

"Go into the parlor and have a rest, Carder. I'll wake you for tea after I finish feeding the children."

"Huh, what, oh, right. You're right, I'll feel better after a short nap."

He got up from the table and went straight to the divan in the cool dark room. He was almost asleep before sitting down, and was out as soon as his head hit the soft cushion.

He woke with a start, still not accustomed to being on land. It was quiet in the cottage and dark outside. He turned towards the kitchen to see a fire burning brightly on the hearth. The smell of a chicken stew wafted into his nostrils reminding him how hungry he was. He looked at the evening lamp hanging over the table, casting its light down about his friend. Sitting there alone, Moore was intently exploring the chart Carder brought back to show him, trying to determine the approximate location of the Shallow Temple.

"I know you are awake, Carder. Come have some tea."

Carder rose and made his way into the kitchen. The overpowering aroma had his mouth watering. He sat down across from Moore, next to the hearth, taking in the pleasant atmosphere here and began to relax.

"Yes, sit down, my friend, sit down! You must be starving. Have some tea and let me get you a bowl of stew. You can finish the lot because I've had mine and so have the children. They wished you a good evening before I tucked them in."

Moore got up from the table and went to the Dutch oven on the hearth. He unhooked the latch on the metal door and opened it. As he pulled out the steaming pot of stew, Carder's mouth began to water again. Moore dished a great bowl full for his friend and set it down in front of him.

"Go easy mate, the stuff will scorch your tongue. Here is some bread, not too fresh, but worthy of sopping up the broth."

Carder started on his meal and John took a rag to grab the kettle wire. He poured hot water into the teapot and placed the kettle on the hook above the hearth. Moore sat down across from his friend and placed two cups on the table.

"This stew is delicious. Where did you learn how to do this?"

"Oh, no you don't. You'll not slip away that easily."

"What are you talking about?"

"You went very nervous when I was going on about the map. I know that you haven't told me the full story. Something took place that scared you or has you worried. Now then, I want it out, every last detail!"

Carder started to chuckle. "Good, you haven't changed a bit. Still the bloody old inspector, aren't you? As I said earlier, I thought it a bit odd that no one else had seen the island. I had not mentioned the quartermaster."

Moore was not in the mood for his roundabout explanation to get to the heart of the story. "I said no you don't, Carder, and I meant it. Now then, what is it about this fellow, the quartermaster?"

"I have the feeling he witnessed everything."

"Come now, Carder, really. The quartermaster you say? Tell me, what makes you suspect him?"

Carder wanted to be very clear about the man he knew was spying on him during the voyage. There were too many coincidences that had taken place and he knew it wasn't going to take much persuading for Moore to believe him.

"He was already aboard ship when I returned escorting the press gangs. That first night they found most of the crew rather easily. Not one of the lads knew anything about him and that in itself was strange. In general, the reputations of the ship's officers and noncommissioned officers would be general scuttlebutt. Yet, our quartermaster had never been seen, had no history with the others. His papers were in order and he proved to be a very capable sailor."

Carder paused while Moore poured tea. "I'd finished putting my charts away, when I knew he was there, I could smell him. I carried on as though I were alone."

"You could smell him? The bloke said nothing?"

"Not a word. I knew when he left, the same way I knew he arrived. He made not a sound."

"You say he has an odor? Not so bloody odd for a man of the sea. What sort of man is he? How is he at sea?"

"I'm coming to that. Unsavory is the kindest description I have for him. When he spoke, which was rare, he had the voice of a serpent: cold and deliberate. He carries with him an odor so foul; it was unlike any living thing I ever encountered. It is certain the crew noticed it, yet no one dared speak about it in his presence."

"Nobody knew anything about him, not even the first mate?"

"Not a crumb. He was adept at giving orders, meticulous and unerring as he went about his duties. He seemed an experienced and able seaman. The men feared him."

"Well then, perhaps then he really knows nothing."

Carder released the bomb.

"He rode in the coach with me to Land's End, Moore."

Moore could not believe his ears.

"What? You always wait until the bloody finish, don't you? Was he following you? Is that why you were looking about the place so strangely? At first I put it to your absence away from home."

Moore unwittingly jumped from his seat and went to the kitchen. He snatched at the closed curtain to draw it aside and looked out the window. It was pitch black out and he could see nothing. He realized if anything, he would be the one who could be seen by someone on the outside and he ripped the curtain shut.

"What name does he go by?'

"Mr. Ontez would be all he gave anyone."

"Ontez? I have never known that name hereabouts. Not Cornwall, St. Ives, nor all of Land's End."

"Nor have I. When he asked me about my business out here, I said simply, calling on an old shipmate. I went on as though I'd never been here before."

Moore was up and pacing again.

"And what was his reply when you asked him the nature of his journey out here to Cornwall?

"He said he was born here. At this juncture I put his charade to the test. I made the remark to him, 'English through and through, eh?' The bloody fool agreed! I had him there, Moore. We both know, were he was from Land's End, he would have understood who the original people of this region are and declared himself Cornish, by God, not English!"

"He knew not that he was Cornish! The bloody devil!"

Both of the men were looking hard at each other.

"Aye! He told me he was coming back to settle some affairs and meet some associates he was involved with. A business adventure."

"He lied to you!"

"As well as I did to him. He knew I didn't believe him, Moore. He seemed to enjoy the hoax and my discomfort with it…and with him."

"There is probably some truth to his talk of business associates and adventure though, don't you agree?"

"I think his business adventure includes you and me, old friend."

"Can this man be looking for the Shallow Temple?"

"You are thinking so, are you not? Time holds no barriers, Moore, as we have found out. Mr. Ontez is onto something and now he has my name."

Moore was up again and at the kitchen window, but, stopped himself from grabbing the curtain. "We have to do something about this, Carder. I fear we had better start making our plans straightaway."

INTERLUDE: BUSINESS AT QUEEN ANNE'S REST

Approximately 10 kilometers northeast of Land's End lay the port town of Penzance. Its strategic location on the southernmost tip of England offered social misfits and privateers the advantage of unseen entry or quick escape because of the surrounding rugged coastline with its many coves and caves; perfect for those who were running or hiding from the law.

At the same hour Moore and Carder were considering alternatives for their future, four sinister men were seated at a long table in the rear of Queen Anne's Rest. Quiet and empty on that night, 'The Rest,' as it was called by those who frequented the place, had a reputation for catering to rough transient characters, pirates, criminals and other vicious types from the underworld with lodging and privacy. This was not a place for the weak-hearted.

On a busy night, if one observed the scene carefully, from one table to the next, nobody paid attention to what was happening at the other tables. Only when someone entered the room did a watchful eye or two take the time to assess the newcomer. An unwanted visitor could disappear in a moment's notice.

Actually, there were only two men seated at the rear table, a Mr. Brass and his associate, Mr. Patch. Patch was a semi-retired privateer and leader of a small community of thieves and loan-sharks. He earned his name from the patch he wore over the hole where an eye had once been. It was cut out of his head in a knife fight. His partner in crime, Mr. Brass, came to his rescue, saved his life and avenged the loss of Patch's eye in one swift blow. Brass had been devoted to Patch since his promotion to the lofty position of chief enforcer and first-rate head breaker of Patch's crime organization. Patch gave him status and a job he loved. He delighted in carrying a brass club, although his immense size was reason enough for those in debt to Patch to pay up on time and without argument. He was dedicated to hurting people, beating them up, breaking their bones and whenever possible, killing them.

The other two seated at the table looked to be men, but in reality, were extra-terrestrials from two different water planets. Brotus Promo, a Martian who retained favor in his boss's eyes because he had a very cruel streak, was second only to his commander Ontez Neuron, who once remarked of Promo, "A man so crooked, he can't think straight." On earth, Promo went by the name Mr. Wright. His name and looks could change at will, as could those of his chameleon superior, Ontez Neuron. For the time being, Mr. Wright's pock-marked face and blackened stumps for teeth made his Earthling identity more than believable. The fourth person in the group was a vampire from the terrorist planet Jam-bo, who was a disgusting, loyal, rat of a yes-man. Ven-Ra was a "necessary evil," Neuron said of him. "He serves me well and has a knack for ferreting out information." The men called him Mr. Irwin.

Wright leaned into the table and addressed his mates, "Welly-well lads, the captain has everything in order, as it were. He has found his man, so it is to our thinking, this job is calculated for extreme measures."

"Damn me bootens but we loves a good kidnappin'," Patch said, nudging Brass, giving him a conniving wink. "Will we be lettin' blood then, says I?"

Brass glowed with hidden anticipation at the sound of these words.

"Nay, Mr. Patch, never for the beginning. Now then, if the captain feels the need for your talents, perhaps then, you shall have a go. You can take this up with the captain."

"Evil is as evil does, Mr. Wright. Surely a man such as our captain who understands evil as his very self, would want naught better than to serve us up some fine wench so we might have a go."

The men had a laugh at Patch's wicked suggestion. The aliens masked their contempt for the earthlings by joining them in their laughter, feigning comradeship.

Revealing his suppressed desire, Brass yelled, "To be sure, I will have my say with the captain, Mr. Wright. Me thinks havin' a go with a wench, then slicing her up right nice, can't be all that bad. Are ye not wantin' to let some blood, Mr. Wright?"

For the first time, the foul little Mr. Irwin chimed in, "Lettin' blood says you? Why that's a fine thing to do, says I."

"A fine thing to do, says you?" Patch asked facetiously. "It's the manly thing to do says I."

Brass looked at his comrades, "Lettin' blood? A fine thing to do, says 'im! A manly thing to do, says you! It's the only thing to do, says I!"

The raucous laughter at the table started up again after Brass's outburst, but stopped just as abruptly when the tavern door swung open. The cold Atlantic wind rushed in making lamp candles flicker. Someone entered, his face not distinguishable, hidden in the recess of his hooded cloak. He moved like a shadow as he made his way along the wall toward the back of the tavern. The presence of Ontez in the 'Rest' caused the thin veneer of ambiance to evaporate and a darker mood saturated the room. The pirates were relieved to see that their captain, who they knew as Billy Bones, was in good humor. He took his place at the head of the table, and his wiry, steel cable body exuded power when he spoke.

"We are in luck, we are! It is him, of that I swear. We will have him to ourselves when he reaches the Bracknell woods in Sussex, close to London. When he least expects it, will be the time to make our move and there will be no one about to interfere. We will be waiting there for him and mark that it shall be in two days. We shall create a diversion that will stop the coach. Then, Mr. Patch and Mr. Brass will tempt our man out into the open by givin' him the opportunity to champion a maiden fair. There will be no thieven' or killin' lads, we just want that man."

Bones turned his look on Patch and Brass. It sent a chill through Patch, but Brass was impervious, still lost in his fantasy of bloodlust. Ontez thought to himself that there might be some hope for Brass. "Agreed?"

The group at the table resounded with a chorus of ayes.

"Now verily, with that said, Mr. Patch and Mr. Brass, we will not have a drop spilled." Then in his serpent voice, Billy Bones smiled and repeated, "Not one drop."

Patch was wondering if Bones had the ability to read minds. He tried not to show his discomfort, but he felt like the captain knew he was trying to hide his thoughts. Brass, on the other hand, could care less if anyone read his mind because he took pleasure in killing and the more people that knew this, the better. Brass joined this group because he thought it would be a chance to hurt someone. He started to think Patch had conned him into this job when Bones made it clear to one and all that nobody was to draw blood and Patch replied, "As it were agreed, eh, captain?" Brass's brain turned red with rage.

Ontez was expert at causing rifts between alliances. His own paranoia about having close relationships demanded that he would always check the loyalties of those under his command.

"Aye, Mr. Patch. Now then lads, this is how the takin' will come to pass." Bones's eyes twinkled as he turned to Brass and said, "Keep in mind Mr. Brass, we do have need for a wench and if by chance she has to do some things that you must force her to do, it may be the only thing for you to do."

Bones statement made Patch blanch because he used the phrase "the only thing," in the exact manner Brass did when he was talking about letting blood moments before the captain joined them. Brass understood who the boss was immediately and now he no longer needed anything from Patch. The smile he gave the captain for the good news he just received could not have made a better impression on his new leader had Brass tried to put it in words. Patch was well aware of what had just happened. He could no longer count on Brass to take orders from him or help him should he have the need for back-up. He knew he was alone.

The vicious rogues sitting there with him, once his trusted partners, were now his secret enemies. He knew his only hope to get an upper hand and come out of this job alive was to do everything he was told and act like everything was just fine. He would not make any moves until the time was right. Little did he know that time had long passed; he was already in way over his head.

Billy Bones reviewed every detail of his plan thoroughly, over and over again, late into the night until he was assured everyone knew exactly what their assigned roles would be for the kidnapping. Quartermaster Ontez and his business associates were ready for 'The Taking.'

EARTH: CORNWALL

It was the morning of Carder's departure. He and Moore, still sitting at the kitchen table, had been up all night, sorting out options for their future. Carder was torn trying to make a decision. It would be easier for Moore to take leave to search for the Shallow Temple on his own. He could always return to his business at Land's End. Lt. Carder had no such option. He yearned to go with his friend, but it meant he would have to resign his commission, ending a career he had worked so hard to establish and leaving the Royal Navy that he loved deeply. He wasn't keen on the idea of losing the means to make his livelihood. By the time dawn started to break they had finally agreed to go to the South Pacific and find the Shallow Temple together, provided Carder encountered no problems with the navy. All night long the men had discussed the pros and cons of their plan.

When the children started to wake up, the men stopped working. John got busy preparing a meal for everyone while Philip stashed all their charts and other papers. There was an unusual silence at the breakfast table that morning causing the children to cast questioning glances at both men, who were lost in their own deep thoughts. After breakfast the children were supposed to be busy cleaning their room. Instead, they were at their bedroom door, listening to Moore and Carder's conversation, hanging on to each and every word.

Before she woke that morning, Jane had a premonition that a significant event was about to take place. She tried very hard to pay attention and perhaps find some clue to the message. The moment Sid heard they were all going to go on a long adventure soon, he could not calm down. Jane was so occupied restraining her brother she was unable to hear the men and learned nothing more.

They continued to develop and organize supply lists with a sense of urgency they could not quite place. They believed time was of the essence hurrying to finish their scheduled tasks. They felt it was imperative to alert the leaders of the wave riders about the ominous appearance of Mr. Ontez on the 'Voyage of Discovery' and in the coach ride to Land's End. Moore and Carder knew these were not coincidences. After reading the diary of Peter Carder and recalling their mutual childhood experience with the Traveler, they reached the conclusion the appearance of Ontez was somehow connected to the Shallow Temple. Ontez displayed an obvious interest in Carder and made no attempt to cover this up. On the contrary, it didn't seem to matter to Ontez that Carder knew he had some sort of hidden agenda and he was positive Ontez purposely encouraged his suspicions.

"Are you sure you wish to travel alone, Carder?"

"Not especially, no. What are you suggesting?"

"I could go along incognito as another passenger on the coach."

"And who will mind the wee ones, old sod?"

"How could I forget that? Well then, if your quartermaster friend appears waiting in the postal station, you will make an excuse for yourself and come back here straightaway."

"You needn't worry, Moore. I'll return in a fortnight with the rest of my things, provided my resignation is approved. First thing when I get back here, we'll plot our course and finish making our arrangements. If it holds true that England may no longer be safe for us, the sooner we set sail to join the tribe of wave riders, the better. Once there, we will learn the secret of the Travelers. I feel the answer to all these mysteries lies with them. In my absence you must start to put everything in order."

"Not another thought about that my friend, I will attend to it. I believe it's time for us to see you off to the postal station."

Moore gathered the children and the small group made their way to the road Carder would follow to the Land's End Postal Station. The moment arrived for him to part company with his friend. Before he did so, Carder distributed the beautiful gold amulets he found in his great-great grandfather's sea chest. He gave each person one: Moore, Jane, Sid and kept one for himself. He put his back into the small leather pouch and tucked it away in his waistcoat pocket. He also gave Moore a copy of the map he made on regular parchment. Moore would be able to locate the Shallow Temple, should any unforeseen circumstance keep Carder from the trip. The two men had burned Carder's original copy in the cottage hearth the night before. He hugged the children and turned to leave.

He yelled back over his shoulder, "Fare thee well, children, take care of your Uncle John!" In a moment he was gone.

Moore and Sid watched Carder walk away; Jane began to feel a familiar sensation. She started to quiver; her eyelids fluttered. She went into a trance and had a vision of a man falling overboard from a ship. She could see other men on the deck of the ship and she was not sure if the man was pushed, thrown, or if he jumped. Were there two men waiting in the water? She tried to center her vision on the man's face to see if she knew him, but her eyes were distracted by an object the falling man held tightly in his clenched fist.

A glittering gold necklace! Before Jane could distinguish anything remotely familiar, he hit the surface of the ocean and disappeared into the water.

The postal station was much like an inn that had an area for receiving mail and a room where travelers waited. Philip was already seated in the carriage anxious for departure to London. The driver was in the station gathering all the outgoing mail bags.

Carder heard sounds and shouts of an approaching rider to hold the coach. He stole a look out the carriage to see if it was Ontez and was not sure if it was him or not. He saw a cloaked figure dismount from an obviously lamed animal and rush into the station house. Moments later the door to the carriage opened and a weather-beaten, haggard looking fellow climbed into the carriage. The man looked tired and smelled of the road, as if he'd been riding for some distance. He clutched a leather satchel to his chest and took no notice of Carder whatsoever. Likewise, Lt. Philip Carder did the same.

THE TAKING

At first, Philip was glad it was not Ontez who rode up to the postal station. He wasn't so sure now. At least he knew who he was dealing with in Ontez and he could remain on guard while keeping a watchful eye on him. This was a different situation and Philip felt that this might be one of Neuron's associates. He decided he would not sleep on this journey.

No one else but Philip and the stranger were riding in the carriage that day and the trip back to London had an underlying air of tension. The man sitting opposite Philip had not looked up once nor did he move during the entire ride, yet Philip could feel the man's presence and he knew the fellow was awake and alert to the change of every nuance of his surroundings. The coach made a last postal stop and was on the final leg of the journey through the Crown's dense woods of Windsor Forest in Sussex, just outside of London proper. Both men were still the only two passengers on board.

The coach entered a clearing and Philip noticed the driver slowing his team of horses. He looked at the man across form him who now was looking straight at him. Philip sensed danger but oddly enough It was not from his fellow passenger. The man seemed to look worried, more for his own safety, as his body language suggested to Philip. Philip motioned to the man to keep quiet and told him, "You will stay in the coach. Do not try to make any untoward movements or you shall pay dearly for it. I will call for assistance from you should I need it."

A woman had dashed out from the woods on the other side of the clearing, screaming out at the top of her voice, "Help me! Please, stop! Help, I beg you! Help me!"

Philip leaned his head out of the coach to see what the commotion was all about while the driver reined in his horses, bringing the coach to a halt. As the woman ran toward the coach, Patch and Brass appeared behind the woman from out of nowhere and grabbed her. The moment Philip saw the lady in distress, he was out of the coach in an instant.

"You there! You scoundrels will remove your filthy hands from the lady!"

Brass released his grip on the woman and started towards Carder. Patch pulled his dagger and put it to the base of the woman's throat. Carder could see her eyes grow wide when she felt the cold steel of the blade touch her skin and her screams stopped. He drew his sword, cutting a more menacing figure than the two thugs expected and they hesitated for a moment. Brass thought better of attacking Carder and turned around to help Patch drag the woman back into the nearby woods.

"You scum had better reconsider while you still have your heads on to do so!"

Patch cackled at the naval officer's challenge.

"A hero says I, come to rescue this stupid wench, have ye?"

This enraged Carder, who decided then and there he would have to kill these men. In a flash it came to him; that smell! He recognized that distinctive, unpleasant odor that permeated his senses; he realized he had been caught in a trap. He tried to turn and face Ontez, but it was too late. He felt the impact from the blow of the musket on his head and felt a black curtain come down around him as he fell to the ground. Carder heard screams and laughter before he lapsed into unconsciousness. Patch and Brass were no longer holding the woman, who was really a harlot brought by Ontez. The three were walking easily over to where Carder lay on the ground at the feet of Ontez. Brass then noticed the coachman slumped over, the fresh blood still oozing from the terrible wound that almost took his head off.

"Beggin thy pardon, captain sir, methinks it were said there would be no blood lettin on this here takin?"

Ontez was staring down at Carder and he was very pleased with what he saw. At last, he had the key that would lead him to the Shallow Temple here on Earth. The smile that came across his face could have easily been mistaken for one of benevolence. The woman read it immediately. She began to scream in earnest.

"Ah yes, me hearties! Tis a go ye are wantin', Mr. Brass? Well then, you shall have it! And Mr. Patch, I'm sure ye have a mind to join in! Have a go, Mr. Patch! Yes lads, have a go!

EARTH: SOUTHERN CALIFORNIA

Pacific Coast Highway, PCH, the fabled Highway 101, was the road to ride for most surfers making their way to check the waves. Surfing and surfers had been around for some time, quietly tucked away in the myriad of small beach communities throughout this famous stretch of coastline. During the 1950's, surfing started to evolve into a counter-culture movement and those in the know understood that surfing was much more than a sport. Surfing involved spirituality, an essence from the life-giving element of water and only those who rode waves were able to pick up on this particular, special vibe, during this particular, special time. Surfing redefined itself by its cultural birth as a preferred way of life. Surfing enjoyed a renaissance that would be reinvented with every new generation of surfers. The rage to surf, to be a surfer was spreading fast. Surfers and their multi-faceted identities were starting to appear everywhere and their numbers were multiplying daily. Just past the small town of Seal Beach and before the equally small town of Huntington Beach, California,

Highway 101 ran parallel with the ocean's edge, skirting back-bay inlets on one side and sandy stretches embroidered with pickle weed on the other.

Sunset Beach, one of those now long gone, idyllic little communities was known as Surfside. It blended into the landscape, hardly noticed by occupants in cars that raced by endlessly on PCH; unless, of course, you were a surfer. Surfside consisted of a few rows of beach cottages and rentals built on each side of the highway and it was here, where one of those houses would become the forerunner of many such renowned, communal lodgings to emerge in the near future along the coast of the golden state.

It was painted pink. It was the reason this particular two-story building, became known as the Pink Party Pad. It housed a can of nuts; four erratic, zany, young surfers. They were part and parcel of a larger, tightly-knit group of people, many of whom maintained friendships throughout their entire lives.

Preacher, a lean, 18-year-old, enjoyed acting out crazy notions in public. His roommate Sow, also 18, was witty, had curly brown hair and a physique Arnold Schwarzenegger would envy. He considered himself an intellectual, yet he loved to portray himself as the ignorant butt of Preacher and Skinny Wally's insults and jokes. Their roommate, Skinny Wally, was the same age as Preacher and Sow. Wispy, extremely bright, he liked to pretend he was raving mad; at least that's what most people who met him thought. The fourth member of the pad was Lester, who was two years older than the others, wise for his age, extremely humorous and volatile.

There were a few other houses like this one, but its notoriety for out and out spontaneous hilarity would be hard put to equal in any age. Its history of wild stories and colorful characters was how it was for most of those types who lived by the ocean along that treasured coastline.

On an early bright Saturday morning, Sow, Skinny Wally and Preacher were exercising on the deck. Dressed in shorts and T-shirts, they did their calisthenics to the staccato rhythms of the famous African drummer, Olatungi. Well into what they called their morning stretch, they were gearing up for their surf safari to Mexico.

Sow's unruly, curly brown hair bounced like little springs as he shimmied his muscular frame to the beat of the drums. He began doing his jumping jacks alongside Preacher and Wally. All three were keeping the beat until the drums finished.

Sow stopped, and said, "Listen."

A horn was honking. Preacher told Sow, "The horn started honking before the drums ended.

Wally added, "Yeah, Preach, I heard it too; it's Lester. The Sow is going deaf, ain't you, Sow?"

Lester continued honking his horn.

"We'd better grab our boards! Wally, don't forget wax! Hey, Preacher, get a spare from my dresser and I'll pull our towels off the line!"

Sow was talking to Preacher about his wine stash. The top two drawers of Sow's dresser never had clothes in them. He kept his gallons of Red Mountain in there; the superb, cheap, rot-gut burgundy that was the drink of choice at the Pink Party Pad. Unless Sow said so, no one dared open those dresser drawers; with or without the boys being home. Nobody worried about locking the doors, visitors were welcome and there would usually be a few people waiting inside when they returned from wherever it was, they went. This was Skinny Wally's brain child. The open-door clause, one of many unwritten laws of the pad. He figured it was good policy if no one had to think about misplacing or losing their house keys.

SURF FU

They ran down the stairs, out into the street and stuffed their boards into the open rear window of Lester's '48 Ford "woody." Sow wanted to change Lester's name to Horny. Les loved the sound of his woody's horn and had figured out a way to stretch and mute the volume of the horn by pushing and pulling on the steering wheel column. Sitting in the driver's seat alone when he was doing it, he looked like a deviate, but he achieved the weirdest sound that ever came from a car. Lester was not finished honking, even after his three friends piled in.

Sow yelled 'shotgun' first, and he would maintain the privilege of sitting in the second-best seat of the woody. Actually, it was the only other seat, because all the seats in the rear had been torn out and replaced with a mattress. Whoever called 'shotgun' would own that seat until the next stop.

What was typical behavior for these surfers might not be the right way to act for others. One had to be cool enough to handle the strange antics openly displayed by those who lived or hung out at the Pink Party Pad. There was no real leader of the pad and depending on the occasion, house rules determined the right person to manage any trouble. Simply put, any member of the pad could be the house boss knowing he would be vigorously supported by the other three. One member of the household was always in charge for whatever happened to be going on at the time.

Visitors sometimes reacted negatively to the radical ideas the residents of the Pink Party Pad came up with. Invariably, those types would be embarrassed into doing something stupid and get 86'd from the house, never to return. There were those lively occasions when a new guest joined in with the group instead of acting uppity. These people would always be welcome. If you were an unreasonable, negative type of person stuck in your own ways, you might not want to party down at the Pink Party Pad.

The woody was cruising down 101, loaded with the surfers, who loved and accepted each other for who and what they were. They were on the way to Mexico, they had their wine, some dinero and good surf waiting for them. Their ETA at '3 M's would coincide with the evening glass-off. Life was short and these four surfers practiced what they preached, they lived to surf and surfed to live. Surfers rule; pray for surf and surfers ole`.

EARTH: LAND'S END

The sound of his mallet rang in the boatyard. He was outfitting a vessel the English would call a carvel; a three-masted full rigged boat which was a basic copy of the Portuguese lateen caravel. John Moore had no idea how his father found the original hull he transferred structural measurements from. It was likely built more than a century before his father had heard news of an exposed hull near the lighthouse out on the Lizard. Part of the hull could be seen in the sand at Housel Bay when the tide was out.

Moore's father seized an opportunity presented by seasonal low tides, unearthed the ancient skeleton and hauled it to the boatyard at Land's End. Rumor had it that it may have been one of nine caravels taken at sea between 1448 and 1455 by the English and the Irish. Others remarked that it was the remains of a secret mission by the Portuguese to capture a renegade who was thought to be hiding in exile in western England.

Moore kept to the traditional standards of measurement for length to beam ratios that would maintain the finer characteristics of the caravel's original design. His decision to keep her hulls narrow was based on demands for acceleration should he need to outrun an enemy. He reconfigured the aft castle to house cabins for Carder, himself and one for the children, just above the pilot's cabin. The tiller was below deck and attached to the whipstaff forward of the pilot's cabin.

Quarters for the crew to get out of foul weather was a small hold just forward of the galley he built amidships. He also borrowed from a contemporary design for mounting the sternpost rudder, a design change in earlier caravels that made the use of steering oars a thing of the past. She had a shallow draught and would have the ability to sail closer to the wind. He had just finished installing rigging for the square sails of the forward mast and main mast which created a basic change in the lateen configuration. His ship was now carrying a square spritsail, fore sail and fore topsail and two lateen sails. Only the lines for a smaller lateen sail for the mizzen mast were left to be rigged. He had built a small harness for the Traveler on the interior bulkhead of the aftercastle. He also had constructed one forward and below the mizzen mast. He had yet to build a block and cradle near the portside after rail for their longboat. Moore tried to stay busy finishing up the list of things he had to do until his friend returned.

There was only one problem; Lt. Peter Carder had not come back to Land's End.

"Don't worry, I will return in a fortnight," he had said.

A month had passed since Moore and the children saw him off. Moore could trust Jane to see she and her brother stayed out of trouble. He kept them nearby anyway, in case he needed one of them to run and fetch something. He wasn't fooling himself; he had to keep them close at all times because of what Carder told him about Ontez. This brought him full circle with his thoughts, the list of things he must attend to, keeping an eye on the children, where was Carder and what was Ontez up to?

Around and around, all day and every night for the past week, the carrousel turned in his head. *"This is maddening! I can't stop worrying about Carder. He will pay for this when he shows up."*

John's thought evaporated! He heard the sound of a coach approaching. *"It had better be Carder!"* He whistled for the children who appeared immediately to this pre-arranged signal.

"You two stay here and see that you make no noise. You will hear the whistle again if you are to come up to the cottage. Jane, you know what to do if I don't signal."

He set his mallet and chisel aside, removed his apron and ran up the hill to find out who had arrived. Moore saw the coach and the monogram on its door that signified it was property of the crown. The driver of the coach was already down and attending to his horses.

"Official business," Moore muttered to himself. He headed toward a well-dressed young man, already moving away from the coach, walking around the cottage. The man yelled out, looking for signs of life.

"Hello? Hello there in the house! I say, hello. Is anybody here?"

Moore braced himself for bad news; he believed his worst suspicions concerning his friend were about to be confirmed. He walked up behind the large man who was dressed in dark colored clothes, obviously a barrister, or solicitor. He startled the man, who whipped around at the sound of Moore's voice.

"Yes? Can I be of service?"

Moore appreciated the man regaining his composure without skipping a beat.

"I am looking for the lodgings of Master John Moore, shipwright. It is my understanding that he lives here in Land's

End. I saw the boatyard nearby and thought perhaps this would be the correct place to ask. Would you sir, by chance, know him or have any knowledge how I may find him?"

Moore reasoned this person was not Ontez or one of his associates because his businessman like appearance said as much. He also admitted the evident reason for stopping here. He remained cautious although sure this man had no reason for being here other than attending to the affairs he had been sent here for.

"I am he. How can I help you, sir?"

The man explained he was in the service of a law firm in the employ of the crown, who dealt with affairs concerning the Royal Navy. The day was warm and the fellow looked over-heated, uncomfortable and tired after his long coach ride.

Moore spied the driver, still feeding his horses; he would offer him tea or water later. He turned back to the solicitor and suggested they go inside where it would be cooler, to the apparent relief of the man.

Before they entered the cottage, Moore let out a strange whistle making the driver look over towards him and stopping the crown's agent in his tracks. Both men were on their guard. As a general rule, Moore didn't trust men from cities and these fellows he would treat no different. The barrister carried himself in a dignified manner and Moore noticed he was alert; keeping a watchful eye in these unfamiliar surroundings.

Moore explained to put his guests at ease.

"By all means do come in. The whistle was for my children. Would you care for tea?"

"Oh yes, quite so. That would be most refreshing, so good of you to offer."

Moore went to the kitchen table and offered his visitor a place to sit. A moment later, the children entered the room quietly. They saw the big man seated in the room and came to an abrupt halt.

"More water, please?"

They scrambled out the door, their squeals fading as they distanced themselves from the cottage. Moore grabbed two mugs from the mantle above the hearth and placed them on the table. He took the kettle from the hearth and poured some hot water into the teapot to steep.

"I take it sir; you have information for me?"

"I dare say you might prepare yourself for disturbing news if you are Mr. John Moore, friend of Lt. Philip Carder."

"Carder? You have news of Carder?"

"Not exactly, Mr. Moore. You have just answered one of my questions, though. That is to say, you are indeed the John Moore who is a friend to Lt. Philip Carder."

"Yes, Carder is my friend." Moore sat down eyeing the man warily.

"Now then, sir, state your business."

"Before we begin, Mr. Moore, may I introduce myself? I know who you are, but you haven't the foggiest notion about me."

Moore made no reply but gestured for the man to continue.

"I am Louis Heart, associate director and barrister from the Temple Inn, at your service." "My pleasure, Mr. Heart..."

The children's timing for introduction was just right as they bustled into the cottage, carrying a bucket of water, the contents of which was more on them than in the bucket. "Children, this is Mr. Heart. He is here on business. Take the bucket down to Mr. Heart's driver for his horses."

Relieved to be dismissed, they were out the door and gone.

"Mr. Heart, I do not want to be rude but please get to the point and tell me why you are here."

"Yes, thank you for the consideration you have shown my driver. Now then, I must report to you that we are in search for your friend, Lt. Carder. It appears he may have been at the scene of a crime that included some very foul play indeed!"

The discussion took a turn that Moore had not expected. "You are looking for Lt. Carder?"

"We discovered Lt. Carder was one of two passengers riding in an official postal carriage of the Crown. On route the coach was waylaid outside of London. The coachman was brutally murdered as was the other passenger, who was an officer of His Majesty's Foreign Service, and found dead inside the carriage. In addition, and to make matters worse, an unidentified female, who by all accounts, may have witnessed the crime. I was told there was blood everywhere. The poor woman, more than murdered, she…"

Moore stopped the solicitor, who he reasoned had been informed of a gory spectacle at the scene of the crime. His anxiety and pent-up emotions from the past weeks caused him to vent with a momentary fit of uncharacteristic anger. He turned on the solicitor.

"Curses and confound it man! Damn the others, what of Lt. Carder?"

Louis Heart was familiar with a variety of reactions that caused people to behave irrationally when he had to deliver unsavory news; it came with the territory. He knew personal tragedy brought out unexpected emotions and Moore's outburst seemed normal to him.

Moore stood and started to pace back and forth, scrambling to put his thoughts in order. "Precisely, Mr. Moore, where is your friend? The authorities at the scene of the crime reported there was no trace of the lieutenant. Not a sign."

Moore saw the direction this conversation was taking. He had to hold a temper starting to flare. Certainly, this man suspected

Carder as an accomplice to the crime and it occurred to Moore that he was now probably suspect as well. He felt insulted by the man's presence in his house and became indignant.

"You think Lt. Carder has some connection to these murders, don't you? Sir, how dare you?"

Moore was thinking to himself that Lt. Philip Carder had been discovered! *"Ontez captured Carder!"*

Moore knew he was not privy to all the information this man had and he must be careful about what he said.

"Robbery is common among the poor, but the assassination of an agent for the king is an entirely different matter. Someone wanted us to believe this was only a case of theft. There is one important lead to follow for whoever would be in charge of the inquiry, and that is the disappearance of your friend. If his body was not there with the others, doesn't it stand to reason that the lieutenant might be involved?"

"Yes, Mr. Heart, but as you noted appearances can be deceptive. What if I told you, I suspect those murders were a ruse to kidnap Lt. Carder?"

"Then you had better explain it to me, Mr. Moore. I hardly believe the lieutenant meant more to anyone involved, save that he may have been an instrument used to accomplish a higher purpose."

It took a moment for Heart's statement to sink in. When it did, Moore had to make sure he heard right. He believed Heart thought Carder was part of a conspiracy to kill the king's man; that Carder was a traitor and a spy!

"Tell me, Mr. Heart. Who must I make an appointment with in order to plead Lt. Carder's innocence?"

"I beg your pardon, Mr. Moore, come again?"

"I wish to speak to whoever is in charge of this inquiry?"

"Mr. Moore, in addition to my regular duties with my firm, I have carved out another area of investigation which appeals to my delight in solving riddles, enigmas and puzzles. This small talent has proved to be of use to my firm and I think it applies to this case."

"Are you telling me, Mr. Heart, it is you who is in charge of the inquiry?"

"In a manner of speaking, yes. I am privately commissioned by the crown to pursue this matter to its end."

"I am hard put to organize my thoughts for the moment, Mr. Heart. Of one thing I am certain though, Lt. Phillip Carder had nothing to do with any murders!"

Moore had an idea! The thought that he could possibly get help from Heart actually enabled Moore to start thinking clearly again. It was as if a wind blew all the other desperate notions he was forced to consider clean out of his mind. His head was back in working order and he decided to focus on Heart, who was rambling on with instructions Moore would be under order of compliance to carry out.

"Will there be anything else, Mr. Heart?"

"It is the wish of our clients, the crown and His Majesty's Royal Navy, you proceed to London as soon as time permits. There, you will meet with a representative of the crown as required by law. If you wish I can arrange to be your counsel. I must warn you, Mr. Moore, there were requests that appeared to be unusual, in light of what has taken place, made on behalf of the lieutenant in the event of his disappearance or ...untimely death."

"Are you suggesting, sir, that I had anything to do with this heinous crime?"

"By all means no, Mr. Moore. It was only just now, sir, that you yourself gave me any indication that the crimes perpetrated against the crown were other than just that."

"But you said." Moore, checked himself.

Well aware of his new interest in what Moore suggested about Carder's disappearance, he had to alleviate Heart's suspicion of involvement with a conspiracy to commit such a deed. Moore's prior knowledge about Carder's movements or future plans could look like he had reason enough to gain influence and property through Carder's demise. He knew Carder had deposited documents regarding such business and from now on, Moore would have to be very careful about revealing what he knew. Moore needed Heart as an ally, someone he could trust. Eventually he would have to confide in this man and reveal their plans to find the Shallow Temple.

"You spoke of written requests? London? I don't understand."

"Oh yes, quite so. The lieutenant left instructions designating you as joint owner, heir and executor of his estate."

"He what?"

Moore's surprise was genuine enough to the solicitor.

"I see, yes. May I ask your permission, Mr. Heart, if it is allowed and would not be an inconvenience to you, that I accompany you to London?"

Moore was pleased to see that his request brightened the solicitor's mood from his somber legal demeanor.

"Oh rather! Good show, that will give us time to talk and perhaps clear up a few questions I now have reason to believe you can answer for me."

"The children!" Moore paused for a second and then continued, "Sir, I apologize. In my haste I forgot that my niece and my nephew are now in my charge, and…"

"The coach is more than adequate to carry all of us and I can assure you that I for one appreciate children, yes, quite so, I do. We shall all travel to London together!"

With the long journey ahead of them, Moore contemplated where he should start his tale to Heart. He was beginning to hatch a plan! There might be a slim possibility Mr. Heart could join him in the search to find the Shallow Temple. He needed to find out more about this man. Did he have any knowledge or interest in sailing?

EARTH: BAIL FOR SKINNY WALLY

The surfers had just returned from their trip to Mexico, without Wally, who got himself thrown in jail in Ensenada. They had already unloaded Lester's woody and were upstairs on the deck making plans how they were going to get enough money to cover bail plus gas to cruise back down to Mexico and get Wally.

Lester came out of the shower and told his friends, "I have to work tomorrow, you guys. I can't drive back down with you to bail Wally out and I'll have to use the woody."

"That's o.k., Lester, me and Preach will use my wheels to go and rescue him."

"The Pontiac? Bitchen! I'll drive, Sow!"

Preacher had a thing for Sow's Pontiac. In his eyes, it was a classic piece of automobile. It was probably the only possession Sow really took care of, that is, besides his surfboard. He kept his car sparkling clean. It was fully equipped, automatic and all electric accessories. Preacher loved to fiddle with the door locks.

"Click, click. Click, click. Yes sir, nothing like the sound of security," he never failed to tell Sow, only adding to Sow's misery when he was forced to let Preacher drive.

"Sure Preacher, I'll let you drive, yeah, you bet! When Wally's dad lets you stay upstairs alone with Judy in her room!"

"Thanks Sow! And you can bet your sweet butt that you're the one who gets to ask Wally's parents for the bread to bail him out of jail, down there in old Mexico. Hey Sow, isn't Mexico a different country than…"

"Wait a minute, Preacher! I thought you were going to ask."

Sow did not want to face Wally's parents and Preacher would never pass up a chance to drive his car. Sow was screwed, he knew Preacher would not give in.

"All right, dammit! If you ask, you get to drive the Pontiac. Only down, not back!" Wally's parents liked most of his friends and because they knew Sow's parents, they treated him more like one of the family. He didn't want to be the one to face Wally's folks and ask for money to get their son out of jail. Let Preacher do it.

They liked Preacher even though they didn't know his given name. He always clowned around even if adults were present. Oddly enough, they trusted his honest behavior, but Wally's dad kept an eye on Preacher anyway. He saw his daughter, Judy and Preacher, giving each other *'those looks'* and he knew something was up. What he didn't know was when Judy's friend Kate had stayed over recently and he went into Judy's bedroom to check on the girls, Wally and Preacher were in the bed too, under the covers. Judy's dim night light helped conceal the boys who were in leg heaven.

"Bitchen, Sow, consider it done! God, I love electric windows, electric seats, electric door locks. Click, click, click."

"Come on, Preacher, don't start."

Preacher had already started.

"Come on, Preacher, don't start." Preacher mimicked.

"I mean it, Preach."

"I mean it, Preach."

"Oh man, what did Wally get me into?"

Preacher went into his bedroom, grabbed his bracero's hat and started for the stairway. He yelled to Sow.

"Let's head on down to Mexico, pardner, and suck up a couple of them there takillyas, after we get Wally, of course."

"Bring 'em back alive boys, and leave the horse."

All three surfers started laughing at Lester's remark about the horse. Preacher was in a great mood; he was going to drive Sow's short.

Wally's parents are going to crap!

"Yeah, just like Wally's horse."

The hilarity started up again. When their laughter died down Sow began to plead with Preacher.

"You're not going to tell them the truth?"

"Sow, how many times do I gotta tell you? The truth will kill you because the truth hurts…but not in this instance. This will be the truth that counts. Yeah, that's the truth I'll use for them!"

"I suppose any of your truths is o.k. with me because I'm gonna be waiting in the car."

"Wait in the car? But Wally's mom likes you Sow."

Preacher started to act like Wally's mom when she greets Sow. His curly hair always seemed to attract her fingers.

"Why hello, Jimmy! Where's Ron? How is your mother? Oooh, your hair is so cute, I just love to put my fingers in those curls of yours. You're just like a big old poodle."

Preacher had his fingers all tangled up in Sow's hair.

"Cut it out, Preacher. I'm not going in with you."

"Oh, come on Sow, they really like you."

"Yeah, that's right, and I plan to keep it that way."

"You mean you are actually going to pass up the chance to get a free scalp massage from Wally's mom?"

"That's different, Preacher, but I'm still not going in with you."

On the stairs, the two surfers met Lester's drop-dead gorgeous girlfriend, Pamela, stopping up to see Les. Skinny Wally nicknamed her, 'Gaggamaggot.' His definition for an ugly person whose looks were repulsive enough to gag a maggot. They gave this name to Lester's sweetheart so he wouldn't get uptight and think they were trying to hit on her.

Wally's idea was Pamela couldn't possibly be interested in any of them if they gave her a crude name. Unfortunately for them, she took to the moniker and started calling herself, 'Gagga'. She was in a class of women Sow called instantly desirable. The first time Sow saw her he started drooling and now, he was pretending to drool on the stairway. Preacher started laughing at him.

"You really know how to turn a girl on, don't you Sow?"

Gaggamaggot was radiant.

"Jimmy, you are so darling and funny."

"Yes, Jimmy, you are so darling and funny, for a poodle!"

Pamela started to giggle at Preacher's remark.

"For a poodle? God, Preacher, that is so mean," but she started to laugh harder.

"Bark goodbye, Poody."

"Arf, arf, gruff, arf, woof!"

Lester could hear all the noise coming up from the stairwell.

"I hear you, Sow. Stop barking at her."

They ran outside whooping it up. Sow threw Preacher the keys and they jumped into the immaculate green and white 1956 Pontiac Chief. Preacher started the engine.

"We have ignition!"

Sow groaned as Preacher put the car in gear. They were headed over to Belmont Shore, simply called the 'Shore' by all those who lived there or frequented the place. Skinny Wally's parents' house was right on the marina.

Sow, sitting shotgun, sank down low and maintained his cool since Preacher wasn't playing with stuff. Sow knew Preacher must be going over how to approach Wally's folks to ask for his bail. He was going to keep his mouth shut and not distract Preacher, leaving well enough alone. They were almost there. Preacher turned into a lane which skirted the boating events marina, separating those houses bordering the marina from the other part of that upper middle class sub-division.

He pulled up to Wally's pad and stopped the car. He took his time getting out, all the while looking up at Judy's room. She was up there all right, staring out the window, smiling at him and giving him *'the look.'*

"Too bad we have to go and get Wally."

Preacher winked at Sow, who was slouching down lower trying to hide. He sauntered up to the front door, rang the doorbell and banged the brass knocker on the door at the same time. Wally's perky, blonde, dizzy, pretty and voluptuous sister, Judy, opened the door. She was breathing hard. Preacher knew she must have run down the stairs just to greet him.

"Hi, Preacher! Did you come over to hide from my dad in my bed with me again?"

"I sure did! Let's get up there right now!"

Judy's bright blue eyes started dancing.

"Do you mean it?"

"Yeah, a week from Tuesday!" Preacher was going to pull a Wimpy on her.

"Why next Tuesday?"

"Because, I would much rather have a hamburger today instead of next Tuesday, and I could pay you for it on Thursday."

"What are you talking about, Preacher?"

"You haven't been keeping up on your Popeye, but that's cool, Judy. I'll tell you all about it later in your bed when I hide from your dad. Is your mom home?"

"Yeah, wait a minute and I'll get her. Do you want to come in?"

"Nah, thanks, Judy. I think it would be better if I spoke to her out here."

"So you can run away again?"

"Today is not a running day. Go get your mom."

Judy was gone for a moment and returned with Mrs. Tosh. Wally's mom was an attractive woman in her early 50's. Some of Wally's friends liked to fantasize about her which didn't bother Wally in the least. Wally claimed he didn't have the room for other people's fantasies, there was hardly enough space for his own.

Mrs. Tosh was smiling at Preacher.

"Why hello, Preacher. Ron isn't here, but you are welcome to come in."

"Neither is Wally, Mrs. Tosh. In fact, that's why I'm here, so I can tell you why Wally isn't here."

"I wish you guys would call him by his real name. What's wrong with Ron?"

"We do call him by his real name, Mrs. Tosh. I don't know what's wrong with Ron, but Wally is in jail down in Mexico."

Preacher was happy with himself. Judy had put him in the mood to lighten up and the telling of bad news about Wally to his mom came off without a hitch. Preacher had thought this might be a bad scene. He wasn't in the clear yet, he still had to ask for some bread to get Wally out.

"Oh no! His father can't hear about this, Preacher! Is he all right? He's not hurt or…" "Nah, nah, he's OK. The federales probably needed some extra money so they just snatched the nearest gringo off the street, who happened to be Wally. They claimed he urinated in public. It's a famous bust, they use it all the time."

"Oh God! He didn't…"

"No, no, Mrs. Tosh, Wally would never do that. When the federales have to hustle up some dinero in a hurry, they just find some innocent young gringo and arrest him under false pretenses. They make sure to arrest his friends too, except for one, who they leave free, so he can make it home to the States and bring back bail money for his pals. Like I said it's a scam."

"This is so sweet of you, Preacher, to do all of this for Ron. How much will you need?" "Probably a hundred and twenty-five…I really don't know."

Wally's mom didn't bat an eye. She told Preacher to wait right there and was gone for only an instant. Again, this turned out to be way easier than Preacher thought, *and I get to drive Sow's Pontiac, bitchen!*

She returned with two crisp one-hundred-dollar bills. Usually, Preacher would have reacted differently about seeing that kind of money. He was pretty nonchalant about it being given to him because he was fantasizing about how Wally's mom got the money so fast; she probably stashed those bills in her bra which led to other thoughts.

"Thanks, Mrs. Tosh. You are too cool."

"No, Preacher, you are the one who is cool. The extra money is for gas and food. Are you going down there alone?"

Preacher could have kicked himself for his crummy thoughts about Mrs. Tosh, not because it mattered that she was Wally's mom, but because she was really cool.

"No, Mrs. Tosh. To tell the truth, I've got the Sow with me."

Mrs. Tosh thought the nick-names the surfers gave to each other were crude but she tolerated them with the idea this was just another passing phase that young people go through as they grow up. She didn't understand these were the names they gave themselves by choice and that they were the never forgotten credentials of life-long friendships which had real meaning to every one of them.

"Gee, I wish you wouldn't call him that. Why do all of you change your names?"

Preacher knew where this question would lead, so he gave her one of his stock replies that would change the subject.

"It's easier than getting tattooed."

"That's not funny, Preacher," Mrs. Tosh laughed.

"Where is Jimmy, I can't see him."

"Oh, he's out there all right, he was dozing when I pulled up and I didn't bother to wake him."

Mrs. Tosh stepped off her porch to get a better view. Preacher told her to look at the window on the front passenger side where she could see his curls sticking up.

"Hey Sow! Sow! Wake up, man. Mrs. Tosh wants to see you!"

Sow finally sat up and reluctantly rolled down the window. He changed the dirty look he was giving Preacher into his best smile when he looked at Wally's mom.

"No, Sow, come up here and say hello."

Sow opened the door, threw another dirty look at Preacher before putting on his shades and getting out of the car. He walked up toward Mrs. Tosh, beaming his terrific smile directly at her.

Preacher positioned himself slightly behind and to the right of Mrs. Tosh so he could not be seen by her if he felt like doing something rude behind her back to make Sow laugh. As soon as she spoke Preacher started to mimic her.

"Hi Jimmy! Come up here right now and let me take a look at you. Goodness, the curls God gave you are so cute! Just like an overgrown poodle."

Sow was having a tough time holding back his laughter because she sounded exactly like Preacher when he was making fun of her over at the Pink Party Pad. Preacher looked really crazy standing there behind Mrs. Tosh, silently mimicking her, crossing his eyes and sticking out his tongue.

Sow started talking in his 'Leave it to Beaver' Eddie persona while pretending Wally's mom was Mrs. Cleaver.

"Wow, really, Mrs. Tosh? The poodle I remind you of must have a pedigree!"

"Oh, Jimmy, you have such a good sense of humor."

"Gee, thanks, Mrs. Tosh. I'm really sorry about Ron. I tried to tell him not to give the horse so much water, the owner said the horse already had the runs."

This caught Mrs. Tosh totally by surprise and Preacher knew that Sow had no idea he had just stepped in it.

"The runs?"

Preacher enjoyed the show as Sow continued with his 'Eddie' ruse.

"Yes, Wall..., I mean, Ron just let the horse keep drinking. Anyway, I couldn't talk him out of that or riding the horse either."

"The horse?"

"I tried to tell him not to, but he decided to ride the horse into Hussongs. Didn't Preacher tell you?"

"Hussongs?"

"Ron was pretty funny actually. He told me he saw a cowboy movie where some guy rides his horse into a..."

Preacher was rolling his eyes towards the sky and Sow suddenly knew Preacher had just RF'd him. He realized he was telling the real story and something totally different than what

Preacher had probably told Mrs. Tosh. Sow dropped his 'Eddie' act.

"... saloon and hitched the horse up to the bar rail."

Preacher started to twitter and Sow wasn't going to try and stop him. He understood that would be useless.

"Don't pay any attention to Preacher and go on with the story, James."

Ooooh, it was James now.

"Well, Ron got inside Hussongs and everybody started cheering Ron and the horse. The horse must've got excited or something and besmirched itself in front of everybody. The stuff even squirted on people across the room and pandemonium broke out! People were laughing and barfing at the same time!"

Preacher was beside himself and even Sow started to snigger.

"Stop it, Preacher! It isn't funny." Sow choked on his words.

"Stop it, Preacher," Preacher repeated, while injecting a farting sound, "It isn't funny."

That was it. The two could no longer control themselves. Preacher laughed so hard; tears rolled down his face. Sow tried to continue.

"Ron didn't even have a chance to get off the horse. The federales…"

Sow broke off in mid-sentence, overcome by the memory of the horse.

"I didn't mean to lie to you, Mrs. Tosh," Preacher lied. "I didn't really know what happened because I wasn't even there."

The situation had escalated and become a bit more serious than Preacher had anticipated. He too, noticed when Mrs. Tosh started calling Sow, James.

"Thank you, Preacher. Please go and get Ronny out of jail now. I will talk to you some more about this later, James. Perhaps we will invite your mother over to join our conversation?"

"We gotta split, Mrs. Tosh!"

"Wait a moment, Preacher."

Once again Mrs. Tosh disappeared into the house and was back in a flash to hand Preacher another crisp one-hundred-dollar bill.

"Take this with you, I know you will probably need it. I have no idea how much more they might want. The charges against Ron are so much more severe than we realized, Preacher. If you need more, find a phone down there and call me."

"Thanks again, Mrs. Tosh. We should be back with Wally sometime tomorrow." Preacher and Sow turned away and rushed down to Sow's Pontiac. They could hear Mrs. Tosh reminding them to call as they climbed into the car to get away. Preacher started it up and punched it. A deafening screech of tires and a wall of smoke was all that was left for Mrs. Tosh to look at.

"Click, click."

"Thanks a lot, Preacher. You prick! You set me up!"

"Now, now, Sow. Our deal was I'd ask so I could drive."

Preacher started clicking the electric door locks.

"Nobody told you to rat Wally out. What have I said to you about telling the truth, Sow?"

The two surfers started laughing.

"Sow, if I told you once, I've told you a thousand times. Never tell the truth."

"You asshole, Preacher!"

Neither of them could stifle their mirth.

"Let's stop and get some food."

"Bitchen! How much did she give you?"

"Three portraits of Ben."

"Far out! How come she gave you so much?"

"I can't really tell you why, Sow. She asked how much I needed and I told her probably one hundred and twenty-five…"

"Not dollars, pesos! One hundred and twenty-five pesos! Man, Preacher, that's only about twelve or thirteen bucks!"

"Gosh, really? Gee willikers, James, how would I know that?"

"Gee, Mrs. Tosh, I didn't mean to lie to you. I wasn't even there."

"I tell you, Sow, when the horse let it go and started making those weird farting noises, all those people started to puke and laugh and howl at the same time, I couldn't believe my eyes!"

Fits of laughter were ringing out of the Pontiac as it rolled down Highway 101.

"That was all time, Preacher! I'm glad you didn't try to talk Wally out of doing it."

"The water story you made up about the horse was hilarious."

"Thanks, Preach. Where did you find the exlax?"

Preacher reached into his pocket and dug out a little box.

"It's the companion's companion, Sow. I always try to have an extra bar or two around with me. Never leave home without em, they really do in a pinch!"

The surfers roared and Preacher gasped, "The horse ate four helpings."

"Wally didn't even see you give it to the horse. That was genius!"

"Remember the look…"

Sow finished for Preacher, "…on Wally's face?"

The surfers were hooting.

"Those horse farts, Sow, oh God! What a sound."

Preacher had to pull the car over to the shoulder of the PCH because they were laughing so hard. The comedy continued as they rolled to a halt.

"How about them apples, Sow?"

"Horse apple pureeeee!"

SURF FU

The Pontiac sitting on the side of an abandoned stretch of highway, in the pickle weed, fronting the ocean was jiggling and shaking. Anyone in hearing distance might have wondered about those muffled shrieks and howls.

INTERLUDE: THE COACH TO LONDON

If Moore thought he was worried about Carder before Heart had appeared at Land's End, he knew he was desperate now. He had no idea which way to turn or who to unburden his thoughts to. Could he trust the barrister, Louis Heart?

There were a few occasions before this one when Moore planned to travel to the great city, but something always came up. He could never manage leaving his work at Land's End. He imagined the reason for his first trip to London would be for a happy, special occasion rather than the dire circumstance that sent him and the children packing in the company of someone they hardly knew.

Moore couldn't have guessed the journey to London would have him believe his current problems were resolved. Heart would become more than a mere acquaintance to all of them.

The children were excited at first, but the monotony of being in a close space over such a long distance soon took its toll and they fell asleep. This allowed the men plenty of time for conversation.

Heart was anxious to learn more about Carder's relationship with Moore. He fought back every urge to ask about it and waited patiently until Moore broached the subject. Heart spoke to him of other things.

He had already made his mind up to tell a tall tale to make Moore open up to him. A completely false story, but Heart had no trouble telling it as he had done so many times in the past. The first lie started with where he was born and raised… just outside London, where he now still lived.

His fiction was that of a young widower who witnessed the sickness, deterioration, and death of his wife and family. All from the ravages of consumption.

This was nothing new to Moore, who had watched members of his own family taken. He was completely deceived. Heart might have seemed a distant man on first meeting, but as their conversation gradually explored facets of each of their lives, Moore was led to believe Heart had fine values, great courage, and the strength to maintain them both in mind and spirit. Heart conquered his grief through hard work and the determination to live.

The moment arrived for which Heart was patiently waiting. He had drawn Moore into his confidence. Moore's eyes locked onto Heart's eyes.

"Perhaps it is a good time I tell you why I believe Lt. Carder has been kidnapped. It began with the appearance of an object we saw float in on a wave. Later in life we would find reference to this object in the journal of his great-great grandfather, a legend in his own right, who sailed with Drake. I'm sure to cause your eyebrows to rise with skepticism, but I swear everything I'm telling you is God's truth! Do not worry, Mr. Heart, I can prove my story and I will not hesitate to do so. You must assure me that the information

I am going to give you remains with you. There are items I can show you that verify…"

"Very well, Mr. Moore. Before you begin, I have a question to ask and I expect an honest answer from you, sir."

"By all means, Mr. Heart, any service to help you with your inquiry, I offer willingly."

"Yes, quite so. I have reason to believe that you have almost everything in place to leave England. Am I correct?"

Moore was shocked! *"How could he know that?"*

Paranoia grabbed him by his guts. *"I don't even know this man"* he thought. Moore did not want to think where Heart's question would lead to. He felt it may be Heart's idea to link him and Carder, to a conspiracy. At once, he became suspicious of Heart. He decided there was nothing to say about future plans. He really had no idea what he would do now that Carder had disappeared.

"Perhaps, when this business in London is finished, I will have a better idea of what is in store for me and the children."

Moore waited out the following silence before introducing Heart to Ontez.

"It started when Lt. Carder and I were just wee lads…"

He revealed more than he meant to, but he didn't mention Ontez's name. Invariably, Moore knew he needed to ask someone questions about Ontez that nagged at him. Opening his plight to Heart seemed to have relieved his stress about the current situation. He changed his mind once again, deciding he had to place his trust in him. Moore supposed Heart would be the obvious person to start with. Heart was a good listener and by the time Moore finished, Heart understood he had underestimated the shipwright. There might be much more to Moore's story than he had first assumed.

"A remarkable tale Mr. Moore, and very well told."

Moore wasn't sure how to take that remark. It wasn't said in a condescending manner. He revealed all he could recall to Heart and now he was determined to get some answers from him.

"Mr. Heart, I need to inquire about certain confidential matters I believe your office is in charge of. I am sure if I find the answer to my question, we will not only know why this terrible crime was committed, but also learn the identity of the leader of those cutthroats."

"Of course, you may ask, Mr. Moore, yes, by all means, but I may not have the answers you seek."

"Do you have access to documents or files about what has been written in ships logs, or duty rosters? Better yet, are you familiar with policy concerning public requests for that type of information?"

"Yes, I see. I know of certain files, hmmm. There is no public access to ships logs that I know of. It would be highly unusual for anyone other than the proper authority to be privy to written logs. All other information unfortunately, is common knowledge quick enough."

"As a solicitor, do people have to go through your office to seek information?"

"That depends, well, of course, often there are times set in my schedule when part of my weekly assignments includes overseeing clerks who provide information for the public. All other documents for public review pertain to those who have established official relationships, and have authorized scheduled appointments. There are others who do this sort of thing in the office too, Mr. Moore."

"Tell me this then, Mr. Heart. By chance, do you recall any appointment where you met or heard of a person who referred to himself as Ontez?"

There! He said the name. He felt instant relief and then a stab of fear lodged itself inside him that wiped away his earlier moment of respite. Moore was overcome with a feeling of dread, making him unsure if he had done the right thing by revealing himself as someone acquainted with, or who knew of the mysterious forbidding man. Again, he felt his paranoia directed at Heart.

Could the solicitor be something other than who he said he was? The spell was broken by Heart's reply. The name came to Heart's recall as though he summoned it himself.

Moore's story about the quartermaster involved with Lt. Carder didn't quite come into sync as he listened, but now that Moore mentioned that man, it brought about a dynamic shift offering a ray of illumination into Heart's mind's eye.

"A peculiar name, oh yes, and a more than peculiar smell, quite so."

Heart knew him! Hearing this helped to put John Moore at ease, but he would not forget the chill that filled him and the strange delusional side-effect overtaking his whole being after he mentioned that name out loud.

"That's it, Mr. Heart, that is it! He requested information from your office! Hold! He wanted to see the names of the captain and crew of *Endeavor*."

"How would you know that, Mr. Moore?

Once again Heart's natural instincts made him suspicious of Moore, but he continued. "Certainly, I remember the man; disturbing and unusual, that one. A quartermaster, I do believe he was, yes. I have to tell you, I found it peculiar for a member of that very crew and terribly odd of the quartermaster, to make such inquiries. Am I beginning to see?"

"I think we have discovered the key to Lt. Carder's disappearance."

"Really, Mr. Moore? How can you be so sure?"

"I dare say I am, if we are talking about the same Quartermaster Ontez, who came to your office."

"It was him all right, of that, I am quite certain. My goodness, now that I bring it to mind, he specifically asked for information about Lt. Carder. He said he had something to return to the lieutenant and that it couldn't wait. I thought nothing of it at the time, until you brought his name to light. Mr. Moore, I'm terribly sorry."

Heart was telling him the truth.

"You need not apologize, Mr. Heart. The fault lies not with you."

"Actually, there was nothing in his request, other than his being a member of that crew to have aroused my suspicions."

"Then sir, we have found our murdering highwayman. I am now convinced he was the man responsible for those deaths and the disappearance of my friend, Lt. Phillip Carder."

"Mr. Moore, we must report this information to the Admiralty at once!"

"I beg you no, Mr. Heart! I cannot allow that to happen."

"No? Come now, Mr. Moore, really? This is a matter of great concern to the Crown. You shall give me just cause not to, sir. It is imperative that I know why the quartermaster became so interested in Lt. Carder's affairs."

"This is what Lt. Carder and I were trying to find out, Mr. Heart!"

"I have a proposition and I only ask you as a form of courtesy, Mr. Moore. I think that we should discuss this matter further, after I hear your tale again and I am still of the mind to take up the chase personally. If so, we shall have to make some sort of business arrangement. If you do not want to make a contract with me and you try to leave England, I shall have you stopped and demand passage on your vessel by order of His Majesty. I assume that you have no one to accompany you, no crew, save, the children."

"You assume correctly."

"The course of action I am thinking of will require some type of a working agreement that can keep the real purpose for the voyage hidden, yet still authorize our itinerary as it were and see to it that all the paperwork is official and in order."

"I do not doubt your intentions are honorable, Mr. Heart, but I should warn you first. You had better think deeply about what you are asking for. Understand that in all likelihood we may not be returning to England and there will be very grave danger ahead."

"I suspected you would say something to that effect, Mr. Moore and I was prepared for it. Now then, it is time for you to explain the puzzle to me once again. London is still far off and as you know, I am a very good listener."

"There is more to this puzzle than meets the eye, Mr. Heart."

"Yes, quite so. I gathered that. You should also remember, Mr. Moore, besides a crew, you will need someone you can depend on to help you with the children."

"You are serious, aren't you? Great God man, you really mean it! I had better re-tell the story."

"There is always much to know and more to learn, I fancy, Mr. Moore. Please do begin. I want to hear all of it, every detail of course."

Moore felt a rush of happiness with the sudden turn of events and the possibility that he would have a person that he could trust to join him. He was unable to stop smiling as he thought how convenient it would be to have official backing from the king, himself, by way of a partnership that could prove beneficial to both parties.

EARTH: LONDON, FLEET STREET

The very name of this street conjures images from many different windows of time and perspective. The variety of stories: fact, fiction, myth and legend were born out of this strand from so many different eras. It was no small wonder when they finally reached London, Moore and the children were entranced by the sights and sounds of the famous world trade center. None of them had ever been to this great city and that in itself was enough to fill their heads with excitement.

Moore had finished his tale for the second time and Heart had questions for which there were no answers. He had listened to John Moore's tale with all his senses. It was a fabulous story filled with adventure and romance completely lacking in his cut and dry lawyerly life.

He now understood Moore to be honest, sincere and trustworthy. He knew of Lt. Carder and he had already met Ontez. By his own estimation, Heart felt at the time Ontez appeared at his office there was something odd about his requests that he could not quite put his finger on. Ontez was seeking answers to questions for different reasons than the ones he gave. One thing for sure, the quartermaster definitely gave him the impression something was not quite right. Why didn't he remember that?

Heart insisted he had to see the Traveler for himself. His decision to collaborate with Moore under the guise of a business partnership along with the blessings of the crown would be determined by what Moore showed him. The Traveler, the No Fear T-shirt and the amulets.

Moore had completely forgotten he was wearing his, and so were the children. Heart was keen to see the Traveler after one look at the gold crests. For the time being, he decided to continue his ruse being a widower. He really did own an estate outside of London and when he arrived at his firm, he would send word to his household staff to set everything in order.

Heart wanted to introduce Moore and the children to his man-servant, Arnon, who knew his every routine and would have the guest-rooms ready when they arrived. He hadn't said much about Arnon, who, in Louis Heart's estimation was a man who could do anything. Heart thought he would fit into the scheme of things perfectly.

Had he been able to see into the future, Heart would have known that it would prove to be too perfect.

Moore felt their return to Cornwall and adjusting to this new situation might not be as complicated as he had first thought. They would set sail for the Shallow Temple. He was sure of this straightaway. Ontez had taken Carder because he needed a guide to the temple. It would occur to both men how this chain of events seemed to have been prearranged; the way some chaotic circumstances fall into place in such an orderly fashion.

Heart took them straight to his firm, situated in that group of law offices known as Temple Inn on Fleet Street. In the very near future this district would become a world center for printing and publishing. The crowded street was also something to behold with the many jugglers, ventriloquists, actors, vendors and of course, the soon to be famous wax works of Madam Toussaud. The men decided during Moore's appointment with the Admiralty, Heart would take the children to look at the sights and perhaps enjoy some street theater. They set a time and place to rendezvous after Moore finished his business.

Heart traded places with Moore, departing to the Temple Bar to arrange all the necessary details for his business partnership with Moore. He sent a message to Arnon to prepare for guests. His associates and staff initiated paperwork for the partnership, under the approval and command of the admiral's office. This would delegate authority for Heart to begin his hunt for Lt. Carder, with John Moore on the *Venus*.

Heart arranged to freeze Lt. Carder's assets unbeknownst to Moore. He made sure Lt. Carder's personal documents and others concerning Moore would be stored together in a safe place until further notice.

Finally, Louis Heart went against Moore's wishes. He retold the fantastic story to the Admiralty. Instantly, orders were sent out to have a ship of the line follow them, well out of sight until they were summoned to Heart by a pre-arranged signal.

It was late in the day, but well worth the time spent tying up loose ends. The children were tired as were both men. Heart hired a coach and driver that waited for them in front of the Temple Bar. They departed immediately to Heart's country residence. Jane and Sid were sound asleep when they arrived.

The servants were there waiting at the door. They carried the children into the huge house to the room where they lay the little ones down for the night. Another servant showed Moore to his room which contained a large, comfortable bed. He wasted no time climbing into it for a long-needed rest.

After a full night of uninterrupted sleep, the guests awoke to the sounds of servants stoking the fires in their rooms. They were all awake by the time breakfast was prepared; a servant led each of them to the entrance for the room. They waited for Heart.

Moore and the children were fascinated by the servants coming and going, setting about the place doing whatever it was they had to do. Never having been in a house with a staff, they were uneasy about how to behave. They entered the dining hall and Heart's man-servant was just finishing the table settings. Louis Heart turned and pointed him out to Moore.

"That is Mr. Arnon, my most trusted servant. He's the one I mentioned to you. He will join us on our, should I say, expedition?"

Moore looked over the man who was pretending he didn't know he was being talked about. Moore understood that was part of his job. Heart continued.

"He has been with me for the last decade. You will find that he is an excellent cook and a very capable sailor."

At that moment, Moore saw something that caused a feeling of uneasiness in him, similar to the one that pervaded his being when he spoke of Ontez Neuron. *"What was that?"*

Heart's man-servant made what Moore thought was a glance containing hidden meanings. Caught off-guard, Moore watched Arnon cast a very quick and sinister look beyond him towards Jane. Moore looked to his niece; grinning defiantly at the servant. A look Moore had never seen before. He turned back to see the servant's reaction; Arnon left the room.

Moore made a mental note to ask Jane what that was all about, but in his excitement for planning the voyage, he would completely forget. It would be remembered quite clearly soon enough.

Everyone thoroughly enjoyed the meal, stuffing themselves with eggs, kippers, toast and a plentiful variety of wonderful things to eat. The children were just able to excuse themselves from the table. They had to slide off their chairs and make it back to their room and rest.

Moore got right to work, retrieving the lists he made the day before. Heart read them over and marked off supplies he already had. The men checked off items that were only available for purchase in London. Heart sent Arnon and his coachman into the city with money, lists, and the instructions, "See to it!"

In their room, Jane was giving very explicit orders to her brother.

"That servant, Mr. Arnon is not real and you cannot trust him. You must never believe anything he says to you. Never find yourself alone with him! Never! You must not repeat what I've told you, Sidney, not even to Uncle John. Is that understood?"

Sid knew that his sister was serious or else she wouldn't have called him Sidney. He couldn't quite understand why Jane didn't like, Mr. Arnon. Sid thought he was a nice enough man, *"What did she mean by saying he is not real?"* Sid hated to look like a fool in front of his sister so he didn't ask her questions about what she meant when she said things he couldn't comprehend. *"The servant was not real?"* Sid was in total disagreement with his sister on that account. After all, didn't he just serve them one of the best breakfasts they had ever eaten?

INTERLUDE: THE TRUSTED SERVANT

Arnon was silent during the trip into London, saying hardly a word to his companion, the coachman and driver for Louis Heart. He was thinking about the little girl. Had he given himself away? How could she know? That defiant grin startled him. He hadn't felt an urge to really hurt anything for a long, long time. By successfully curbing this natural instinct, he suppressed it to the point that he presented himself as a weakling. He could have skills; he could be intelligent but he had to be regarded as a defenseless old Earthling man.

Thus, it felt good for him to stir up that wonderful untouched reservoir of hate; a mixture of profound cruelty and strength. He would win her over and then deal with her. That little imp would pay for her rudeness.

He read off the items and gave the list to the driver. He had already memorized it. Arnon gleaned every bit of data he could before sending it to Neuron. By now, Ontez had beings in place throughout England, France and Spain. This small network served him in a number of ways. Ontez needed a system that afforded him the ability to get away from Earth immediately if need be.

Surveillance was the priority for the group and Arnon was the perfect spy. His plan to make himself available to someone who traditionally worked as a solicitor or barrister was genius. He wished to keep abreast of current military and political intelligence without revealing

himself or his intentions. His choice to work as a man-servant for Louis Heart was pure chance. Luck of the draw more than anything else and he was very proud of this.

Arnon's real identity was Non-Ra, older brother of Ven-Ra, a.k.a., Mr. Irwin, who was the traveling partner of Neuron himself. Non-Ra was the founding father of the school of *'Techniques for Treachery and Deceit,'* a highly regarded criminal learning institution by the sophisticated outlaws from his place of origin.

A great number of his former adversaries were either dead or wished they were dead because they suffered the techniques personally administered by the master himself. He personified the quintessential evil of the terrorist planet, Jam-Bo; home of the notorious Ra family, a known clan of vampires.

Non-Ra knew he would be well rewarded for this prize. Neuron had made it clear. "Whoever brings me Carder's accomplice will never have to worry about anything again."

Profound as the nature of this villain's duplicity was, Arnon could not recognize the double-edged sword of Neuron Ontez's oath. He was so busy thinking about the lavish gifts that would be bestowed on him, he was actually startled when the coach came to a halt. The driver pulled the team alongside the now familiar entrance to a back alley behind Whitechapel Road.

Arnon cared not at all for conventions of the day, especially those rules concerning hierarchy of staff. Normally, an upper servant or major domo would have never permitted a staff member of the rank of driver to go alone or unattended to make any purchases for the master.

Arnon hissed at the driver.

"You shall see to that list. Leave out not a single item. Pay the least price and your share will be half the remaining difference at days end, agreed?"

The coachman nodded his head in reply. He was used to this routine and the rule for shopping. He always scraped off the top before he returned anyway and since today's list was enormous so would be his profit. He also reminded himself today he would return to the alley sooner than he had from past shopping trips.

He reasoned Mr. Heart's loyal servant was skimming off the top before they even set out for London. He made note of the door at the bottom of the steps in the rear of the alley, by observing Arnon from a hidden viewpoint. He was sure Arnon kept his extra loot behind that door. He had a happy little tune playing in his head: *"Today is the day, today is the day."*

Yes indeed, today would be the day alright.

"At dusk then, no sooner, no later."

The order never changed and at the sound of the hissing voice, the driver came out of his reverie, snapped his black snake at the horses and they were off. Arnon turned and made his way down the alley where he could enter the communication center unseen.

The communication center was larger than one would expect, containing machines that utilized technological advances not to be seen or produced on earth for centuries to come. Simply described, these machines included a duplicator for swift identity change. A data processor with data storage components and a relay teleport that could send and receive messages, images and small objects. There was also an emergency transport module just in case anyone had to leave the planet in a hurry. Finally, there was a spacecraft inside an underground hanger beneath the relay center.

Ten other extra-terrestrials and three duplicates, all from the planet Rollon, who were called Rollers, served at this station and never left the building during daylight hours. There was always someone awake and at the screen in this room. It had been this way for the past century.

The driver finished purchasing the last item on the list and still had much of the afternoon free before he had to pick up Arnon. *"Good,"* he thought, *"Plenty of time and nothing to stand in my way for a chance to surprise the old fart and take the extra money."*

The driver could have stopped for a few drinks, as he normally would, but greed made him hurry back across London. He had made prior arrangements to meet a friend who would hold his horses for him until he returned with the promised fee.

His team safe, the driver set off for the alley, nonchalantly turning into it and acting as though it was something, he did every day. He was thinking how pleasant the afternoon was and he had no bad feelings about what he was going to do. He walked quietly to the rear of the alley and went down the steps leading to a door. He turned the latch without a sound, thankful it wasn't locked and pushed the door silently inward.

Something with enormous strength yanked him into the room and he heard the door slam close. He wished his eyes were closed because what he saw made him lose control of his bladder and bowels simultaneously. *"What are those things?"*

"In the name of..." was all he got out before Non-Ra pierced a hole in his jugular vein with his needle digit. Efficient as a modern-day surgeon, he sucked the life out of the coachman by re-placing his tube digit in the hole where his needle digit had been seconds before.

"These Earthlings seem even more refreshing if you know them." Non-Ra laughed as he tossed the sagging mass of meat to the Rollers stationed at the communication center.

"I knew this day would come," he bragged, "now I can return and place Carder's friend into the hands of Neuron."

Non-Ra stepped outside into the bright sunlight. He lifted his nose, sniffing for the scent of the coachman's horse team. He found them immediately.

"Close," he said aloud. He was lucky the driver had left the coach nearby and he also knew there would be only one Earthling to deal with when he got there.

"Should I pay him or serve him to my friends here?" the Jam-Bon asked himself, walking away from the sounds of flesh being ripped apart and eaten. *"Decisions, decisions."*

EARTH: RETURN TO CORNWALL

Arnon made sure he was late getting back from the city. His lie to his master explaining the disappearance of the driver was simple and to the point. He apologized for not returning with him, but he feared the coachman would beat him for interrupting his drink.

He knew he would not be questioned; he was Heart's most trusted employee. Heart had no time to worry about the coachman and made note to have a replacement for the him the next day.

It took the men two more days making delivery arrangements for everything sent on to Land's End. Arnon would go ahead, staying with the shipment until he met up with Heart on the *Venus*, at Land's End. Heart finished seeing to the caretakers, outlining their responsibilities and paying them their wages.

John Moore, Louis Heart and the children were anxious and ready to return to Cornwall.

They reached Land's End to find everything they shipped to the boatyard there waiting for them, as was Louis Heart's man-servant.

Heart saw to it that all their purchases matched their lists before they were put aboard the caravel. The ship needed only a few lines of rigging to be secured and then she would be ready to sail. One of the last items sent onboard was done in secret and placed in the special hidden harness Moore had designed. He fitted the Traveler into the caravel's forward deck.

On their arrival, Moore took Heart aside and showed him the Traveler. Heart had never seen anything like it. He wondered if this was a trick of some sort to fool him. Moore told him to touch it. Louis Heart was absolutely dumbstruck! Visibly shaken!

Moore refreshed Heart's memory about why they had to find the Shallow Temple. They were planning a mission to find answers for questions they didn't even know, then Carder disappeared. Now they must find the Shallow Temple in hope Carder would be there or people at the temple would have news of him. Moore also warned him.

"No one, including your servant, must know what this is about, Mr. Heart."

The tingle Heart felt was a revelation he had never expected, and the touch put him in awe of the Traveler. The board seemed alive! Heart may have believed some of what he had been told in good faith, but now he knew that he was meant to be here.

Jane and Sid would stay below and aft in the special cabin John had constructed by dividing what was essentially the pilot's cabin immediately below decks of the aftcastle. He halved that space, leaving plenty of room for the children and enough area for his own privacy. Below that was the great cabin, aft of the mizzen mast and the capstan. It was converted for Louis Heart with a small side room for his servant.

Moore was making his way down from the aftcastle to check on the children. He stepped down the vertical ladder easily and he could see Sid's shadow outlined in the companion way leading to their quarters. Moore watched Sid run into his cabin yelling to Jane. Sid is always so excited, Moore thought, maybe the voyage would calm him.

He made his way into their cabin and found Jane kneeling on her bunk; bent over a beautiful chart he had never seen before. Moore knew what it was. Jane was looking down at a Mercator projection drawn by the Dutch map maker, Willem Blaeu.

To develop reasonably accurate maps that depicted curved lines of a globe on a flat or two-dimensional surface, the Flemish scholar and cartographer, Gerhardus Mercator devised a system of elongating and distorting the extreme northern and southern regions of the globe to allow for accurate and undistorted views of regions in the temperate zones where trade routes for maritime traffic were widely used.

Blaeu's maps were spectacular. Ships appeared on the surface areas of the oceans to indicate key routes of trade. The borders were highly decorated, often portraying the sun, moon and planets along with the four seasons or the four elements. The discovery of this map was a godsend.

"Jane, where did you find this?"

Actually, it was Sid who found the map in one of the old wrecks the children played in at the boatyard. As a child might, Sid thought he was going to get in trouble, hoping Jane wouldn't tell on him for finding the map.

Before Jane could reply, Moore made an intuitive decision right then and there.

"That question needs no answer, my dear Jane. I want you to take this map and hide it for safe keeping. If I need to check something on the map, you can bring it to me if I ask you to fetch my pipe."

Sid sighed with relief.

This resolved a recent unforeseen problem John Moore and Louis Heart had not attended to. How would they plot their true destination on their map without eyes of a possible spy gaining access to it? Now, they could use this map to chart their way to the Shallow Temple.

Jane already knew this map must remain secret. Moore was about to return to the poopdeck, then remembered the episode in the dining room between Jane and Arnon. Fixing his eyes on his niece, knowing full well she was not going to tell him, he had to ask.

"Jane, what was it you saw when Mr. Arnon turned and stared at you?"

Jane and Sid exchanged glances. Sid was all ears. He wanted to know too.

"It was nothing, Uncle John."

The answer Moore expected.

"I noticed he dropped some silverware and I think he may have been angry I caught his mistake, that was all."

Moore stepped back into the companion way. Jane winked at her brother before she crawled underneath her bunk, returning the map to its secret place.

EARTH, CORNWALL: FARE THEE WELL

The day of departure was near. *Venus* lay off the town of Penzance, filling her water casks and receiving deliveries of livestock for fresh meat. With the stipend from the crown, Moore and Heart posted notices from Plymouth to Penzance; a call for able-bodied seamen.

Every man who wished to sign on would be interviewed by both Moore and Heart. All were told that this was a voyage of exploration; a voyage that may not return to England for years. Each man was highly scrutinized and would have to sign a document testifying he was single and had no immediate family before his name was placed on the list for the ship's complement. Signing such a contract was not an unknown practice during this period but these stipulations still caused rumors to circulate throughout Cornwall.

Spies in the employ of that villain, Captain Billy Bones, were supposed to get word to him immediately if any prospect of a voyage of this type should be announced. It was ironic they could not locate him anywhere.

Finding thirteen men did not take much time, especially when those who went to be interviewed first learned that the wage being paid was twice the amount earned for any other regular merchant sea duty. Word about double wages spread like fire and many sailors who had not wanted to go back to sea were found waiting in line to be interviewed. The final complement on board *Venus* would be narrowed down to fourteen men.

The thirteen men hired from the long list of applicants, included the first officer, a stern and weathered sailor named Gevens Collicott.

Collicott's papers proved he had sailed in the West Indies. He remarked in his interview he knew the names of several good pilots who were familiar with the east coast of South America; this in itself made him a welcome addition to the crew.

Murdoch Ford, former bosun's mate, would be first mate. He had a reputation for a short fuse and fast fists after consuming too many jars. Also, a master sail maker, he would be counted on to serve as acting master-at-arms.

The man at the helm called himself Gawen Berryman and both the first officer and first mate spoke up for him as the best man for the job. The two nine-pounders on the aftcastle would be maintained by Myghal Atwood and Trystan Bickle, both former gunners' mates. They would see to the care of all small arms, taking charge of gunnery duties in times of confrontation or possible boarding.

Moore had often asked the help of an acquaintance, Morgan Arundell, a shipwright and carpenter who he picked to be responsible for maintenance and construction of anything wooden. His master apprentice, Davy Brokenshire, was also chosen to join the crew.

Cador Smythe was selected as surgeon's mate because of his genial manner and education. He proved himself to be the most knowledgeable about contemporary medical care out of all those who applied.

Pasco Donithorn and Colan Jolly, foretopsail mates, also carried reputations as men who had absolutely no fear of going up into the yards in any type of conditions at sea. Rounding out the ship's crew was a knowledgeable seaman named Petrok Chellew; a quartermaster who would be assigned extra duties as the ship's clerk and bursar. He understood paperwork and ship's records that had to be maintained and the correspondence the job demanded. After all members of the crew were notified, the total complement on board, *Venus* amounted to fourteen men and two children.

The earliest known caravels were ships used from the 13th into the late 15th centuries, throughout western North Africa and the Iberian Peninsula. Although these vessels were used to transport merchandise and supplies, or for fishing, they also played an important role in the voyages of exploration and discovery. They were used in the charting of the coast of Africa south to the cape of Good Hope, in all of Columbus's expeditions and much of the east coast of South America.

The small crew was filled with mixed emotions when it finally came time to set sail. There was elation among the members of the crew, fueled by dreams of riches they might discover. Anticipation always marked the beginning of an adventure into the unknown. There was also the sadness of farewell, another goodbye to the land of their birth.

It was late November and the long dark clouds making their way across a grey-on-grey early morning sky matched the general mood of melancholy for this occasion. The sea change caused by the outgoing tide meant only one thing; it was time to weigh anchor. The crew turned its attention to the sea and set into action. Men went up the rigging to unfurl the sails while others on deck were busy hauling and securing lines as the brisk ocean breeze filled the canvas, setting *Venus* in motion.

First officer Collicott set their course and stood on the half deck calling down to Mr. Berryman, helmsman at the whipstaff, while he watched the sails draw and grow taught from the prevailing north easterly winds. By nightfall they would be long out of sight of that ancient island outpost, bearing east southeast toward the European continent where, at Ushant, they would change their heading south, southwest for the Canary Islands. It would be at that latitude they would again change the ship's bearing and with the help of prevailing seasonal westerly winds, claw their way across the Atlantic towards the western horizon.

The beginning of their long journey was filled with storms, strong winds and cold weather, but weather would not be the problem encountered by the crew of this small sailing vessel. During the third week under sail, the first man disappeared.

Mr. Chellew had just been relieved of his evening watch by master apprentice carpenter, Davy Brokenshire, who drew the midwatch for the second two weeks of the voyage. Young Davy was trying to see through the moonless dark when he first heard a sound aforedecks. There is always noise on a wooden ship, but the sounds grow familiar to a sailor's ear. The rustle and flap of a sail with the intake or release of a breeze; the beating of lines against the bulkhead or wind-blown harmonious vibrations singing through the rigging, but this was different.

He made his way forward, not sure of what he might find. There! He saw something move past the main mast toward the starboard bow. *"That was really fast,"* Davy acknowledged. Perhaps he should make his way back and alert Mr. Collicott, but he really didn't know what he had seen. Davy didn't want to arouse suspicions of the crew that he might be a coward so he thought better of his notion to get help and inched forward alone.

Davy's eyes were growing accustomed to the darkness. He was fully awake, and his night vision had made adjustments. Yes, now he could make out the form of someone leaning over the ship's side. It was probably one of the mates being sick. *"Funny,"* he thought, Davy didn't hear any retching. He walked up to the cloaked figure to see if he could be of any assistance when it turned around to see who approached. Davy stared into the face of the devil himself! Without time to cry out, the poor lad was so frightened by who he saw, he fainted on the spot.

Non-Ra cursed himself for being spotted in his real form. He didn't need any replenishment; the coachman would last him another ten months. Vampires of Jam-Bo could exist on any regular diet, as long as they supplemented it with four or five quarts of blood every year. There were other misrepresentations about vampires on this planet, such as not having reflections, melting in sunlight, silver bullets and wooden stakes through the heart. All rubbish, but if that is what the Earthlings wanted to believe, so be it.

He was not one to waste blood, yet he was forced to leave trace amounts of it on the deck, before throwing what was left of the earthling overboard. Davy's unconscious form jerked when Non-Ra forced his needle digit through the opening between the young man's left and right pectoralis major muscles, to reach his pulmonary artery. He spilled blood near the spot where Davy would disappear. Non-Ra immediately reinserted his tube digit into the artery and in less than five minutes he sucked Davy dry.

It was quiet enough for the splash in the water to alert the first officer. *"That was not a good sound,"* Mr. Collicott thought. He yelled for the watch on duty, who did not appear; another bad sign. His yelling woke the first mate, Murdoch Ford, who made his way topside heading straight abaft for the aftcastle. On his way, he wondered why the watch had not come to call him.

"Mr. Collicott, how come your voice interrupts my slumber? There will be the devil to pay when I find the unlucky man who is on this watch!"

"To be sure, Mr. Ford, I wish you luck in your search. I heard an unfortunate splash only moments ago. Lord have mercy for him who met the sea on that note."

Ford checked the duty roster. Davy Berkenshire, the watch on duty, was nowhere to be found on the ship. Chellow vouched for Davy, telling Ford that he had relieved him on time for his watch. Negative scuttlebutt could ruin a voyage and it was obvious some of the crew did not like this situation when all hands were called on deck. One of the gunner's mates, Trystan Bickle started to bemoan the missing man as a bad omen. He had just begun his litany.

"It's not a good sign…"

Ford overheard Bickle and made sure he caught Ford's extremely dark look as his voice boomed out a warning for all to take note.

"Belay that notion, Bickle."

"Aye-aye, Mr. Ford," was Bickle's wise reply.

He was not about to get on the bad side of the first mate, who made it known to all on board that he was the ship's jaunty. Nobody wanted a taste of the cat by way of Mr. Ford.

Morning light started to filter through the dark and Ford noticed something out of place on the deck near the forward starboard rail. A loose line brought his attention to a cleat that was no longer secured to the deck. The mount had been lifted up to one side and on closer inspection, Ford found a blood smear on the end of the cleat. Blood drops splattered the surrounding surface of the deck underneath the cleat. It looked like the unfortunate young man tripped in the dark and fell headlong onto the cleat. Probably dizzy when he stood, he lost his footing and pitched over the rail. Ford hoped this would put to rest any superstitious notions the crew might concoct, allowing that nothing out of the ordinary had occurred. Accident or not, this was still not good.

Sometimes days at sea become long, seamless periods of time where strangers living in close quarters have to learn how to get along. Relationships within a crew can strengthen or perhaps the opposite will occur. Certain members of a crew might have conflicting personalities and find the only way to resolve their differences is by confrontation and violence. John Moore and Louis Heart tried very hard to avoid the latter by taking this into account when they assembled their crew.

INTERLUDE: THE SHALLOW TEMPLE

Gnarles was unsure why he was asked to report to Master Cylinder. He had just finished his paddling exercises and was going to catch a few waves when Master Flow called him to the water's edge.

"Gnarles, something of great importance will keep you from the surf this afternoon. Master Cylinder wishes to speak to you; he says it is urgent."

"You mean, don't even go out for one wave, right?"

"You are learning, aren't you Gnarles?"

The Gnar had to laugh, because the monks constantly worked to suppress students desires to go surfing. Gnarles wasn't the only student at the temple who ditched classes to go catch waves. One tried not to disobey the rules of Shallow, but everybody there surfed! There isn't a surfer alive who hasn't called in sick for work or ditched school on that day the perfect swell came to town.

Gnarles would not dare risk missing this personal call from the great master of Shallow. He didn't even bother to put his

Traveler in the rack. He held on to it and walked straight to Master Cylinder's cottage at the opposite end of the lagoon from the temple.

Master Cylinder was sitting on the front lanai of his simple beach cottage, looking out at the waves. He followed their breaking crests along the reef to where the swells flattened, then softened into the channel. The Gnar was greeted by him.

"Shallow, Gnarles."

"Shallow, master."

"Those waves look very special, Gnarles, thank you for being so prompt. If there is time, that is, if we finish soon, we could paddle out together for a session."

Master Cylinder smiled at the Gnar and actually chuckled. Wow, the Gnar thought, *"I have never heard that before."*

Gnarles knew the situation must be serious. Master Cylinder's body language and his outgoing affable attitude betrayed his known stern nature which didn't go by unnoticed. What it really told Gnarles; this was more important than he thought.

"That's a great idea!"

"Yes, it is, Gnarles, if we have time. Let's go inside. shall we?"

The Gnar set his Traveler down in the shade, and walked into the cottage. What occurred next blew the Gnar's mind. Master Cylinder used his *'Voice'* to pose a question.

"What group of beings come to mind when I mention the terrorist planet?"

Gnarles remembered his studies from *'The Commonalities Among Shape Changers'* class. He detested those creatures.

"You are talking about the Ra family of Jam-Bo, master. Specifically, you want me to recall that they are vampires."

Master Cylinder switched to his regular voice.

"Forgive me, Gnarles, I had to get right to the point. The Niele announced that a very serious threat to the temple has already been set in motion. We must attend to this matter now."

"We will need to send a Katana to put a stop to it. Master Ed-Eye and I have chosen you."

"I am honored, Master Cylinder."

Gnarles was a practicing Katana. He had been groomed since childhood for this super elite group of warrior assassins. They were a secret sect of the 'Brotherhood of the Tree,' who were viewed as a separate community from the wave-calling drummers and time transcending wave-riders. They gained their powers through their special connection with the species of tree that sponsored their rights of initiation to the brotherhood.

To activate their magical powers, they would drink an elixir made from sap and leaves donated by their sponsor tree to carry out their duties. Only the Shallow masters knew of the guardians of the temple, *'Spiritus Gladius,'* the spirit of the sword.

"This will be extremely dangerous, Gnarles, and we don't have much time. The *'Severance'* is Non-Ra. He is ready to compromise our trap for Ontez by delivering the friend of the person we chose to ride the Traveler at Land's End to him."

The ever-confident Gnarles wasn't so sure of himself now. He knew who the *'Severance'* was. Non-Ra was big. Very big. If anyone ever found out about this assignment or who Gnarles really was and what his duties were for the masters of Shallow, his time might be cut drastically short by someone looking for a reputation.

This great adversary could also bring a quick end to his life, if he was not prepared. He was not going to be able to surf this afternoon or many afternoons to follow.

Master Cylinder began to discuss their immediate plans. He placed a small box on the floor in front of him.

"I have a present for you, Gnarles. Please open it."

"This is for me, master?"

"Go ahead, Gnarles, this is not a joke."

Gnarles removed the lid and peered into the container. He did not recognize what it was although it looked like a drum. It had to be 18 inches in diameter and the band encircling it was almost four inches tall. There were marks like scars on the surface of this object that looked like borders around several forged sections. Gnarles had no idea he was looking at a musical instrument of the future. It was a steel drum.

Sometime after World War II, steel drums evolved from metal beating instruments played by musicians throughout the islands of the Caribbean, a development resembling the ancient methods used to forge the great gongs for the gamelans of Southeast Asia. It was discovered by percussionists who beat metal surfaced objects. The tone of the metal changed by pounding repeatedly in one spot over periods of time.

The first steel drums were made by cutting the ends off steel barrels, then forging the metal end of the barrel top into a sophisticated tonal surface for island musicians to play their special brand of music.

"Lift it out, Gnarles."

Gnarles grabbed hold of the drum and pulled it from the box. Underneath, he saw two drumsticks with leather knobs on their ends and removed them.

"It's beautiful, master. What is it?"

"It is exactly what it looks like, Gnarles. It is a steel drum."

The room exploded into sound. Loud, it filled the air with indescribable harmonies of percussion. Master Drummer entered the room playing what looked to be an exact copy of the steel drum Master Cylinder had just given Gnarles.

"This is what you will use to call Non-Ra to you. What does this have to do with a common quality among vampires, Gnarles?"

Gnarles understood immediately.

"They have extremely sensitive hearing, Master Cylinder."

"Precisely! Very good, Gnarles. You can begin your lessons as soon as I activate the audio zone perimeter. No one from the temple will hear. I will return as the sun sets. I have to apologize to you, Gnarles, I'm going to borrow your Traveler. Like the tide, I believe I'm going out."

EARTH: PASSAGE TO TRINIDAD

Venus made good time after the disappearance of Davy Brokenshire. The men worked easily together and there were no other incidents for the moment. Jane was forced to stay in her quarters at the beginning of the voyage. The storms they encountered in those first weeks caused her severe dehydration from sea-sickness. She remained ill for a second week, suffering from alternate bouts of high fever.

On the other hand, Sid had no problem with traveling on the ocean. He was all over the ship, and going against his sister's strict orders, he made friends with Louis Heart's man-servant, Mr. Arnon. He knew how to do lots of stuff. He fashioned a sling-shot for Sid, showing him how to shoot it. Arnon spent time telling Sid stories about things that sounded like they were from another world.

Sid couldn't understand why Jane didn't like Arnon. He was a good guy. Sid almost told Arnon about Jane's warning but thought better of it and kept it to himself. Arnon knew Sid had something he wanted to say to him but he also knew it was not safe to pry; he was creating an alliance with the most important person in the world of his enemy.

On most days after the slingshot was made, you would find Sid way below decks going through the holds searching out rats and make-believe monsters. He was a very happy lad, until that early morning when the ship was nearing Jamaica. The Atlantic crossing was well into the ninth week and it would be one more week before they sighted land.

Jane had remained reclusive during the time after her sickness with only occasional visits topside for fresh air. The rest of the time she stayed in her cabin trying to piece together the meaning of her visions and the feelings she had about what was to become of her when they reached their destination. It was early morning and still dark out when Jane had a nightmare. She started talking out loud to herself, struggling to make sense of a puzzle without seeing all the pieces. Keeping Sid awake, he got up and decided to go hunting.

Before he did so, he would say good morning to the first officer and tell him roughly where he was going to play. This was a rule his Uncle John made after the young carpenter fell into the ocean. He climbed up the ladder to the half deck and then scrambled up the steps to the poopdeck.

The first mate was not very fond of children but he had taken a shine to Sid and greeted him warmly.

"Top o' the morn to thee, Master Sidney."

"Hullo Mr. Collicott. I'm going hunting, I am! I'll be making my way below toward the forward hold if anyone should want to know."

"Aye-Aye laddy."

Sid was dressed warmly. He had on a black wool coat and a black knitted wool cap pulled down over his ears. The sight of him reminded the first mate of some kind of midget sailor which made him laugh. Sid's head disappeared down past the ledge of the poopdeck.

The sun was rising over the horizon but the sky was filled with storm clouds and the sea was at her surly best, tossing up and down causing the ship to pitch and yaw; first starboard and then port, up and lean to starboard, down and pitch to port. Jane hated it; Sid loved it.

Sid raced forward along the rail of the half-deck and flew down the ladder to the main deck. He made an about face and headed aft past the capstan and descended to the gun deck, used mostly for storage and an area for the crew to come in out of the weather. Sid became quiet down here. He crept forward silently and looked into the storage holds. He neared the galley where he perpetually tried to sneak past Mr. Arnon.

Sid couldn't figure out how the man always knew he was there. Try as he might, Arnon never failed to speak out to him.

"Well, well, if it isn't the little hunter. Going to slay rats, Master Sid?"

On this day he didn't move without the ship making an accompanying sound. The planking of the bulkhead would creak and Sid would use the sound to camouflage any noises he thought he might make. He let out his breath after he passed the galley and climbed down into the anchor lines forward hold.

At last, he did it! This was the first time Arnon didn't catch him! He was about to go back and surprise the older man when a thump sounded in the boatswain's stores hold which was the last forward hold. Sid calmed himself as Arnon had instructed him to do before locating one's prey. He went toward the sound.

It was pitch dark down there, but Arnon taught Sid a trick about how to adjust his eyes in dark places. You allowed things to appear by closing your eyes, opening them as you practiced easy breathing. Sid knew about an opening in the bulkhead on the starboard side underneath the anchor windlass, where he could crawl unseen into the boatswain's stores hold. He heard the sound again and crawled through the small space. Sid wasn't afraid of the dark and since he'd been here many times before, he knew the worst thing he would find was a big rat. He had something for a rat; no rat was going to scare him. Sid peered into the dark hold. It always smelled of wet lines and damp sails mixed with animal excretions, but there was something else this morning that was kind of old and rotten. Sid was determined to do as Arnon told him, breathe softly and grow accustomed to your surroundings with all your senses, not just your eyes.

It was really dark in here but Sid was starting to recognize stacks of coiled lines, folded sails and boxed items that were stacked on shelves his Uncle John built. *"What was that?"* Sid heard that noise again, that thump, but this time it was followed by a low squeaking sound like wood being pried apart.

Rats couldn't make that sound, even Sid knew that. He leaned forward, straining his eyes to see into the area where the sound came from. Then he heard something different, a long, soft, deep intake of breath through the nose, just like Arnon said to do, but this was very deep and really long. Sid started backing out through his crawl hole, he didn't like this. He climbed out of the store hold as fast as his little arms and legs could carry him. He raced up the ladder from the anchor lines hold and shot up the vertical steps aft of the anchor windlass making the main deck on the run. There was no time to lose, he had to get back to Jane and tell her. There was a creature on board the ship!

At the same moment Sid was trying to get out of the forward storage hold, his sister was having a dream about him. Jane was looking for Sid. She told him not to run and get lost, but off he went anyway. He was just a short distance away in front of her, in that crowd up ahead. It was bright out until a large dark cloud moved in above her and the group turned to look at her.

Suddenly it was very cold and dark and the crowd parted. Jane recognized Arnon standing before her. Although his back was to her, she knew it was him. She watched as he plucked Sid off the crowded street and pull him tightly to his chest. He was going to do something to Sid and Jane could not stop him.

Slowly, he turned his head to look back at Jane and what she saw horrified her. Arnon's face had changed into some hideous mask of green and yellow slime. His orange eyes glistened as did his magnificent chromed, pointed teeth. He held Sid for Jane to see and then the sound rang out. What kind of sound, Jane could not imagine, but it was as bright and colorful as the tropical Jamaican atmosphere.

Arnon dropped Sid! Holding his head with both hands, he looked about to see where the noise was coming from. Immediately behind him, a golden aura illuminated the whole street as it moved toward him. The sound was coming from the walking sunshine. The bright yellow gold apparition started to fade away as Arnon, in a rage, charged into the bright light.

Someone grabbed her!

"He's a creature, Jane! He has turned himself into a creature!"

Jane woke up looking into the anxious face of her brother. She put on a smile for him although she could tell, Sid was really afraid. She knew that Sid had seen the hideous other side of Arnon for himself, discovering Arnon's true identity. Whatever happened, Jane was thankful that it brought his friendship with the master of deceit to a close.

"It's alright Sidney, catch a breath and relax. Rest a moment and then tell me everything."

Sid was safe. He was with Jane and she would know what to do about the creature. He didn't have to worry because Jane would fix it. He answered her happily.

"Yes, Jane."

INTERLUDE: SID AND THE CREATURE

John Moore and Louis Heart were just forward of the main mast talking with Ford and Collicott. Their discussion was quite heated and Murdoch Ford was livid. Jane had Sid go and tell Collicott that there might be something wrong in the boatswain's stores hold. Collicott and Ford had just come up from below decks and were reporting to Moore.

"We have a saboteur aboard, Mr. Moore."

"Aye." added Collicott, "and he means to sink the ship. We have men covering the hole with a tarpaulin and wedging oakum into the seams of the surrounding planks. Arundell is of a mind the patch will not hold for long. He is shaping a batten for a brace and readying some pitch to keep the oakum secure. A quarter plank had almost been torn out!"

Moore was astounded at this news and his mind raced, thinking of all the possible implications as he assessed the situation. He began to experience that odd feeling of dread and as it seized him, he fought hard to shake it off. One of Ontez's men was aboard and Ontez was possibly in the near vicinity.

Venus had to be close enough to land if the pirate were to try to make his way ashore by stealing the longboat before the ship went down.

Murdoch Ford approached Louis Heart menacingly and told him straight to his face.

"It's your man, Mr. Heart, of this I swear. I know my crew. It's him, to be sure."

Louis Heart held back; he could see murder in the first mates' eyes, yet he felt he had to protect Arnon until he could get at the truth of the matter. It was a hopeless feeling because there was no reason not to trust Ford and Collicott, yet he knew if the men aboard this ship were to learn that Arnon had anything to do with the sabotage, all hell would break loose.

Moore could not allow this conversation to escalate or go beyond these four men and said so.

"There will be no idle talk Mr. Ford, Mr. Collicott, do you understand?"

"Aye Mr. Moore, Ford and me won't breathe a word. It wouldn't do for that fella to be hanging about though."

Collicott was looking up toward the yardarms.

"Would it, Ford?"

Both Heart and Moore acknowledged the first officer's meaning and understood that these men didn't want to see Arnon above decks again. He would have to be confined to his quarters, which also meant he would have to be put off the ship when they reached land.

Heart was going to tell Arnon not to worry because he'd be safe once they reached Trinidad. After all, he had His Majesty's Royal Navy close at hand.

"I will inform Mr. Arnon of your suspicions personally Mr. Ford."

"Thank you, Mr. Heart, you have our word."

Louis Heart started to leave the group, Colan Jolly's voice rang out from the fore topsail, "Land ho! Land off the starboard bow!"

The men raced to the starboard rail and Collicott declared.

"We have sailed in beneath the Indies, Mr. Moore, and those islands are Tobago and Trinidad. The small one is Tobago and just around the corner comes Dragon's Mouth and Port of Spain."

Heart was torn about the situation with his servant and wanted to discuss it with Moore, but when he saw that Moore's grim face was set, he went on his way aft and turned down the companionway towards his servant's quarters. He knocked at Arnon's door but there was no answer.

"This is Louis Heart, Arnon, don't be afraid. I do have regrettable news, please open this door."

Heart could hear no movement in his servant's quarters so he made his way below to the galley. He found no one there and he didn't see Arnon. He started to panic. Had the men taken justice into their own hands? He hurried above decks and looked for John Moore. Ford told him that Moore was looking in on his charges. It was calm on the water as well as on the ship and this alarmed Heart even more. Something was amiss, and he had to get to the bottom of it now.

As quickly as possible he made his way aft again, turned down the companionway toward the children's cabin. The door was open and Moore was in conversation with Jane.

"I can't find Mr. Arnon, Moore. He is afraid and hiding, or he is dead."

"Hold on, Heart, you had better be sure before you make such unfounded statements."

Heart appreciated what Moore had said and it gave him pause to think that perhaps Arnon was guilty of the sabotage, but why?

Jane's face lost color and she shrieked!

"Where is my brother? Where is Sidney?"

Both men looked at Jane. They ran out of the cabin and up the companionway. Moore spotted the first mate and shouted.

"Mr. Ford, have you seen my nephew? Call all hands, on deck."

The crew appeared on deck at once except for the four men at work patching the gash in the forward bulkhead of the boatswain stores hold. Ford called out to the first officer.

"All men accounted for, Mr. Collicott."

Collicott repeated the report to Moore and Heart. At that moment, Moore saw it, and his heart sank. He lost control and screamed at the men.

"All men accounted for? What of the ship's longboat? Is it accounted for Mr. Collicott? Have none of you eyes? Look there! Look! The longboat is gone!"

Moore was beside himself and Heart came to him to try and calm him down.

"Easy now, Moore, easy."

He turned to Collicott.

"Head straight for Trinidad. Have Mr. Ford report to us about the damage to the ship. Order the crew return to their duties."

"Aye-aye, Mr. Heart."

Arnon was an expert sailor and he was making good time in the longboat Moore had rigged for sail. He placed Sid just forward of the mast where he could keep an eye on him while he sat at the tiller. Sid tried to keep still and pretend he was asleep. He was very afraid and his fear compounded when Arnon told him.

"I can smell your fear little Earthling, just as I did when you came snooping into that hold. Maybe it was for the better, you finding me in there. Now I have control over what direction your uncle has to take to come after you. Don't worry boy, I won't eat you, not yet anyway."

When Sid heard Arnon talk about eating him, he cried out, "You are a creature and Jane told me someone will kill you!"

This thought enraged Non-Ra and he would have struck Sid if he didn't have to maintain his grip on the tiller. He had wondered about that little Earthling girl and he thought to himself, if he got the chance, it would be her life that would end. He put those thoughts aside, and concentrated on the island just ahead.

By this time every man on board *Venus*, would know about him and his evil deed. He would arrive at Trinidad before Ontez now, but that would be just fine with him. They would be waiting together for Moore, when he sailed into Port of Spain.

EARTH, TRINIDAD: THE SEVERANCE

The Gnar accelerated out of a barrel of a mighty portal. He leaned forward and put a slight pressure onto the inside rail of the Traveler. It responded immediately and climbed vertically towards the lip of the wave. Gnarles had been practicing this maneuver at the temple and since nobody was around watching him, he let it all hang out and pulled a 180 back into the lip, releasing the Traveler from the body of the wave. He banked into the lip as it pitched and rode the outside edge of the lip to the bottom of the trough. He leaned back putting pressure on the tail of his Traveler, the nose lifted and he separated from the exploding water to re-enter the bottom face of the wave. A successful new move!

He powered his board off the exploding fountain behind him and streaked ahead of the cascading curtain once again. Gnarles was going off. He was already thinking about the sequence into the next move, where he would ride the inside of the lip above the foam ball. He believed it was possible. He rode the wave as far as it would take him to the inside, and then the swell disappeared. Gnar was near a beach on the windward side of Trinidad, west of Galeota Point, where Columbus had first anchored before sailing into the Gulf of Paria. He named that entrance to the port, 'The Serpent's Mouth,' because of the narrowness of the passage.

Gnarles stashed his pack and Traveler there, before crossing overland on the peninsula to Punta del Guapo; later to become known as Point Fortin. Wearing only an old pair of cut off trousers held up with a rope, he had his steel drum on a belt looped over his shoulder and enough food for three days. He would have to hurry; the pressure was on.

Non-Ra met up with one of Neuron's spies on the outskirts of the port. Along with Indian guides, they traveled overland to a vantage point near the entrance to 'The Dragon's Mouth,' also named by Columbus, because of treacherous currents and natural hazards.

The spy swore to Non-Ra that this was the only route for a ship to enter Puerta de la Hispaniolas or Port of Spain. Regardless, every ship had to go through the Dragon's Mouth by day, if they had any sense. He could observe the coming and going of every ship. The spy wasn't sure of the time Captain Bones would show his face, but he told Non-Ra not to worry, he would be there soon. Non-Ra worried anyway.

Three days had passed since his arrival, and matters were getting complicated for Non-Ra. Sid wouldn't eat. Non-Ra needed the boy as bait for his uncle. He was going to have to take Sid into Port of Spain and find a doctor to treat him. The sun was just breaking on the horizon when Non-Ra started off for the Spanish capitol, carrying Sid over his shoulder in a large burlap bag.

He had a notion to look back at his campsite and saw *Venus*, just barely afloat but struggling through The Dragon's Mouth, heading for Port of Spain. He was amazed the ship was still making way, and he realized they would all be there at the same time. *"Where was Ontez?"*

Aboard *Venus*, manning the bilge pump in shifts had brought the men to the brink of exhaustion; they had reached their limit. The sight of Port of Spain was exactly what they needed to boost their spirits. A last burst of energy gave them the strength to make it to the seaport.

It was Collicott who spied their longboat moored alongside an old broken wharf, off in the distance. Ford volunteered to go get her and no one argued. Ford invited Jolly to join him. The top foresail man gave the first mate a wide grin and the thumbs up sign. Both men were rough and ready to crack some skulls if need be.

Jane demanded her uncle take her with him and Heart. She had told Moore she would recognize the street where they would find Arnon. Heart did not want her to go with them, yet he had to agree with Moore's reasoning; they needed Jane to find Sid. There would be five men aboard ship at all times and the first officer would be in charge of the rotation to go ashore. Shore liberty would not begin until the bilge could be pumped to a safe level and the temporary patch put in place.

Sid wasn't feeling good at all. He could no longer trust his former friend because he turned into the creature. He didn't dare eat the food, or he would get fat; Arnon tried to make him eat. He was drinking plenty of water, but that didn't help his terrible hunger. Sid knew he was becoming very sick. Maybe he would die before the creature ate him; that wouldn't be so bad.

He was inside the bag again, with his body stuffed down into it head first. The creature was carrying him someplace. Sid found the unraveled strands of burlap in the bottom corner of the bag that he had been chewing on. He planned an escape so Jane would be proud of him.

He started chewing at them again, pulling gently on the frayed ends with his teeth. He managed to pull one of his hands down in front of his face and he poked his finger into the area he was working on. Every time he tried to poke through before, he couldn't do it, but this time his finger went through easily. He pulled his finger out and tried to look through the hole but couldn't see anything. He began chewing a little more and this time when he pushed his finger into the hole, his whole hand went through the bottom. Sid could see out now, but only downward. He was being carried along a cobblestone street. He could hear a variety of voices chattering all about him and the creature.

Jane saw the crowd up ahead and it was déjà vu; she recognized both the crowd and the street. She spun around to tell her uncle, but somehow, Moore and Heart had gone ahead, straight towards the center of town. She turned up the avenue of her dream, the large dark cloud overhead moved in front of the sun. It was going to happen!

Sid was loosening the seam along the bottom of the bag. Finally, he gave a hard tug with his free hand; the bag split open and dumped Sid out on the ground behind Non-Ra. There was a sudden hush among the people standing next to them, who started moving away, frightened by the man who dropped the little boy out of a sack he was carrying. He turned in a flash, bending down to grab Sid. He looked up and saw the little Earthling wench, standing in the middle of the road, staring directly at him, with that insipid grin on her face. He decided he would kill her brother right now, before her eyes. He started transforming into the hideous beast he was. Jane was there for the taking, to replace Sid, as bait to capture their uncle. He scooped Sid up off the cobblestones as the outrageous noise began.

Non-Ra grimaced as the metallic cacophony pierced his head. What torture was this? He had to put the Earthling boy down again to hold his ears shut. This didn't help to keep the sound out and what made it worse was the deafening noise was having the opposite effect on the people around him in the street.

No one had ever heard anything like the music from the steel drum, which had the crowd smiling and dancing. Non-Ra faced the direction where the noise was coming from; it was approaching him. He knew this was not an ordinary situation when the realization hit him.

The instant he understood an enemy was attacking him, he counter-attacked! Non-Ra burst toward the noise-maker who had just enough time to lift his metal drum, protect his chest and parry the first thrust of the charging vampire from Jam-Bo.

Non-Ra's excellent reflexes held back his digits from possible injury. In a single leap he jumped over Gnarles, spun around on landing and grabbed Gnarles around the throat with one arm while he thrust his needle digit into the Gnar's jugular vein. The pain was immense, yet the Gnar had to stay calm if he were to succeed. The hideous Jam-bon hissed through his chrome teeth into the Gnar's ear, "Good-bye fool."

Non-Ra pulled his needle digit out and Gnarles almost missed it. *"Now,"* he thought and during the split second it took for Non-Ra to re-insert his tube digit, the Gnar changed his body size. His mouth was now where his neck had been and the vampire could not retract his tube digit in time. Gnarles chomped down on Non-Ra's tube digit severing it cleanly. He spit it out and it landed near the vampire's feet.

There are only three ways to kill a vampire from Jam-Bo. Gnarles chose the one which required the vampire be in his indigenous body form. He would be vulnerable when he exposed his tube digit that only appeared after he used his needle digit. The tube digit must be cut cleanly and totally removed from his digit system. Non-Ra never knew what bit him.

The vampire screamed over and over, grabbing his tube digit off the ground, trying in vain to stab it back into his digit system. He looked on in horror.

"No! What have you done? This can't be! No! No, no, no!"

He sank to his knees watching the red faucet that could not be turned off. The creature spilled himself out all over the old cobblestone road that wound away from Port of Spain. The Gnar looked at him with disgust and replied, "Good-bye, Non-Ra."

EARTH, TRINIDAD: PRISONER OR PILOT?

Jane ran to her brother who was sitting up and staring at the pool of blood and bile that was once the creature. Sid had a real hero now. That man had saved him from the creature and as long as he lived, Sid would never forget what he just witnessed. He didn't quite know how the man did what he did. He could vaguely recall how it happened. Of one thing he was certain, the musical drummer man couldn't have shown up at a better time.

Jane spoke to the man with a tone of respect and admiration that Sid had rarely heard his sister use for anyone.

"Sir, I dreamt of you some days ago and I knew you would be here to save my brother."

Gnarles looked down at the twins and a flood of memories washed over his senses, reminding him of his early days when he was a child without parents. He recognized it in these two children and knew how they felt. A great wave of affection poured out from him to Sid and Jane.

"At least they have each other," he thought as he gave a hand to help Jane stand up. He bent over and picked Sid up out of the road.

"So, you were dreaming about me, eh?"

At last, Sid was able to speak.

"You are a great hero, you are! You killed the creature. The creature said he was going to eat me and then he was going to eat Jane. Now, he will never eat anybody again!"

Sid's voice worked like an analgesic soothing the Gnar like a salve was being rubbed on his numbed psyche, calming him down from the mindset he had to use to destroy another being, especially one as great, although immensely evil, as Non-Ra.

"That's right young man, his eating days are over."

The crowd that was listening and dancing to the music of the steel drum, until the violence erupted, had all but disappeared. A small black youth stood nearby, only a few feet away, tried to get the Gnar's attention. When Gnarles noticed him, the boy stepped forward. "You had better get away from here. The soldiers will be on their way, and they will arrest you. You will be hanging in front of the governor's mansion by tonight!"

Gnarles had forgotten! He would be thought of as a slave who killed a white man. No matter the circumstances, he would automatically be sentenced to death. Suddenly, John Moore and Louis Heart were running down the narrow street.

Moore spotted Jane standing next to a man, who was holding Sid's hand. He ran straight at them, shouting out his obvious concerns.

"Sid, you are safe! Are you all right, boy? Jane, where did you go? We turned around and you were gone! We were so worried; the whole crew has been searching everywhere for you! Who are you?" He demanded of Gnarles.

Jane motioned to the lump of clothes and the remaining bits of Non-Ra, who was almost finished evaporating. Heart, who was still approaching, didn't hear her say, "That is what is left of Mr. Arnon."

Sid cut her off in mid-sentence and pointed towards Gnarles.

"This musical man is the hero, Uncle John. He saved our lives! The creature was going to eat us and then it attacked the musical man! He killed it, he did!"

Louis Heart, upon hearing Sidney call Arnon a creature, spoke in his defense.

"Here now, young man. Mr. Arnon may have taken you against your will, but that is no reason to call him a creature."

Moore looked at Heart and was sad for him, because he understood the man's loyalty to his long-time servant, even after his foul deeds.

Heart continued. "Where is Arnon, anyway?"

Moore repeated what Jane told him, directing his gaze to the lump of clothes and the dried, sticky, now yellowing ooze on the cobblestones. Heart looked over at the puddle not quite comprehending what had happened.

"That can't be Arnon. That isn't even human. If this man has murdered him, we will have to take his story into account and hold him until we can deliver him to the proper authorities."

Moore could not believe what he was hearing and he knew there was no time to waste. There would be too much trouble if they remained there longer. They had to get back to the ship immediately. He didn't know if there were spies about or even if Ontez, himself, was nearby. Moore wanted to grab Heart and shake some sense into him, but he simply replied, "We will talk later, Heart! We have to get away from here, now!"

Moore turned to Gnarles and told him it would better to go along with them. Gnarles was thankful for the consideration. The small group hastened up the road and quickly turned into the first lane they came to. Without a second to spare, all of them had moved out of sight.

A small column of Spanish soldiers turned up the cobblestone road and marched directly to the spot where the lump of clothes lay. The sergeant-at-arms told his men to stand at ease. He looked around the nearby area for signs of the reported disturbance and the men stood in the quiet, sweltering, tropical afternoon heat.

The disgusting smell coming from the clothing on the ground made the men wish the sergeant would hurry and be done with it. They could see for themselves that whatever the trouble was, it happened and everyone went away. At last, he returned to the column.

"Another false alarm, men. There is nothing here but those smelly clothes!"

The sergeant gave his commands. The column closed ranks, did an about face, and marched back to the stockade, near the governor's mansion, relieved that they were getting out from under the glare of the hot sun.

Moore had no idea if they were in jeopardy from any local judicial repercussions. Their ship's flag was recognized as one on a scientific mission which meant they would not be bothered by the French, or the Spanish, under present maritime law. If Heart was of a mind to take matters into his own hands and notify the Spanish authorities concerning the fate of his man-servant there would be problems. Moore led his small group back down toward the dock where most of the crew was anxiously waiting word about Sid. They let out a cheer when they saw both children returning with Moore. Heart followed closely behind Gnarles making sure their 'prisoner' would not try to escape.

Moore did not trust the Spaniards, so when he saw that the longboat had been brought back and secured in its cradle amidships, he was thankful that they wouldn't have to tarry after returning to the ship. He called the first officer, ordering him to go into town and find the rest of the crew.

Afterwards he sent for the ship's physician to attend to Sidney. He turned to the first mate, thanked him for the return of the longboat and told him to call all hands.

"Make ready to sail." He instructed Ford to report to his cabin, along with Collicott, within the hour. Moore had no time to waste; he had to get *Venus* under way. His orders were to head due south, leaving the islands by way of the Serpent's Mouth. Turning to Gnarles, he ordered him to, "Follow me!" Louis Heart trailed behind.

Moore was seated at his small desk in his quarters wondering where to begin his questions. The Gnar remained quiet. Heart could only wonder about the death of Arnon. He stood up, pointing his finger at Gnarles accusingly.

"You have murdered an Englishman, and you must not think for one minute that you will escape justice!"

"Hold on Heart, let's be a bit more civil and begin by asking this fellow what happened."

"Oh, I know what happened, Moore. We knew Arnon would face the gallows for his crimes, but this man still murdered my most trusted servant and friend."

"That will be quite enough, Heart. I will add that you had better reconsider what you have been accusing this man of. Perhaps you might follow your own advice concerning such matters, until you know all the facts. Arnon tried to sink our ship! He stole the longboat and kidnapped my nephew!"

Louis Heart had to acknowledge Arnon's treachery and decided to retire to his cabin. He was mentally and physically exhausted. For the past six days he could think only of reaching Arnon before any of the crew found him. He was on the verge of firing the flare he had secretly brought aboard. It was the prearranged signal to the Royal Navy's ship as a summons to rendezvous with him, but the temptation passed.

Arnon committed those crimes and Heart needed an explanation why he stole the boat and kidnapped the boy. It didn't make sense that he would try to sink the ship! He had not considered any of the events leading up to the kidnapping or anything else. He was spent and he knew it. He went to his quarters, climbed into his bunk and fell asleep instantly.

After Heart left the room, there was a knock at the cabin door. Moore got up to answer, but the door opened and Jane entered the cabin, closing the door behind her.

"May I stay and talk to you, uncle? I have something important to tell you about this man who saved Sidney. He appeared in my dream."

Gnarles, smiling at Jane, remained silent.

"You dreamt of him? Why on earth did you not tell me, Jane?"

"I did tell you. I said I knew where to find Sidney."

Moore told Jane he wanted to discuss this with her privately, later. He did not doubt Jane's gift and her ability to *'see'* things. He understood that without Jane's presence in the landing party, things may have ended very differently.

"How is Sidney?"

"Mr. Smythe said he needed rest, some nourishment, and then he will be as right as new."

"I think it might be best for you to go back and stay with your brother. Keep an eye on him."

Jane acquiesced, but stopped to thank Gnarles again, for saving her and her brother before she went back to her cabin. As soon as the door closed behind her, Gnarles spoke his first words to Moore.

"She told me that she dreamt about me after my fight with the kidnapper."

"How did you know about Arnon? Were you aware he kidnapped my nephew?"

Gnarles had to be careful about what he said. It wasn't the right time to reveal where he was from, or his knowledge about John Moore and the Traveler.

"No, sir, I saw the boy fall from the sack the man was carrying. I called the man a scoundrel and he attacked me with a blade of some sort. I was fortunate to fend him off and turn the blade on him. That was it."

For the first time John noticed the wound on the Gnar's neck.

"I think we are finished for the moment, sir. I will see you to the surgeon's mate and have him take a look at your wound. We can gather fresh clothes for you and after, I will show you to your quarters. Tomorrow will give us plenty of time for more questions and answers."

"Thank you, sir. I just need some rest."

"First, the surgeon's mate and then to the pilot's cabin for the time being."

With Arnon gone, Moore had to hire a new cook immediately. He stopped Gnarles on the spur of the moment, and asked him if he knew how to cook? Of course, Gnarles could cook. He learned how to prepare a multitude of tasty dishes from his, *'Water Planet Cuisine Primer'*. Every student at the temple had to include that class in their studies.

He admitted to Moore he had some training as a cook's apprentice. Moore hired him on the spot. The meals he would prepare would never be forgotten by those lucky enough to be on board during the remainder of their short time together. Moore took the young man to see the surgeon's mate, and both returned to their cabins. Moore had one more important hire.

The following day they reached Serpent's Mouth and Gnarles would volunteer his services. He was talking with Ford and

Collicott on the poopdeck and ventured some information about the treacherous currents that would work against them if they tried to escape through this very narrow passage.

He explained how they would have to wait for the outgoing tide accompanied by easterly off shore winds that crossed the great land mass, reaching out to the Atlantic. It was either that, or come about and struggle past Port of Spain to face the submerged rocks of Dragon's Mouth, an equally treacherous strait of water to navigate.

"I know this coast and Magellan's passage quite well. I could see to it that we gain the Pacific safely."

The news reached Moore; he couldn't believe his ears! He was ecstatic as he eyed the young man with a new perspective. Gnarles was a Godsend, but there was yet, one great concern. They had to repair the starboard bulkhead. Ruminating about Arnon's sabotage, Moore questioned Gnarles if he knew of safe harbor where they could run the vessel ashore, to lay her over for repair.

Far beyond John Moore's wildest expectations, Gnarles claimed he knew of a spot near the southeast tip of Trinidad, outside Serpent's Mouth, where they would find everything they needed. For the moment, Moore could put his worst fears out of his mind. He forgot he had yet to thank the new man for saving his nephew.

In the most formal phrasing he could muster, he acknowledged Gnarles.

"I have not even asked your name. Be that as it may, I wish to thank you for your gift. You have my sacred pledge to grant you anything in my power to offer you; just say the word."

Moore had no sooner said his thanks to Gnarles, when another rap sounded on the cabin door. Moore replied to the knock, "Enter!"

In came the first officer and the first mate. Moore's relief was visible.

"Mr. Collicott, Mr. Ford, we no longer have to seek a pilot. Our cook here, Mr. er, what did you say your name was?"

"The name is Gnarles, Mr. Moore."

The Gnar winced and chided himself under his breath. He hoped Moore wouldn't recall he had not given his name to the Gnar. Gnarles figured he could say he heard the other fellow, Mr. Heart, use his name if asked.

"Yes, Mr. Gnarles. Mr. Collicott, the first officer and Mr. Ford, the first mate. Please see to it that our pilot has some decent clothes. That will be all."

Murdoch Ford was the one who told Moore the new man had the knowledge to gain passage to the Pacific. He already knew the scuttlebutt about Gnarles, and Murdoch was very pleased to know it was Gnarles who had taken care of that rat, Arnon. He would see to it personally that no one on board this ship would bother the pilot.

INTERLUDE: PORT OF SPAIN, THE RED TIDE

Venus left port the day before the *Red Tide* dropped anchor. The few wharf rats who saw her hobble into port, witnessed the ship's jaunty claim their longboat. Repairs were made, search parties went scavenging about for a lost boy, or some such story. Cheers were heard aboard her after they returned and then they were gone; in and out with the tide.

"Something is not good!" Ven-Ra could feel it in his bones.

Ontez didn't want excuses. He wanted Carder's associates.

"This is no time for a blunder! Your brother promised me he would be here with Lt. Carder's mate."

"Accept my apologies, sire, I fear this is far worse than a blunder. I should be feeling him; his pulse is absent. There is only one reason for this; he is dead."

"You don't know for sure yet, do you, Ven-Ra? Take Promo with you. The meeting is arranged, you know where to meet them."

Promo accompanied Ven-Ra to the meeting. It was the same location, where the spy last met with Arnon.

"He was having trouble with a sick lad, Mr. Irwin, and went off in search of a doctor. He did not return that night. It was the last I saw of him."

He pointed out the direction Ven-Ra's brother, Non-Ra, was walking towards, after their last contact. They set off back towards the town and it didn't take long for Ven-Ra to pick up the scent. Promo, following behind, hurried to keep up with the vampire. Ven-Ra ran directly to the square where Non-Ra fought with Gnarles. His howl shocked Brotus Promo. The vampire from Jam-Bo fell to his knees and crawled to the spot where Non-Ra died. He had deteriorated to the point of wind-blown dust; all of him was gone. Promo had no idea how to console the vampire for the loss of his ancient, older brother.

"How was this done? No one on this planet stood a chance against him! It had to be one of those monks from the temple, who the master is after. Somebody powerful helped those Earthlings and their wretched little boat!"

Ontez was furious. There was nothing he could do. There was no trace of the ship Arnon had orders to sabotage outside Port of Spain. He had no room for empathy, but he did promise Ven-Ra he could take his vengeance out on the lieutenant. After all, wasn't it Carder's friend, or his accomplices, who killed his brother?

EARTH: THE SERPENT'S MOUTH

The passage through Serpent's Mouth was even more dangerous than the Dragon's Mouth. The very treacherous currents running north and south would have been impossible to navigate without Gnarles to guide them.

Heart fully realized that Arnon was solely responsible for his heinous acts, and acknowledged that Gnarles had indeed saved Sidney from a terrible death. He was still having trouble dealing with the complete about face of a once trusted servant. He began to wonder if Arnon was associated with Ontez and the disappearance of Lt. Carder. No, that was impossible. He was uncertain about Gnarles, yet admitted his guidance through Serpent's Mouth was an admirable accomplishment. Gnarles brightened the general ambiance of the ship. The food he prepared made the men wonder why, while at sea, they had never eaten fish before. What finally won Heart over came on the day to repair the bulkhead. They had run the vessel ashore in grassland west of

Pt. Galeota, in the Gulf of Paria, only miles east of the entrance to Serpent's Mouth.

Gnarles requested Moore and Heart to join him in search for the right piece of wood to mend the bulkhead. Both men wondered why Gnarles took them to the place he did, not knowing that was where he left his Traveler. He ran into a small copse of trees where it was hidden. He retrieved his pack, hanging on one of the lower branches. As he walked out of the thicket with the Traveler under his arm, the two men could not believe their eyes. They exchanged looks and then looked back at Gnarles; they were speechless.

Gnarles began his tale.

"I couldn't allow any chance we would be overheard, further compromising your mission."

Gnarles gave Heart and Moore a moment to let his words sink in.

"I had to let you believe the worst about me, Mr. Heart. If somebody were watching they would have to believe I was not a member of your crew, or part of a conspiracy aboard your ship to kill their man. I had to have it thought I would be delivered to the proper authorities when the time came."

Heart could not take his eyes off the Traveler and Moore had a hard time comprehending what this all meant. Moore was certain of one thing. Gnarles, if that was his real name, was a member of the tribe of wave riders from the Shallow Temple.

"I am on my word of honor to my superiors and a code of martial conduct not to reveal anything else to you except that I will take you to my home."

"You mean the Shallow Temple?" Moore asked excitedly.

"Yes, Mr. Moore, that is exactly what I mean."

Louis Heart felt like a fool for his terrible misconceptions about the Gnar, especially after practically bragging to John

Moore about his superior powers of deduction. As if Gnarles were reading Heart's mind, he admitted this.

"Mr. Heart, I am very sorry for taking the life of your servant. I can only tell you he was not who he seemed to be. You should be commended for your loyalty and your steadfast belief in the long-time friendship you maintained with him."

"Can you tell me who he really was, Mr. Gnarles?"

"I am aware of your quest. I know that you two men are now involved with the mysteries of the Shallow Temple. I will tell you this. He was a very powerful being and an ally of Ontez Neuron. You should never talk about him again."

"What do you propose to do with your Traveler, Mr. Gnarles? I have no extra room where I hid mine." Gnarles smiled at Moore's reference to the Traveler as his.

"I have already spoken with the Traveler you stored away, Mr. Moore. We have agreed that it would be best this Traveler is used to repair the damage to the ship."

Once again Moore and Heart were bowled over. They knew there was some sort of life manifestation coming from Moore's Traveler when they touched it. After hearing Gnarles say he spoke with it, both men stared at Gnarles with awe and respect. They felt like little children before this man.

Moore began to grin foolishly as he looked at Heart and then at the Gnar. Heart was grinning too, and so was the Gnar.

They returned to the ship and the men noticed the change in Heart's demeanor towards Gnarles immediately. Whatever it was happened they did not ask; they were just glad that it did. The ship and crew were whole again. For the moment.

Morgan Arundell had just finished preparing the area around the damaged bulkhead. He had to pound wedges to lift the step plank strake above the missing piece in order to re-insert a new strake. They would have to steam the wood and bend it to form, in order to refit the piece. Afterwards, they would have to caulk the seams.

Gnarles approached Arundell and told him that he would see to finishing the job, but Arundell argued that it would be impossible for Gnarles to do the work without the aid of a couple more men. Gnarles insisted he could take care of everything and thanked Arundell for his fine preparations. Morgan Arundell went to speak to Moore about the situation. He expressed his concerns about finishing the job properly. In the short space of time he took to speak with Moore and return, Gnarles had performed the unimaginable.

The new planking strake had been refitted perfectly. Arundell felt more than surprise. The task could not have been completed by one man, and not in the brief period of time he was away reporting to Moore. This frightened Morgan Arundell to no end. He became very suspicious of the new man.

He imagined Gnarles might possibly be one of those island *'witchdoctors,'* he'd read about. Perhaps he was from a head-hunting tribe, making plans to 'take over' the ship.

Hadn't he single-handedly guided the ship safely through the Serpent's Mouth, without the aid of sounding leads? Was it not he who changed the crew's diet to things unknown or unheard of? Didn't everyone seem to be under his spell of amity? What about Mr. Heart? The new pilot brought him and Mr. Moore back from their search for the strake, all in smiles! Heart had hated the man only days before. Arundell was terrified when he ran his hand over the new strake. It felt alive to his touch and he jerked his hand back! This only meant one thing: The board was bewitched and the new man was a sorcerer! Of this, Arundell was sure, and it was his righteous duty to inform the crew of his suspicions. He approached every member of the crew except the ship's officers; Cador Smythe, Murdoch Ford, and Gevens Collicott.

Arundell was angered by Colan Jolly, who was the only one who laughed at him when he invited Jolly down to feel the plank. Jolly told him if he heard another word, Mr. Ford would know Arundell was leading the crew toward a mutiny.

It didn't take Arundell long to persuade the others. Sailors are a very superstitious lot in the first place. One by one, he took them down to the forward hold to touch the strake and feel its magic. Each man heard Arundell's litany of suspicions and each one of them became a believer there was a demon aboard their ship. Before they reached a quarter of the way down the coast of South America, not one other person besides Heart, Moore, Gnarles and the children, would still be on board *Venus*.

The men were too afraid of the pilot because of Arundell's claim that he was a sorcerer. Secretly they voted in favor of a mutiny and decided to take the long boat, make their way back to Trinidad and join a ship returning them home to England. Real scientific exploration was all right, but they would have nothing to do with witchcraft.

Not long after their secret council, the men gathered together in the darkness. Moore, Heart, Gnarles, and the four aforementioned officers and the children slept. The mutineers collected enough stores to make it to Trinidad, and then lowered the longboat down onto the ink black sea. Quietly, they took in the sails; no one made a sound as they climbed into the awaiting longboat. Silently, they pushed off and away from the ship they would never see again.

EARTH: FINAL DESTINATION, THE SHALLOW TEMPLE?

If any of them had been thinking about the length of time this strange voyage was taking, little did they know it would be another 70 days before they reached the place where an incredible mind-boggling event would alter their lives and change their way of thinking forever.

Gnarles awoke first. Strange, he thought, he heard no one moving about on the upper decks. He instinctively knew they were gone. He dressed and made his way forward to wake Murdoch Ford. Ford was up and he told Gnarles to wake Collicott and call all hands. Ford would get Mr. Moore and Mr. Heart.

Heart was awake, coming out of his cabin.

"I say, Mr. Ford, it's terribly quiet this morning, is it not?"

"Yes sir, Mr. Heart, it is. Perhaps you had better come topside to see the reason why."

Ford turned and rapped on Moore's cabin door.

"Mr. Moore, you may want to report to the aftcastle and join me and Mr. Heart. Something has happened."

"Where is everybody?"

Moore asked Heart when he came above deck. Only the children were still in their cabin. Moore looked around at everyone assembled, the first officer, the first mate, the surgeon's mate and Colan Jolly.

"My question exactly, old man!" Heart said with a disheveled look. "What do you suspect, Mr. Collicott?"

Colan Jolly answered for him.

"They have abandoned ship, sir."

"Abandoned ship?" Both Moore and Heart asked incredulously.

"Mr. Arundell was spreading the word there's a sorcerer on board."

Murdoch Ford had to protect his first officer and himself.

"Collicott and me knew nothing about this, Mr. Moore."

Heart couldn't believe his ears.

"A sorcerer? Did you know anything about this, Mr. Gnarles?" Heart asked pointedly.

"I can only tell you that after we refitted the strake to repair the bulkhead, the crew treated me with a courtesy mixed with hostility and fear."

Moore inquired heatedly. "Bloody hell, man, why didn't you tell me?"

"I really didn't suspect anything other than the fact I was a newcomer, Mr. Moore."

"It was more than you being new, Mr. Gnarles," said Colan Jolly. "I think they believed you were something other than you appeared to be, if you don't mind my saying so."

"Please explain yourself, Mr. Jolly," Murdoch Ford demanded.

"By all means, Mr. Jolly," Collicott blurted. "Please tell us."

"Yes, right. After Mr. Gnarles, here, patched that hole in the bulkhead, I watched Mr. Arundell talking to the men one at a time. He would take them down into the forward hold. They'd come back up, the looks on their faces was fear. He come and took me down to touch the strake Mr. Gnarles replaced. He started gibbering all sorts of crazy stuff and I just laughed at him. He didn't say another word. I would have said something but Mr. Ford warned us about such talk."

Moore addressed the men.

"I hadn't imagined it would come to this. They have deserted the ship."

Heart let out a nervous laugh. He thought it was he who was the most suspicious member of the crew. He laughed again, shaking his head.

Moore didn't get it. "What is it, Heart?"

"It's quite simple, Moore. They suspected our friend here as an agent of the devil. I believe when Arundell took the men down into the hold, he had them feel Mr. Gnarles's special plank for themselves. They touched it. There was no explanation for it other than what Arundell probably told them. I say, I would probably have joined them too, had Mr. Gnarles not taken us aside that day. Thank heavens for that!" The barrister was amused.

Moore paced the deck of the aftcastle, mulling the situation over.

He realized the other four men had no idea what he, Heart, and Mr. Gnarles were talking about. It was time to tell everyone aboard what this voyage was really about. He told the men they were searching for a place called the Shallow Temple. Before they could react or complain, Heart then revealed to Moore the admiralty knew the whole story before they left London. They were being followed. Another betrayal! This was too much for Moore. He wanted to attack Heart. Heart then told the small group; he had a signal flare to use when he needed assistance from the Royal Navy. He explained he could signal them to call for help. The remaining crew could transfer as soon as the ship caught up to them. Safe passage back to England for whoever wanted to leave the ship's company.

Moore had only one question. He asked Gnarles.

"Can we sail this ship on our own?"

A thoughtful glance back at Moore, before he answered.

"I would have to refit an extension from the rudder that bypasses the tiller and whipstaff. We can use both those instruments on the exterior of the bulkhead, so the helm will not be hidden below decks, eliminating the need for two people to steer the ship. The old tiller could be refitted as an attachment from the rudder to extend straight up the exterior aft bulkhead to the aftcastle rail where I can attach the former whipstaff as the new exterior tiller. I think our only difficulty will occur when we have to enter and navigate the Straits of Magellan. After, we will be home free."

This turned out to be true.

Moore wanted Heart to leave with the rest of the crew. Heart argued they would no longer be in jeopardy of being noticed by any spies once the remainder of the crew returned to England. He apologized profusely for not believing John Moore. He said he had no doubts about anything now that he had met Mr. Gnarles. He said he would leave the ship if Moore absolutely said so.

Moore knew he needed this man and that knowledge was instrumental in his decision. "You can stay. The rest of you must return to England."

It took a day for the Navy to reach them. Heart accompanied the four men to give the captain sealed dispatches with information about the mutiny and reports regarding their mission for the Admiralty. He paid the men their wages, took his leave and returned to the *Venus*.

Finally, they were on their own.

Thirty days had passed since they entered the Pacific Ocean. The small group was beginning to show signs of despair; the men grew despondent. There was the added stress of Moore being unable to trust Heart.

The children began to voice their worries about leaving home. Although they had Gnarles with them, none of them were sure they would ever see the mysterious island that was home to the Shallow Temple. What if they couldn't find it? What next?

Moore could not return to England without giving his message to the leader of the wave rider tribe even though one of the tribe members was on board. Gnarles was perplexed also; he was stuck aboard the ship with them.

The usual routine for the day began with assigned duties and chores. The same as they had for the past 113 days, since hoisting anchor in Trinidad. The days were long, hot and dry. They encountered no danger since rounding the Horn.

There was something different in the air on that day of change. It conjured up a feeling of positive energy in John Moore, who remarked, "This is the day, I can feel it in my bones."

His good humor was contagious and a mood of well-being spread to everyone on board.

"I know we are close, Heart. Mr. Gnarles, let's have another look at the chart!"

Jane and Sid were below playing in their cabin. Gnarles stepped down into the narrow companion way to retrieve the chart from an overhead locker near the children's cabin. They watched him as he rifled through some papers and located the chart. They ran out to him as he went up the companionway, he turned his head and gave the children a smile.

"Not now, little ones. We shall play cards after I give these notes to your uncle. We are going to estimate our approximate location and compare it to where we think we our destination is."

Gnarles thought he left the children behind as he made his way above, but they followed right behind him. Heart joined Moore at the aft castle. Gnarles spread the map out on the deck where all three could see well enough to check their progress according to the chart.

Heart looked around, his senses picking up abnormal changes in the surface of the ocean and in the atmosphere. Moore's eyes were fixed on the chart.

Gnarles excused himself to check the lines.

"From what I make of it, the island should appear soon, Heart."

Heart was mesmerized by the ocean behind Moore. Sid took one glance in the direction Heart was occupied with and decided to go below, straight to his cabin. The men were too occupied to notice Sid's rapid departure, or that Jane had made her way forward of the main mast, to sit in the sun.

"Yes, Moore. Although, I have to admit, I feel rather apprehensive about it."

"Really, Heart? What's wrong?"

Heart could not take his eyes off the movement on the ocean all about the ship. He cleared his throat in order to get his words out.

"Have you noticed, there is only a slight breeze that is barely filling the sails, yet we are starting to make way at a rather highly increased rate of speed?"

"You are finally getting the hang of it, Heart. I didn't notice, but you are right. Perhaps we are in some sort of current."

Moore was facing forward towards the bow, opposite the direction of Heart's gaze.

"You are correct, in a sense, Moore. It's causing me some worry. My, my, it has been some time since I've been in such a state, quite so."

Heart's thoughts were engaged with the great mass of water slowly gathering speed as it grew. Were he and Moore talking about the same thing?

"I can only pray, dear fellow, this doesn't give you too much cause to worry. It is this very nature of things that I explained to you when I first told you about the Traveler; this mystery we are involved in."

"I see now, I certainly do see. I will try to remain calm."

"Good on you, Heart, that's the spirit."

Jane was at peace and happy. She saw the remarkable wave that was forming behind them and it really didn't seem to bother her. Her attention jumped to the forward starboard side. She yelled out.

"Uncle John, look! An island! Over there, I see an island!"

Moore heard her shout. He forgot about everything; Sid, Jane, Heart and Gnarles. He clamored about to get a better view of where Jane indicated the island was.

"By heavens, she is right! There is an island, Heart! Have a look!"

"Incredible, absolutely astounding!"

Heart's voice sounded distant.

"Mr. Heart, you are looking in the wrong direction!"

In that instant, Moore realized that the boat was being lifted and it felt like the surface of the water was dropping away, producing an incline getting steeper by the second.

At last, he understood what Louis Heart was raving about. Every hair on Moore's body stood on end. He was stupefied by the monstrous wall of water.

Jane observed Mr. Gnarles who had taken her uncle's Traveler. What was he was doing? The board, now free from the lines that secured it for so long was in the hands of its brother. Jane continued to watch the Gnar set the board down on the forward portside deck. Gnarles didn't know Jane watched him. He went aft to tell the men he was going to return the Traveler to the temple.

Meanwhile, Jane sat down on the Traveler, her legs crossed comfortably without a care in the world.

"That wave is monstrous! We have to come about!"

"I doubt sir, we have little enough time for a prayer!"

"Heart, the children! Where is Jane? Bloody hell! She was here only a moment ago! Where did our pilot disappear to?"

Moore spotted the Gnar coming aft toward him, who turned around abruptly.

Heart shouted, "I'm going below to find the children! Godspeed, Moore!"

Heart went below where Sid was alone in the children's cabin. He held onto him, trying to comfort him; Moore stayed where he had to be, at the helm. Desperately looking about the ship for Jane, his eyes followed Gnarles, hurrying forward, when he spotted her sitting on the Traveler! It was impossible to retrieve her without leaving the tiller and jeopardizing the safety of the ship, and every soul on board. He yelled as loud as he could.

"Mr. Gnarles, grab my niece! Save her!"

The Traveler was near the forward rail, leaning over the edge of the bulkhead. Moore screamed at the top of his voice for Jane to jump off the Traveler and for Gnarles to bring her back to him. He watched in horror; the Traveler seemed to leap off the deck of the ship on its own…Jane sitting on top of it! The Traveler moved to position itself alongside the ship, maneuvering into the slot of the gigantic wave while Jane was beyond her uncle's pleas.

"Great God, no! Jane, hold on to the Traveler no matter what! Don't let go of the Traveler!"

Gnarles was over the rail already, diving into the face of the monstrous wave. He popped up next to the Traveler and effortlessly climbed on top of it and it started to race downward, gaining momentum. Jane briefly caught her uncle with the strangest look on his face. The smile she returned to him was one he would never forget.

She sat there on the Traveler as casually as she would on a carpet, in a lotus position, with her little legs folded in front of her. Gnarles stood behind her on the Traveler. The last thing Moore saw of them, Jane was sitting just beneath and forward of Gnarles. The Traveler screamed down the face of the enormous wall of water.

The ship was moving at an incredible rate of speed and the wave started to pitch out over all of them. Jane and Gnarles disappeared out toward the opposite end of that great tunnel, underneath the lip of falling water that Moore was trying to avoid. With no chance of exit and speeding through a huge hole in the ocean, all he could do was try to hold the caravel on an even keel and look at the glorious sight of flying through the portal of the most enormous barrel he had ever seen.

Heart was below sheltering Sid with his large body. Sid couldn't have moved if he wanted to. Moore's excited shouts turned into a different exhilarating sound. Heart felt a wave of energy emanating throughout his body; What a sensation! Did he turn into liquid? He wondered if Sid felt it too?

"Steady, Moore, hold on! I have Master Sidney, Moore, hold on!"

INTERLUDE: THE SHALLOW TEMPLE

Master Drummer relayed Master Shaper's message to Master Carver and Master Flow, who immediately began to prepare for any emergency they might encounter out in the water. Master Drummer rejoined the troupe out on the beach, leaving Master Flow and Master Cylinder to their warmup exercises. They would be ready when they paddled into the epic swell called by the drums.

Word spread through the temple like wildfire, monks and novitiates were making their way down to the beach in small groups. The air was punctuated with excited conversations and predictions about the great event scheduled for that afternoon. Most of them were aware that Master Caver and Master Flow had their Travelers with them and were getting ready to paddle out.

The temple community was under the impression they were going to have the pleasure of witnessing a rare demonstration of surfing prowess by two of the more accomplished masters of big wave surfing. No one was going to miss this show!

Outside, cloudbreak sets were maxing at 40 plus feet, yet the wave-callers continued the beat. The on-going percussion caused the wave size to increase. Things started happening fast!

The crowd on the beach was so focused on the huge waves, Master Carver and Master Flow slipped into the water unseen. Somebody spotted them and yelled, "Look, there they are, almost halfway out!"

A different voice shouted!

"I don't understand it! Check the outside! There's a ship or something headed straight into the impact zone!"

The spectacle unfolding in front of the Shallow Temple gripped them all with suspense and disbelief. Many who gathered on the beach that day assumed disaster was about to occur. A Traveler leaped from the vessel and someone was sitting on it! The moment arrived with an occasion far greater for viewing than everyone previously imagined.

The crowd roared! Someone else dived off the boat and climbed on the Traveler. A little girl sat there as if glued to the board. They were accelerating at terrific speed; the wave jacked up when it hit the reef of the perfect wave. The man positioned the Traveler along the face of the wave, underneath the lip. There was a moment of hushed silence on the beach, even the drummers had stopped.

Everyone's focus turned to the boat heading away from the point in an unbelievable barrel. The surfer and girl on the Traveler went left in one direction; the boat on that same monster went right in the opposite direction.

The throng on the water's edge oohed when the lip pitched out over the entire ship going right and the tiny pair on the Traveler going left. All disappeared behind the immense curtain of water and the wave broke.

Master Carver and Master Flow appeared on both sides of the man and his companion. The three Travelers faded away from the huge wall of white water and emerged from behind the stupendous onslaught. The impact of the breaking wave shot foam a hundred feet up and out, making them look like miniscule dots. Bouncing and leaping against the backdrop of that mountainous turbulence behind them, the Travelers raced out in front of the soup towards the safety of the channel.

The ship was gone!

Master Cylinder was talking story with Master Shaper. He was on Earth especially for Gnarles's return to the temple. He excused himself early from a council on Nalu because he was not going to miss this. He planned to be in the water himself had there been time for him to prepare.

He was pleased with the protection provided for the arrival of a very important little girl.

He was further gratified that Gnarles returned to the temple safely, his mission accomplished.

Master Cylinder's belief in the Shoal prince, as the only one who could have completed those tasks, brought an immense feeling of love, pride and respect for the great Katana and future Shallow Master.

He commented to Master Shaper, "The Travelers do not forget water conditions, do they? Behold the ordinary! An examination of the ordinary illuminates the extraordinary."

"Ahh yes, Master Cylinder, an astute observation."

"We both know beings who inhabit water planets can't afford to lose consciousness of the spiritual nature of water. It is the element directly related to the development of all life forms and therein, creating environmental systems to sustain those life forms. It's tragic the Martians lost sight of the elemental nature of water, corrupting themselves with greed. They putrefied their water systems, introducing toxins and waste into their seas without remorse. They destroyed the very soul of their planet."

"This is why we are here, is it not my lord? Behold the natural. For it is within the natural that you shall participate in the supernatural!"

"A brilliant meditation, Master Shaper. It gives me hope, knowing the information we have garnered can be shared when those who will join us to continue our work. The meditations recorded in the book, such as the one you just mentioned, will have considerable impact on those students who were present here today. It was a perfect living example for them and it was you who was responsible for putting it into their minds. A wondrous way to instruct, I commend you."

The monks placed their attention back on Master Carver, Master Flow, Gnarles, and Jane, paddling towards shore. It wasn't until they arrived on the beach, that the students became aware of Master Cylinder's presence. The buzz of their conversations ceased altogether.

They watched him wade out to meet Gnarles and the young girl, who rode the largest wave any of them had ever seen. Every person there was in awe of the surfer who delivered the child safely to the Shallow Temple. It was a great surprise when they recognized him. It was their classmate, Gnarles!

Master Cylinder embraced Gnarles, something no one had ever seen the master do. He bent over to lift Jane up off the Traveler, and held her close. She whispered something that came to her while riding the enormous wave.

Waving his free hand to the entire group, whose rapt attention was focused on Gnarles and the young girl, the great monk introduced Jane with his special *'voice.'*

"Behold everyone, I present to you, Marina Clearwater!"

Shouts of welcome burst out on the beach and everybody gathered round to say hello to the newest member of the temple. The green flash blinked, the pale green sky turned dark blue and the bright evening stars sparkled above the procession of students and monks going back up to the temple. The ship was all but forgotten.

EARTH: DOWN MEXICO WAY

Months had passed since their last trip south of the border. The call to go back and surf primo waves, appreciate the uncrowded conditions and discover a new all-time surf spot to rave about on their return, was irresistible.

A surfer from across the street stopped by to borrow some wax. The boys were out on the sundeck getting gear together for another adventure in Mexico. He asked Wally if he wasn't afraid of getting arrested again. It was the way Wally laughed at the guy, as if it was the stupidest question he ever heard, embarrassing him and ultimately, pissing him off. He split without the wax, yelling out a special curse for Wally.

"I hope they bust your dumb ass again, and throw away the key!"

Wally continued laughing at the guy. He told his roommates, "People like that never learn."

Wally could care less that he wound up in jail on the last trip and understood that it didn't matter if he ended up behind bars down there again. Wally believed in the here and now; living in the moment. He figured if you were the type of person who stopped going someplace because of an unfortunate experience from the past, out of fear of the same thing repeating itself, then you probably didn't learn from your mistake in the first place. It wouldn't matter where you went, the fact remained that you were still the same imbecile who ended up behind bars where ever you went, anyway.

"That's why I laughed at him so hard," Wally explained, "The guy is a moron."

Lester joined them on the deck.

"Synchronize your chronometers, gentlemen."

The other three nodded their heads in unison, looking at their wrists as though they wore watches, examining their wrists for the time. Lester was the only one wearing a watch.

"Is the emergency duffel bag packed? Wax? Wine? Mesquito nets?"

Preacher answered Lester while Sow and Wally continued to nod their heads.

"Yep, yep, yep, and yep!"

"Preacher, got the cash? Sow, got the stash? Wally, tent, sleeping bags and extra blankets?"

The exuberant head nodding continued as the surfers stood up and shimmied out the door, down the stairs, skank lining out to Lester's woody. Four tail blocks were sticking out of the rear window opening, two skegs up and two skegs down.

Wally yelled at his pals.

"Hey, we have to split over to PCH, first."

They followed Wally down to highway 101, where he stopped, bent down off the side of the road and dug up some sand crabs for the four of them. He told Sow, Lester and Preacher to each take one. They copied Wally, knelt down at the edge of the highway waiting for the occasional traffic spurts to disappear. They placed their crabs on the ground facing the ocean on the opposite side of the road and Wally announced.

"The first crab across PCH gets the first wave of the day!"

The last of the cars passed and the surfers readied their crabs, focusing their attention on the squirming little critters. The empty road gave Wally his cue.

"They're off!"

The surfers released their crabs and Sow screamed at his crab to go faster and Wally cheered, "Go, go, go!"

Preacher screamed, "More cars are coming!"

Lester shouted. "Mine is winning!"

He was right only for that split second. The cars came and went in a crunch. Thwop, thwack, fwhup; cracked crab a la tarmac. Sow's crab survived, making it to the other side.

They didn't realize Wally's idea was an event of epic proportions, marking the dawn of a new era. The first "Sacrifice for Surf." The surf trip was officially underway. Bitchen!

They hooted all the way back to the woody. Wally yelled shotgun. He would be in charge of radio until the next person claimed the cherished seat. Lester started the engine, drove the woody along the canal, made a left turn, crossed the narrow bridge and came to a stop at the highway. One more left turn onto PCH and he headed south. There was a new wine shop at Dana Point that sold a fine dry muscat for a reasonable price. Beer and wine were preferred to the drinking water in Mexico, and they had Red Mountain for partying.

Les noticed the woody needed gas, so they stopped to fill the tank. No problem! The price of gas was 26 cents a gallon. That was the beauty of living in Southern California, so close to the international border. A tank of gas got you into a different country to surf and back again for less than five bucks.

SURF FU

Sow took over shotgun after a quick go out at Poche'. He maintained his seat until they made it to Mexico. It was noon by the time they crossed the border. They took a vote on whether they should stop at the Long Bar to quench their thirst and smartly elected to move on; the surfers knew their bad habits too well. Their agenda would change after they entered the Long Bar. One beer would lead to another, those beautiful Mexican senoritas would appear, day would turn into night.

Tijuana night spots would call, they would want to see what raunchy entertainment the Blue Fox had to offer. All their money would disappear, someone might get popped and end up in the Tijuana jail. The surf trip would be over without even one glance towards the huge waves at the Tijuana Sloughs, or the mackers rolling in along Rosarita Beach.

Instead, they stopped at a liquor store. Lester went inside with Wally and bought two cases of Carta Blanca, two styrofoam coolers and a couple blocks of ice. They returned to the woody, and Sow told his friends he had stashed two six-packs of green ones somewhere in the back. "Maybe Wally should put a couple of those bottles under ice too."

Lester found the quickest route out of town and Sow turned on the radio. He moved the tuner band, seeking out the only station available for sounds south of the border, other than the fine Mexican music. He zeroed in on the Wolfman! Sow leaned back knowing that the audio radiance for this radio audience would be very cool indeed. "All right, Baby!"

There was no wind; the sky was cloudless. Days like this in Mexico were scorchers. One could see heat waves rising out of the road in the distance, creating melting road mirages. They reached the end of the paved road a few kilometers past San Miguel and before Three M's.

The cervecas were ice cold and the surfers were ready for some thirst quenchers. Bumps and holes permeated the surface of the dry dirt road, that otherwise provided a pretty smooth ride as long as you avoided them. Lester was a good driver and navigated most of the bad passages by just pulling off to one side or the other, using an alternate trail until it was best to get back on the main path. Those times that he did hit something, the four heads inside the woody would rise up and bang the roof in unison.

The woody looked like a wild animal during those moments bucking up off the land and touching down in a great cloud of dust, bursting into the air around it. Wally passed everybody a beer and as each bottle cracked open, the suds blew up out of them imitating the billowing clouds of dust outside,

Lester was hauling ass to make it in time for the evening glass-off. It wasn't far now, but Les was not about to slow down. He knew they had to set up camp and have it done before they went out; they would not leave the water until dark.

Lester turned onto the beach access trail that would take them down to the new surf spot they discovered on their last exploration. Wally got a view of the water. He could see some pretty decent surf and a mad grin appeared on his face, stretching ear to ear. Sow saw Wally's face and he knew.

Lester parked where they would make their camp. It was quiet enough to hear the waves the second the engine shut off. They spilled out of the woody to stretch their arms and legs before trudging up over a small dune to see if what Wally glimpsed was true. Sow ran back to get his board.

One by one, heads appeared over the rise of the dune. The waves were epic and the conditions couldn't be better. Lines were marching in from the horizon and the surf was a solid four to six feet.

Only a hint of an off-shore breeze from out of the desert, cooled the afternoon down, adding the perfect touch to those glassy sets rolling in one after another. The others chased after Sow, to grab their boards, unpack some of their gear and change into their surf shorts. They were all sporting new canvas trunks they bought from a woman they met in Surfside. She set up business next to Crow's shop. Crow was a trip! As far as anybody being in the know about contemporary ideas and changes in surfboard design, it was Crow. Sow said he saw him the day before they left for Mexico and he was busy hiding his new laminated skeg designs.

One look at his friends told Lester the campsite wasn't going to get set up until they finished surfing. The others disappeared back over the dune and were probably paddling out by now. He located the Coleman lantern and set it down under the rear of the woody and hit it for the waves. He hollered at his friends.

"All right porpoise lips, who has the wax?"

Wally, turned to look at Sow.

"Soooow?"

Sow replied to Wally.

"Waaaally?"

Lester was impatient.

"Tell me it ain't! We walked all the way out here and no one brought wax?"

He was looking down at his board, working this over in his head. Sow and Wally were showing Preacher the two fresh bars of paraffin they had purposely hidden from Lester, to piss him off for fun. Wally laughed at Lester.

"It ain't!"

Preacher's smile turned into a grin as he looked on. Sow called out to Lester.

"Ain't not!"

Wally made a loud coughing sound, followed by another throat clearing noise. He spit on Lester's board. Thwopp! Fritters of laughter from Lester's roommates. He spied the gob on his board. He couldn't help it; he started chuckling too. He knew what he would see when he looked up. Each of them had a bar of wax in their hands. Wally had the extra bar for Lester.

Lester threw some sand on the gob, turning it into a pasty. This was the simple way to remove Wally's gift. Lester knocked the pasty into the sand and all four of them looked at it thinking the same thing.

Preacher had met a pretty, tall, lanky surfer girl at the Rendezvous and brought her back to the Pink Party Pad. He introduced her to his roommates and in turn, they all became good friends. She was the one who showed them how to make a pasty; that's why they named her, Pasty! The moment Lester made the pasty, each one of them thought, *"I wish she was here."*

They were all bent over their boards waxing them furiously, stopping at the same time to look at one another. Nobody said a word. Smiling, they knew the same thought was going through the paces in each one of their horny minds.

They scrambled into the water, kneeled on their surfboards and paddled out. Sow may have won the crab first wave contest, but being the strongest, he paddled hard to get outside and catch the first wave, contest or no contest. This was always the best. The other three would hold back to watch Sow's wave. They could see him stroking into a wall and dropping in. Sow knew they were watching him and that turned up his stoke.

He flew down the face of the wave, powered a bottom turn, launching past the exploding foam. He charged underneath a section and found a little barrel. Out in front of the shoulder, he cut back, turned and casually walked up to the nose for five. He stood on the nose for a few more seconds, stepped back, cutback and stalled while the inside wall jacked up. He was coming down on his friends who were hooting for his classic first wave of the day.

He raced by in front of them, dropped his shorts around his ankles, and threw a B.A. They roared at his ugly butt display. The group's sense of humor was an experiment in what was allowable. They were in their element.

"Yeeaahh Sow!"

"All right Sow! You'll need your mouth washed out with soap, after a dirty crack like that!"

Lester and Preacher began paddling past the impact zone and Les leaned over to tell Preacher he saw a bigger wave way outside.

"Check the cloudbreak, Preach! Bitchen!"

There was no way a wave that size could be showing itself! They watched the monster outside jack-up. Wally was a short distance behind them, looking to see how far Sow rode that first wave inside to know where to exit when he caught one.

The wave was so big even Preacher could see it.

"What a Bitchen wave! Lester, can you tell the size of that sucker?"

"It's really big, Preach, check it out!"

Lester was pointing at the gigantic wave. It was transforming into a much larger wave. The surfers tried positioning themselves to get a better view. It didn't make any difference to nearsighted Preacher, who always needed glasses for his terrible vision. The water was the only place he was comfortable without them. *"I feel the water,"* but he still couldn't see diddley when he surfed.

Lester described a wild image to Preacher,

"It's outrageous, Preach! A wooden ship!"

The vessel looked to have been built in a different era, exploding out of the enormous barrel, exiting up over the shoulder.

"That wave was bigger than anything I've ever seen."

Lester watched intently. The boat, at least that's what Lester made her out to be, made it up and out the back of the wave. It sat in the safety of deeper water far beyond the outside reefs. After that monster, things started to settle.

"I don't believe it. We're in for it, now." Lester sagely remarked.

From what little action Preacher saw, he also, was visibly moved.

"Did I really see that? This blows my mind!"

Lester was ecstatic. Both he and Preacher were ramping it up!

"Bitchen! Sow, Wally! Come out here! Did you see it?"

Wally paddled out to see what they were yelling about. He noticed a boat floating easily outside. He paddled for a wave.

"Hey, don't lose it. It ain't like a Mexican fishing boat. Like I've never seen one. Never! Not!"

Disregarding their calls, he paid them no further mind, gliding into a hot glassy bump. He caught a perfect wave, thinking this is what his pals should be paying attention to. He didn't know Lester and Preacher were in a trance, paddling out to the vessel that had just appeared out of nowhere, right in front of their eyes.

EARTH: MEXICO

John Moore was perplexed, looking out to sea where he thought the island he just saw was supposed to be. Heart came up from the companionway holding Sid to his chest, the danger passed.

"You did it, Moore! You saved us!"

Yes, Moore had somehow brought them through it all, alive. Obviously, they were no longer in the middle of the ocean. They had no idea where they were or how they got there.

Sidney squirmed to get down. Heart let him loose; he scanned the deck for any sign of his sister. His heart told him he would not find her and as her twin, he physically felt their separation. He knew she was gone.

He said softly, "Jane is not here."

Moore, in his shocked state, called her name out, although he knew she went on the Traveler with Gnarles. "Jane…Jane."

"Jane is not here!" Sid shouted.

"I don't see her, Moore. She wasn't with us in the children's cabin."

Sidney screamed, "She is not here! Jane is gone!"

The men looked down at Sid, who had stopped yelling. He sank to the deck, alone in his grief. It all came back to Moore, the look Jane gave him as she sped off in the brilliant sea tunnel with Gnarles, who commandeered the Traveler along that spectacular mass of water. He vaguely recalled his own experience at the tiller, instinctively holding the ship in the wave as it raced toward the opening tunnel and beyond.

Moore experienced something inside that huge portal; some sort of travel through an energy mass he felt! *"Did everything turn into water, even me?"* His recollection of what happened seemed real and instant. *"That was not a day dream."*

All aboard *Venus* were lost in their own thoughts. No one saw Lester and Preacher paddling out to them. Lester could see the looks of anguish on the faces of the three people on board the ancient wooden ship. He could only imagine the circumstances that put them in that situation. He thought it was probably because the ride they just had was so hairy.

They reached the ship and Lester hailed the men on deck.

"Ahoy, captain of the ship! You have accomplished the impossible!"

Lester's surf intellect took over.

"That was totally bitchen! Where is the takeoff spot out there? How did you ever manage to pull into that wave? What made you do it?"

Preacher, added, "Lester's right, man, you made that wave! That was too much. In fact, that was the bitchenest thing I've ever seen, that was all-time! You are Captain Hair Balls!"

Moore snapped out of his reverie, not believing his eyes or his ears.

"You are on Travelers? You speak English? Where did you come from? Are you members of the wave riders tribe?"

"I don't think we're your version, Captain Balls." Preacher replied.

Lester explained, "We speak American English," and then he asked, "What kind of tribe are you looking for?"

"He said wave riding Les, wave riding. Let Captain Balls know we're surfers who want to join his tribe."

Sow ended his first ride on the inside and kicked out in time to see the old wooden ship exiting the tube. He started scratching as fast as he could to get out there with Lester and Preacher. Wally was on the nose of his board, nonchalantly hanging 10, arms casually hung by his side and totally immersed in his ride. In a flash, Wally cutback and aimed right at Sow. Sow urged Wally to kick out of the wave.

"Wally, come on! You gotta come and see this! Lester and Preacher are already out there! It's insane!"

Wally pulled out of the wave, exiting smoothly over the shoulder with enough momentum to glide over near Sow and paddle alongside his friend.

"This had better be good, Sow. I was just setting up for an inside juice hole."

"Wally. I swear to God! What I just saw was totally bitchen! That old wooden ship roared out of the biggest barrel!"

"Yes, of course it did, Sow. I'm sure it's probably Peter Surfing Pan, come looking for his shadow again."

"I ain't lying, Wally, let's get out there!"

Wally and Sow watched someone drop a rope ladder over the rail. Lester started climbing the ladder and stopped halfway up the exterior hull. Preacher handed him his board and Lester passed it on to someone on deck. After Preacher relayed his board, they both climbed on deck.

Wally and Sow started paddling faster, they didn't want to miss out on anything. They thought maybe the cold ones were getting busted out. They reached the ship and Preacher stuck his head over the rail and grinned down at them.

"Did you guys see it? It was so righteous."

"Hey, Preach, like don't flip out." Wally continued with the Peter Pan metaphor.

"It's not like you've never seen an old wooden boat. Like never, not the Petrus."

"Toss the ladder, Preach."

Preacher dropped the rope ladder over the side.

"Here you go, Sow. Did you see it?"

"Yeah, I saw it, Preach. It was all-time, but Wally didn't and he doesn't believe it. I tried telling him, but he thinks it's a put on."

The boards and Sow were on deck. Wally was last, hesitating at the base of the ladder, pleading.

"Shmeee! Shmeeeee! Pull me up! The ticking! I hear the ticking! It's getting closer! Shmeee!"

"Who is that? Who is yelling like that?" Sid ran to the railing, his head popped out over the edge, to peek down at Wally.

"Is that you Pan? Not! It ain't the Petrus Panus!"

Sid wasn't sure if the person on the ladder was talking to him. Wally climbed aboard and everyone but Moore sat on the aftcastle deck staring at each other. Moore looked over the surfboards, searching for the Shallow Temple Crest. He couldn't find any!

"Heart! These people are imposters; they are not members of the wave rider tribe. See to it they depart at once. These are not real Travelers."

Moore had Preacher's board in his hands. It was the first one he tossed over the side, into the water. He leaned over to grab Sow's board and repeat what he just did, but Preacher was already up and on the larger man. He shoved Moore from behind, sending him sprawling on the deck.

"Hey, asshole! What do you think you think you're doing?"

Moore jumped up, grabbed hold of Preacher and lifted him up to throw him in the water.

For the first time, Moore saw the Mexican coastline. He stared in disbelief, astonished he and his ship were no longer in the middle of the ocean. This was beyond his grasp. He set Preacher down, who immediately dove off the boat to retrieve his board, pulled himself up on it and paddled away.

Wally and Lester called for him. Preacher flipped them the bird without looking back. He caught a pretty good wave and worked his way to the inside barrel. Sid watched Preacher in amazement, forgetting about everything. Sid remembered the liquid feeling that went through his body when *Venus* traveled through time. He wanted to ride on a wave. Heart was there at his side. "It's time for your nap Master Sidney."

He tried to take hold of Sid's hand but Sid refused to leave. He was going to stay right there and watch the surf.

Moore, mesmerized by the sight of land, uttered, "Where are we?"

"Not we butt breath. Where are you. Adios."

Sow was really angry with Moore, and was not about to explain anything to him. He did take the time to tell Moore he should have never touched Preacher's board. Preacher was not done with the man on the boat. Sow was the only one who could calm him down, make a joke of it. The good surf would help. It was a very bad sign Preacher flipping him off. It meant no playing fair.

Sow took his board and lowered it to the water. Lester spoke up.

"Hey Sow, try and get Preacher back here will you?"

Wally walked past Moore, put his board under his arm, gave Moore the finger and jumped off the boat.

Wally waited, calling Lester.

"Let's go Lester, Pan or no Pan."

"Wally! Something heavy is going on here. Don't you guys split without me! Tell Preacher and Sow, Captain Hairballs wants to apologize. If you decide not to paddle back out, wait for me."

Wally could see Preacher and Sow surfing primo waves, shredding them. He stroked over to his friends as fast as he could. Lester scanned the waves, torn between surfing, or staying on board to learn more about these strange dudes. Moore stood there motionless, not knowing where he was or what was happening to him. He searched for the right words.

"I didn't stop to think we were so close to land, even when I saw you paddling to us. I have offended you and your friends after inviting you aboard my ship. I..."

"You really pissed them off is what you did, but they'll get over it. It's no big thing. Don't sweat it, worse things have happened. You shouldn't have put your hands on Preacher's surfboard. You're damn lucky Preacher stopped you from tossing Sow's board in. It would've been all over."

Moore could not comprehend what Lester was talking about. He did grasp certain words because they were a type of English, albeit sub-standard and bastardized. It was spoken so fast; with a different cadence. He couldn't get the gist of the surfer's jargon.

"Pissed them off? Don't sweat it? All over?"

"You were begging for it. Even though you are bigger than Preacher, he simply doesn't care. And, he's nothing compared to Sow. If you don't set things straight with Preacher, he is capable of doing something really shitty to get even with you for tossing his board off your ship."

Moore was miserable. Not only lost, he had no idea he traveled to the future. Jane was gone, and he had made enemies with the first people he had come in contact with. He remembered Heart and Sidney. He walked past Lester to look down the companionway below the aftcastle. He could see that Heart had finally put Sid to sleep.

Heart nodded to Moore, who went back above to talk with Lester.

"First, I offer my deepest apologies to you. Please, allow me to introduce myself. I am John Thomas Moore, master shipwright at Land's End, Cornwall, England. I am in the company of my nephew Sidney, and my business associate Mr. Louis Heart. We set sail from Cornwall, one hundred and eighty-nine days ago, in the year of our Lord, 1771 and the 11th year of the reign of His Majesty, George the Third."

Lester started going off the rails hearing what Moore said. He put his hands up to interrupt Moore.

"Hold it right there, captain! What year did you say?"

"The year of His Majesty, George the Third, in the year of our Lord, 1771."

"Did you bang your head, man? I'm here to tell you that you are off by a couple hundred years. You are in the 20th century, Captain Hairballs! The year is 1962."

"Surely, sir, you jest! Heart!"

Heart had almost dropped off to sleep with Sidney, despite all the commotion, he was exhausted. He arrived above deck and Moore questioned him.

"Heart, would you please tell this gentleman what year this is?'

"Certainly, Moore. Sir, this is the year of our Lord, 1771."

"Both you guys banged your heads!"

It hit Lester like a bolt of lightning. He instinctively knew something cosmic happened the moment the ship appeared out of the tube. At first, he didn't think their clothing was authentic, now it was serious and his attitude changed toward these voyagers. He apologized to the two lost souls standing in front of him.

"You fellows really don't know what has happened to you, do you?"

Lester explained slowly.

"Your ship now lies off the west coast of continental North America. That land in front of you was once known as Nueva Espana or New Spain. The Spanish have been here for centuries and this country is now called, Mexico. Perhaps you know of Sir Francis Drake and New Albion, which is further north of here."

Sow, Preacher and Wally were back, calling for Lester.

"Lester, the waves are really bitchen! Wally and Sow said Captain Hairballs has something to say to me and it better be good."

Lester held Moore back from the rail, to coach him on what he should tell his friends.

"Don't be offended by the name Preacher has given you. It's a compliment. Don't call him sir, that will piss him off even more. Say something like, hey, Preacher, I'm sorry for grabbing your board without asking. That will work fine; keep it simple."

Moore nodded his head and walked slowly to rail, expecting foul looks, thinking they would be angry with him. He was surprised to see them laughing and goofing with each other. Their anger had all but disappeared because of the great waves they were catching. When he spoke, it felt like he was talking in a foreign tongue.

"Hey, Preacher, I'm sorry for grabbing your Trav… your surfboard, without your permission. It was a fool's mistake."

That was all Preacher needed, just as Lester had predicted.

"Everything's copacetic, Captain Hairballs, let's forget it happened."

The mood the surfers were in was contagious. Their good vibe reminded Moore of Gnarles. Moore began to loosen up. Reminded of the night he and Carder talked about fate and destiny, he couldn't explain it; he felt these surfers were people he was supposed to meet.

"Would you gentlemen care to come aboard? I believe it is time we made proper introductions."

Heart dropped the rope ladder down for the boys to come aboard; Lester relayed the three surfboards up to Moore. They assembled on the forward deck and Lester had to warn his buddies.

"These guys are formal, calling each other by their last names, but were gonna have to change all that, eventually. The captain here is Mr. John Moore. That big dude over there is his business associate, Mr. Louis Heart. All right then! Moore, Heart, these are my best friends and roommates, Preacher, Sow and Skinny Wally.

"We are honored to meet you, gentlemen. If it's permissible I would like to ask you some questions,"

"There aren't any real rules, Mr. Moore, you don't have to ask permission to speak, but sometimes it's better to hold your mud and not interrupt. When its obvious, certain things aren't done."

"Yeah, like messing…"

"Cool it, Preach, it's over."

"Sorry, sometimes I can't resist. Besides, I get envious, man. How did you manage to get in that wave?"

"Mr. Lester er, I mean Lester here, thinks Heart and I have banged our heads. That monstrous wave brought us here, truth be told."

Moore elaborated, how he and Heart set sail from England on a quest to find the Shallow Temple. He told the surfers their quest had come to an abrupt halt, with their destination in view. He tried to reconstruct how he had come through a portal where time holds no barriers. He, his nephew, Louis Heart and the ship were living proof of this. He went on to explain the connection between the Traveler and Lt. Carder's great great-grandfather.

Heart told how he became involved with the quest. His former occupation, the king's coach, the murders, Lt. Carder's disappearance, and the search for a criminal named Ontez.

Finally, Moore answered Preacher's question of the great wave in front of the Shallow Temple. He explained how he lost his niece, his Traveler and the pilot, Mr. Gnarles, who they believed was a member of the wave rider tribe.

The surfers were in absolute awe of the men and what they had experienced. Everyone heard Sidney calling for his uncle John. Moore excused himself to go and get the boy. When he returned, he held Sidney in one arm, and a keg of Royal Navy rum under the other one.

Wally broke the ensuing silence.
"Not! It ain't Peter!
Then, Sow.
"Couldn't be the Panus!"
"What did I tell you Sow? Couldn't be Petrus Panus.
Lester interrupted. "Knock it off you two, this is serious."
"This is serious Lester, Pan lives!"
Preacher spied the rum container, "Check out the keg, Sow. I've never seen one like it."
Heart was more than ready for a grog ration.
"Good show, Moore, rather!"
Moore called everyone's attention to his nephew.
"Gentlemen, I would like to introduce you to my nephew, Master Sidney Alexander Moore, who..."
Still sad, Sid finished the sentence for Moore.
"We all know and love as Sid."
There was a good round of laughter. The surfers looked at Sid and cheered in one voice. "Sid!"

Their cheer actually made him feel happy! Sid spent a long time watching them riding waves today and he knew he wanted to ride waves too. He wiggled loose from his uncle's hold and went directly over to Sow, the one he watched the most. Sow smiled benevolently at the boy. Little kids were drawn to Sow because he loved little kids. He didn't care what anybody thought and he would play with them like he was one of them. They seemed to know this and gravitate to him.

Sid asked Sow, "Are you going to stay with us?"

"I'd like to, Sid, but we have to get back to our camp on the beach before it gets dark."

"Sow's right, we had better head in to collect some wood to start the fire. Hey, Captain Balls, do you guys want to come to our camp for something to eat?"

It was difficult for Moore to call people by their first names, it was simply not done where he came from. Although considered extremely bad form, he felt surprised that adjusting to some of the easy-going customs of these new acquaintances seemed to make him forget about Jane and Carder.

"I think we'd better stay on board tonight, thank you, Mr. Preacher."

"That's cool, Captain Balls! Let's hit it, you guys. Don't finish that keg without us, you two."

Lester grabbed his board along with his friends and turned to tell Moore and Heart.

"We have enough sunlight to make it back to our camp and get organized. You'll be able to see us from out here. We'll get up early, have a surf and then all of us can eat a good breakfast. We'll head back North in a few days, so we have plenty of time to help you make plans and consider your options. Sleep well, fellas, see you in the morning."

The four surfers dropped their boards into the water, diving in after them. They climbed on them and started paddling towards shore. Sow stopped to wave to Sid.

"I'll see you on the morning Sid! If your uncle says its o.k., I'll take you riding on my surfboard with me."

Sow told Sid earlier, to call him Sow and as he waved at Sow he yelled.

"Bye-Bye Mr. Sow. I will see you in the morning."

Moore put his hands on the rail and watched the surfers paddle towards the shore. They laughed as they splashed each other with water. The sun was gone and the twilight of this special evening gave Moore pause to think about everything that had happened. His mind reeled as the steady flow of recollections poured into his head. It seemed like only yesterday that he and Carder had found the Traveler. Then came the twins. The story from Carder's great great-grandfather about a different Traveler from a different time. Was Mr. Gnarles involved with that tale? Enter the navy, then Ontez, then Heart and Arnon.

Moore saw a campfire blazing on the shore. The surfer's voices and laughter carried out across the water to him. He wished he was over there laughing with them but his heart was heavy and he would not be good company. Was Jane safe? Moore shoved his fingers through his hair and rubbed his eyes,

"Wishing you were here, Carder."

Where was Lt. Philip Carder? Would they ever meet again? It was right then and there, Moore decided all that happened was not mere coincidence. There was a reason for all of these events and they were linked together. He would follow this path to the end no matter what; he would find the Shallow Temple.

EARTH, 18TH CENTURY: PRISONER OF THE RED TIDE

Carder had been drifting in and out of consciousness for weeks. Ontez had hit him hard enough to kill him, but instead, gave him a very serious concussion. It was extremely fortunate for Carder that he didn't slip into a coma and die. His good health and strong physical condition allowed him to be able to regain his senses. He took his time, examining events that took place since his kidnapping. He had been drugged many times.

He sensed there was someone else down in this filthy hold with him.

"Welly well, if it isn't his lordship makin' his return amongst the living. The captain declared you would make it back; odds had it among the crew you wouldn't."

Patch was going on about the crew's wager and Carder couldn't help but recognize his voice.

"You are the scum who had the woman."

"Ah, tis good of thee to have us remain in thy lordship's thoughts, but you must be careful not to be so brave in the company of our captain."

"Do you mean that scoundrel Ontez?"

"Now there goes thee, driftin' about. You had better hold your tongue, or perhaps it may be taken by the good captain's blade. There's but one captain of the *Red Tide*, your lordship, and it wouldn't be the likes of someone with the name Ontez."

"You have no idea who your captain really is, do you? Then and again, why should you?"

"Feelin' right smart about yourself, are you not, Mr. Philip Carder? Oh yes, says I. Knowin' is knowin' and I know all that needs to be known about you."

Patch wanted to show this arrogant Royal Navy officer that he knew a thing or two himself. He was on the verge of leaking information to Carder that would make things very dangerous for both of them if Ontez were to find out. Carder determined now was not the right time to egg Patch on. He would question Patch later, perhaps find out more about Ontez.

"Yes, I can imagine you know a great deal more than I…"

Suddenly, a hatch cover was removed and daylight poured into the dank, cramped quarters. A voice called out for Patch to come up on deck. A rope ladder was lowered down into the hold and Patch grabbed it to climb up. Carder tried to watch the man, but was forced to look away from the bright, piercing daylight. He rolled away into a shadow in order to glance up again. A shot rang out and Carder instinctively covered his head with his hands. Patch fell through the opening, landing on the wood floor with a great thud, his head just inches away from Carder's. He took his hand away and saw the gaping hole in Patch's forehead, one as big Patch's surprised open mouth.

Light beams streamed down into the hold and Carder heard that hideous voice.

"Now then Lieutenant, I hope this serves to explain why there will be no more mention of the name Ontez. I'm sure you understand."

The hatch cover slid back into place and darkness swirled around Carder, who slipped back into unconsciousness.

Carder awoke later in darkness and it was cooler in the hold. He waited for his eyes to focus, filling in the form of the dead man lying next to him. Rats were already nibbling on the corpse. Carder sat up and some of the rats fled. He decided he would search Patch's coat pockets; the remainder of the rats ran away. He reached into the deep pocket, startled to find a familiar chain and amulet. He pulled out his own golden necklace. Patch had robbed him while he lay there unconscious!

He checked the other pocket. Stuffed deep down inside, he was not surprised to find his copy of the navigator's chart location of the Shallow Temple. Carder assumed he was very lucky; Patch had not yet shown his loot to Ontez.

Carder heard the sounds of bare feet running towards the hatch cover above him. He flattened himself face down on the deck of the hold, back turned away from Patch, and pretended unconsciousness. The hatch cover slid open and a rope ladder was lowered back down into the hold. Two sailors climbed down; Carder could barely hear their whispers.

"Tis a waste of a good man here, Robert…" Carder recognized the voice of the other highwayman. To say Brass had changed was an understatement. Captain Bones and his henchmen Irwin and Wright, made Brass realize what evil was really all about. It was an eye-opening experience for Brass, witnessing what Irwin, Non-Ra's brother Ven-Ra, could do to a man. Due to those unearthly scenes, his terrible treatment of other people underwent a complete turn-about. Thomas Brass now hated violence.

"Aye, that it was, Tom. I liked old Patch, too. We shared some good times. I trust you Tom, enough to tell you the cap'n shouldn't a done this."

"Has there been any other talk?"

"Plenty o' whisperin. just like this, but nobody will say a word. Those other two, one of the three of them always seem to appear or be near..."

"Shhh. Someone is makin their way forward."

"You down there, what is taken ye?"

It was Mr. Irwin. Tom Brass signaled his mate to be quiet with a finger to his lips. He shouted up to Irwin.

"Patch here fell on top of the prisoner, Mr. Irwin. We was just checkin' to make sure he was still alive."

"The prisoner is no business of yours dead or alive. Let's have Patch up here now. The captain is callin' for every man on deck to hear his words over Mr. Patch, and then we'll have done with him."

"We secured a line so he can be hoisted up."

A different voice called down to the men in the hold.

"Throw that line up to me and be quick about it!"

The voice sent chills through the two sailors down in the hold. Every man aboard the ship feared and despised the captain's wicked first mate. Brotus Promo, known only as Mr. Wright, had made a name for himself for being a vicious, merciless cutthroat.

The other sailor in the hold with Brass, Robert Turnan, yelled up to the first mate.

"Here's the line, Mr. Wright."

Turnan threw the line into his waiting hands. As soon as he had a firm grip on the line, Wright yanked Patch up fast, as though he was weightless. Both sailors gasped at the speed of the ascending dead man. Patch's head cracked against the side of the opening as he was pulled through the hatch and out of sight. The laughter of the first mate made Brass's blood boil. Brass was still a large man and looked as formidable as he ever did, but he knew he was no match for Wright or Irwin. That unhuman recent display of strength by Wright, told him as much.

"You two get up here now. There will be no talkin' to the prisoner."

From the corner of his eye, Carder watched the sailors climb the rope ladder, disappearing into a night sky, just a touch lighter than the hold. They wasted no time sliding the cover back into place, closing off the light and leaving him alone in the dark to contemplate his future.

EARTH: MEXICO

As the sun was lifting above the horizon, the surfers sat around the embers of last night's fire. They were thinking about the fantastical story Moore and Heart told them. They were trying to wrap their minds around the concept of time travel through the waves. This was epic and they were now a part of it. That notion really got to them.

They agreed the first thing their new friends should to do is get some new identification. They were hiding from other time travelers! They had to arrange places for them to live and be safe from danger.

Preacher wondered where they might hide Moore's boat. It must change its appearance, and soon. Sow believed they were telling the truth. The unopened official royal navy keg of rum was all he needed for extra persuasion.

"How was that navy issue keg, Preach? I bet they have more than one! I'd love to buy a full one! I wonder if I can get an empty from Moore?"

"Sow, forever the opportunist. We still need to figure out where they can hide their ship and I don't think it would be a good idea to ask Wally's mom and dad."

"I don't know, Preacher. I could tell my parents some men I recently met who sailed over from England are willing to trade secrets with the colonies for a safe haven."

"You could say you met them in jail in Ensenada."

"Yeah, Wally. You could tell your dad the horse…"

Preacher laughed at Lester

"You're losing it, Les, Wally's dad doesn't know about the horse or Ensenada."

"I thought they knew the truth, Preach."

"Half the truth, Les. I only told Wally's mom…"

Wally's face lit up. "I got it!"

"Where?"

"Yeah, Wally, where?"

Lester smiled at Wally. "I think I know. the prince, right?"

Preacher ran it through his head. "Bitchen! I forgot about the prince."

Sow lost track. "The prince?"

"Yeah Sow, the prince of motors."

"You mean in Surfside?"

"Yeah! His shop is before the canal, right? We could put Moore's boat in the canal in front of the pilot's house."

"I think Ed will go for it just to have the boat nearby. Hide it in plain sight!"

Preacher stood up and walked over to grab his board. "I'm jumping in the water!"

"Preacher's right! Let's hit it!"

They knelt down alongside their boards, waxing them to charge the surf. The waves weren't as big as the day before, but the swell was still rideable and looked like fun. Sow slipped into the water taking a glance out toward the boat; Sid was there at the rail waving to him. He decided to paddle over and get him. After all, he promised to take him surfing, didn't he?

Wally eyed, Sow. "Can't wait to see the Pan, eh, Sow?"

"Come on, Wally, let's teach Sid how to surf."

Preacher joined them. "He's right Wally, imagine if we had the same opportunity when we were Sid's age?"

"Right, Preach. We'll train him to be a champion surfer!"

"Bitchen! Let's get out there. C'mon Lester!"

"I'll be right out, I gotta dump first."

Preacher shouted back, "The toilet paper is under the front seat, shotgun side."

He ran to the water and skipped his board on the surface like a paipo board, jumped on it, standing and gliding out a couple of yards before he knelt down to paddle and re-join his friends. "I'm stoked! Let's get Sid into some waves!"

Moore and Heart were on deck with Sid, waiting for the surfers, stroking their way out.

The men had been talking over their plan of action, and decided that it would be best to follow the advice and go with whatever the surfers worked out. They were in over their heads, and out of their depth. There was more than a great deal to learn, and they had to do it quickly. They tried addressing each other by first name, to try and fit in, but they couldn't get used to it. It would be slow going.

"All right Moore, er, John, I'll go by land with these wave riders."

"Surfers, Heart, ah Louis, they call themselves surfers."

"Yes, quite so, surfers, indeed. I will travel with the surfers by land and we shall ask one of them to accompany you and Sidney by sea."

"I'll need at least one of them if you are to go along by land. I feel it will be the one called Lester. He was the most observant, knowledgeable about the country, the water around here and sailing in particular."

The surfers reached the boat and Sow called up to Moore for permission to take Sid surfing with them. He assured him the boy would be safe. He explained Preacher and Wally would be right alongside them. They didn't know Moore surfed and was well aware of their prowess in the waves. He was not worried, but told Sow he had to ask Sid first.

"Would you like to join your friend, Mr. er, Sow to ride a wave?"

Sid, only in a pair of trousers, didn't waste any time hanging around to answer, he jumped right off the boat into the water. Sow grabbed the boy before he started sinking. Sid's eyes were bright with excitement and wonder. The surfers were cheering Sid and he was ecstatic! Sow positioned him on his board in order for him to paddle easier, and Moore asked him, "By the way, er, Mr. Sow, where is Mr. Lester?"

Preacher answered for Sow. "He's taking a dump, Captain Balls. He'll be out in a few minutes."

"A dump? He is taking a dump?"

"Yeah, you know, dropping the kids off at the playground."

"The playground?"

"You got it, Captain. Les is squeezing the cheese."

"The cheese?"

Wally couldn't resist, "Yep, he's pinching a loaf."

"A loaf? Pinching a loaf?"

Preacher got off on Wally's last remark; he hadn't heard that one before. The surfers were cracking up at Moore's expense. Heart, standing next to him, taking it all in, started to chuckle.

That took Moore by surprise! He could not recall hearing Heart ever laugh.

"I believe they mean Lester is looking for the privy, Moore."

"Moore's dry wit allowed him to break into a slight smile. "I get it now. Pinching." The crude imagery bombed his mind. He thought about what the surfers had said, causing an occasional laugh to rise out of him for the rest of the day. Moore, lifted his hand to his brow, getting a better view of the surfers taking Sid to ride his first wave. *"His first wave!"* The very thought brought a sensation of pure delight to Moore. He knew the feeling.

He concentrated on every move the three surfers made to get into the wave. Sow, in the middle with Sid, had Preacher and Wally on either side of them. Moore followed them riding wave after wave after wave. Sid traded places to ride with Preacher, and then with Wally. He was standing easily now, and the three surfers agreed he was a natural. Finally, Sow asked Sid, "Are you ready to ride one by yourself, Sid?"

"Can I really, Mr. Sow?"

"You sure can, Sid. Wally and Preacher will be right there beside you. Ready?"

"Yes! I am ready!"

Sow paddled them into a wave with his two friends. Both he and Sid stood simultaneously. Sow jumped off the board without Sid even noticing it. Preacher was out in front of Sid, hooting.

"Bitchen Sid! You are surfing it!"

Wally was right behind Sid and he was hooting for him.

"All time, Pan! The Pan surfs!"

Moore almost panicked. He saw Sow fall off the surfboard, riding with Sid. To his relief he watched Preacher, Sid and Wally ride the wave all the way to shore. Lester waited there on the beach. His trust in these new people was growing. The surfers surrounded Sid on the beach, treating him like a king.

Lester set him down in the warm sand. Sidney still had his sea legs and wobbled about while Wally and Preacher ran up to the campsite. Preacher returned with a large beach towel, wrapping it around the little boy. Sid was in heaven. It's interesting how easy it can be for a young person to transition into a new environment and seemingly, forget their worries. Sid was at that perfect age where reality turns to fantasy. Sitting there in this new land with nice surfers, all he could do was repeat his new mantra over and over again. "Surfing is so bitchen, I rode the most bitchen wave today. It was really bitchen."

Lester smiled down at the boy. "Hey, you guys keep an eye on Sid Bitchen. I'm gonna paddle Sow's board out to him and catch a few myself. I'll talk with Moore and Heart afterwards. There's bread, peanut butter and jam, in the cooler. Why don't you make him a sandwich, Preach? Oh yeah, there are some cold 7ups in there, give him one of those, too."

Sid did not know what a sand witch might be, but he knew he would like it; it would be bitchen. He liked everything here with his new friends. They were bitchen. Lester paddled out with Sow's board in tow and Moore watched the two of them catching waves, longing to go surf himself. He would have to wait until Mr. Sow and Mr. Lester finished when he realized they were paddling towards the beach.

Both Moore and Heart started yelling at the surfers, thinking they were being ignored.

Paranoia hit Moore fast and hard. Sid might be in danger! Then he saw Preacher and Sow heading back out to the boat with surfboards in tow behind them. By the time the boys reached the boat Moore and Heart were anxious to go ashore.

Sow yelled out to them, "Hey, Captain Balls and the first mate! Let's go grab a few waves."

Moore called down to Sow. "I thought you had forgotten us." He jumped into the water. "Jump in, Heart, the water feels wonderful."

"I'm not sure I can do the surfing."

Sow reassured him. "Don't sweat it Mr. Heart. We will be right here with you. Nothing is going to happen to you. You saw Sid, didn't you?"

"That was wonderful." Moore responded. "I was quite concerned at first, but I can see the four of you are very capable and know what you are doing."

Sow agreed. "In the surf we do, that's for sure. By the way, Lester gave Sid a surf name. We are going to call him Sid Bitchen from now on, and when you come ashore, you'll understand why. Wally likes to call him Pan. The waves are waiting, let's go surfing!"

Moore made a final check on his anchor lines, and the four men paddled into the line-up. He stood up on his first wave and got a decent ride which surprised the hell out of Preacher and Sow. Preacher remembered he told them about a Traveler, and he was happy for Moore to do so well on his first wave. Moore paddled back out with a grin on his face.

"What a wave! That was superb, Mr. Preacher! This Trav... um, surfboard doesn't fight me like the Traveler did."

Heart was not so lucky. He was a pure kook through and through. It was all he could do managing to stay on top of the surfboard. It felt to him as if he were trying to balance himself on a log. Sow helped him maneuver into a wave with a push, but like so many before him, he stood up and fell immediately. Nobody thought to ask if he could swim, but it turned out he was adept and could swim after his board, not reaching it until he was almost to the beach. He struggled to get back outside, caught some soup and proned all the way in. The others made their way to shore and Wally was there with some towels. They walked up to the surfer's camp. It was time for amazement and discovery for the men from the distant past.

Moore reached the campsite, setting Lester's board down carefully in the shade next to the others. He joined his nephew who was sitting next to Sow under a small Mexican mesquite tree. Sow made sure there were no thorns about, showing Sid at the same time what to be aware of with Mesquite. Sid looked happier now than Moore had ever seen him.

"Well, Sidney, how was the wave riding lesson with Mr. Sow?"

Sow got up to move one of the coolers into the shade.

"I don't know if you were watching Captain Balls, but Sid here, is what we call a natural. He rode a wave all the way to shore by himself."

"I knew you would ride all the way in too, uncle John." Sid declared.

"I take it you enjoyed the lesson then?"

"It was bitchen. Surfing is so bitchen. The food called peanut butter is also very bitchen. Everything here is bitchen, uncle John."

Sid was obviously stoked. Then came the expected questions.

"Peanut butter? Bitchen?

Wally tried to explain. "Bitchen is word that means something is good or great. It covers a whole range of what is the best of the best. It can be boss, cherry, groovy, copasetic, the whole spectrum."

Lester added, "Yeah, it's the cat's meow. It's tits!"

Preacher said, "It is the current metaphor for cool, although it will never be as cool as cool. My guess is because it's bitchen."

The surfer's got a laugh out of that and then Heart spoke up.

"It was refreshing to be in such delightful, warm water, I must say. I have never felt anything like it. Hopefully I will learn to surf bitchen."

The laughter continued. Sow opened the cooler and offered another soda to Sid. Moore was in awe of the blocks of ice in the styrofoam cooler, it blew his mind. To top it off, Sow grabbed three beers and handed one each to Moore and Heart. Ice cold beer inside a bottle with a cap on the top! Unbelievable! Preacher grabbed three more, passing one to Wally and one to Lester. He raised his bottle.

"Here's to bitchen!"

"Tell me it ain't," Wally chimed in. The four of them clanked their bottles together and toasted, "Tell me it ain't bitchen."

Moore and Heart were still staring at their unopened, ice cold beers. Neither of them had ever experienced anything like this. They drank ale at room temperature. Wally caught them staring at the bottles.

"What, you guys don't like beer?"

Sow laughed. "Hey, Wally, lighten up. They've probably never seen a bottle of beer like this, or the cooler or…"

Preacher interrupted, "Or any of this stuff. It's all brand new to you guys, isn't it, Captain Balls?"

"You are right, Mr. Preacher. We will have to learn as much as we can, to not stick out. It is as I told you, time holds no barriers. We don't know who or what Ontez is and he must not be able to recognize us."

"Well, lemme open your beers gents, and we can go over those details later. Hey Preach, where's the church key?'

Preacher tossed the opener. "Here you go, Wally."

Heart inquired, "Are we going to a church?"

"Nah, Mr. Heart," Wally told him, "A church key is a utensil that opens cans and bottles. See this? Dig."

"Dig?"

Wally took the beer bottle from Heart and popped the cap off.

"Dig means look at what I'm going to show you, check it out, or, look at this. It can mean that you really appreciate something and you dig it. You'll get down with it after a while. Here's your beer. Let me have your bottle, captain."

Moore passed his bottle to Wally, who opened it and handed it back.

"We're going to call you, Captain Balls, Mr. Moore, and Mr. Heart…"

They were going to goof on Heart. Sow and Preacher backed Wally up in unison, "Shmee!"

Wally patted Heart on his shoulder, "That's right, Shmee, you're him! Pan lives!"

INTERLUDE: THE SHALLOW TEMPLE

Jane was thinking about her brother. She was everything to him, yet she already knew they were going to separate. She sensed he was happier now than he'd ever been in his life and she knew they would meet again. A darker premonition had to be discussed with Master Cylinder.

She approached the four masters during their daily afternoon discussion.

"Hello, Marina." Master Flow offered her to join them. "We know how hard it has been for you. Are you beginning to recover from the separation from your brother?"

She thanked them for their concern, telling them Sid was quite happy where he was and there was no cause for worry. Marina directed her attention to Master Cylinder.

"I had another dream about the bad ship."

"Let's talk this out, perhaps the four of us can be of help."

"This time I recognized one person in the dream. I also know there is a terribly wicked being on the ship."

"Would you like to explain what happened in this dream? We might be able to teach you how to use your dreams."

"How can you teach me if I am the only one who sees these things?"

Master Shaper spoke next. "All of us see through different eyes, Marina Clearwater. We may be observing the same thing, but our different minds offer different versions of the same instance. Studying these interpretations, we are able to create a well-founded learning base."

Master Drummer continued. "We are simultaneously teachers and learners when we see. We must live with respect and trust for one another's individual perceptions. We share vision as a function to enhance our learning skills. This basic concept enables us to free up our ideas and share them willingly without ego, in a mutual quest for learning and insight."

Master Flow completed the thought from these teachers.

"We hope you understand, my dear. Simply stated, we are here to help you, as you are here to help us."

"I know that I have entered a special bond of trust, Master Flow. I knew I was coming here, yet I'm frightened. He is getting closer. He is trying to find you. He hates you."

"What happened in your last dream, Marina?"

"The boat sits in front of the temple where we were, and it is getting dark. There are monks near the boat on their Travelers. The evil man is searching the water, looking for the person I recognized."

"Who is the person, Marina?"

"He is my uncle, Lt. Philip Carder."

Master Cylinder asked the next question.

"You are positive it is Carder, Marina? Not someone else?"

"I never see faces clearly in my dreams, Master Cylinder, yet I feel who people are. There is a man falling off the ship, and I recognize him because I see the necklace dangling from his hand. The necklace has an amulet attached to it that looks exactly like this."

Marina pulled out the necklace beneath her robe. This was the first time since arriving at the temple, she revealed it to the monks. All of them wanted to see it. They were rarely surprised but astonishment was visible on their faces. Beams of sunshine bounced off the golden crest of the Shallow Temple.

Master Drummer was first to ask.

"May I have a closer look, Marina?"

Marina removed her necklace, handing it to Master Drummer.

"This is beautiful, Marina Clearwater, where did you get this?"

"I received this gift from uncle Philip, who also has one. My brother, Sidney, has one and my uncle John does too."

Master Flow questioned Master Shaper, "The lost Traveler?"

"I think not Master Flow. I believe these were made before the Traveler was sent out to Marina's uncle, John Moore."

Master Cylinder smiled. He had the distinct feeling he should make note to ask Gnarles if he knew anything about the amulets.

Master Flow recalled the day of failure for the young monk's departure, long ago. The surfing monk had been set up to fail!

"So, it *was* you. I saw you put something in the water that day. You knew all along the Traveler would go alone into the future."

"I couldn't let anybody know, not even you, old friend. It was a delicate matter."

"I understand Master Shaper. I know that ultimately your decision for secrecy was for the good of the temple."

"Uncle Philip said he found the necklaces left by his great-great-great grandfather. I am not sure if there is supposed to be another great."

This brief moment of levity came at a good time and the monks had a chuckle over the reference to age. Master Flow asked again about Marina's recent premonition.

"Marina, can you give us any more details from your dream?"

"I saw uncle Philip falling, holding on to his necklace. The evil man is in a rage and he is screaming. They are almost here, Master Flow. I'm very afraid."

"Don't be afraid, Marina. In fact, I think Master Cylinder has planned a little trip for you. You are going to travel to a safe, faraway place. You will meet the mother of Master Shaper and Master Drummer, Queen Fura. She has a daughter who will be like a sister for you. You are going to live with them."

"I will be leaving soon, won't I?"

"Yes, dear Marina Clearwater, you will. There is still plenty of time before that journey. Go get something to eat and then off to your room for some well-deserved rest."

Master Flow excused himself and escorted Marina to the dining hall.

Master Drummer took up the conversation.

"I think it's a wise move, sending Marina to Nalu. My brother and I have to prepare for the rescue. It is too dangerous to grab Ontez here. He must not suspect we have found him. Gnarles must deliver them to their oblivion somewhere in the future."

"My brother is right. Ontez is close, but we can't have a severance of this magnitude here. I suspect he will have others with him. We know Brotus Promo has never left his side. It has also been reported, Ven-Ra is with them."

Master Cylinder, ever thoughtful, made his recommendation

"Master Flow will rescue Philip Carder, who will join the 'Brotherhood of the Tree.' He will finish his studies and travel to Nemi for initiation rites. Gnarles will take Ontez and his men into the future."

"Isn't it too dangerous to have Ontez experience transcendence? Won't he know too much?"

"Yes, if he survives. It will be a humbling lesson for him. He will know too much and too little. This is exactly how we will go about shattering his immense ego. The knowing will consume him like a disease. Master Drummer, you must assemble your troupe to begin calling the waves. Ontez will arrive here tomorrow night and be dealt with in the future. Gnarles will begin our search for Moore, and Marina's brother."

EARTH 18TH CENTURY: THE ESCAPE

Carder was fully conscious and wide awake. He had no idea how long he had been at sea. There were a few lucid moments intermingled with suffering in a darkness mixed with a crazy vortex of unearthly images. He heard voices, footsteps, and felt the pitch and yaw of the ship. He began to wonder if they would ever allow him above deck again.

He asked himself, *"how long has it been since my farewell to Moore?"*

Abruptly, the hatch cover was moved away and a line was tossed down to him. Someone shouted orders.

"It's time for you to pay your respects, lieutenant. Grab the line and hold tight."

Carder vaguely remembered how Patch had been ripped off of him, flying up through the narrow opening. He recalled the sound of Patch's head cracking into the side of the opening.

He secured one foot in a loop near the bottom end of the line, keeping his eyes fixed on the opening above to avoid the same fate as Patch. He could not sustain such a blow and live, especially so soon after the concussion Ontez gave him.

Carder called out, "I'm ready."

"I doubt that, lieutenant."

Carder was yanked up so fast, it was as if he had been catapulted out from the hold. Wright snatched him out of the air as he cleared the opening. He was angry Carder secured himself in a loop, fashioned at the end of the line. He chuckled to himself earlier, planning to burn Carder's hands, ripping through his flesh by pulling the rope faster than suspected.

"It thinks it is pretty high and mighty, does it not? It had better hope to fare as well with the captain. Follow me."

The difficulty for Carder to walk let alone keep up with Wright took his breath away. Carder caught up to him waiting near the companionway; leading them below and aft to the captain's quarters. Although, not as distinct as before, Philip could smell Ontez before he entered the room. Wright knocked on the door.

"Send him in and leave us alone."

Carder entered the captain's quarters, and was taken aback by the polish of the spotless, well-kept quarters. Carder had no idea who he was really standing in front of. He couldn't know Ontez Neuron was an ancient, evil being; the destroyer of Mars.

"You have been very sleepy on this voyage, Lieutenant. At last, we are face to face once again."

Carder wanted to anger Ontez. He would address him as an inferior and treat him as an officer would a rating.

"A moment I give no meaning to, quartermaster."

"I doubt that, Carder. We couldn't find your old grandfather, but that is no longer important, is it?

Carder and Moore had suspected it was Ontez who murdered the goldsmith more than a century ago.

"Quite right, Ontez. You were not important then, and you are not important now."

Infuriated, Ontez was out of his chair in a single leap. He cleared his desk with that move, slapping Carder so hard, it lifted him into the air and slammed him into the bulkhead.

"You stupid Earthling! I could easily have you dribbling about for the rest of your meaningless life."

Carder had to catch his breath both physically and mentally. He did his best to keep from blacking out. He realized Ontez was more formidable than he could have imagined. *He called me an Earthling!*

"Spoken like the true scum you are, Ontez. Only the unenlightened are drawn to using force…"

"You came to the right place to die, fool! But first, you will hand the chart over to me. It was on this very day a few years back that you and I first saw the Shallow Temple."

Ontez almost spat the last words out of his mouth. Carder remembered the odor of Ontez giving himself away. He wanted to antagonize Ontez about his anomaly, but he decided it was better not to acknowledge witnessing anything on that day.

"I have no idea what you are blithering on about, Ontez. You have been at sea much too long."

Ontez seized Carder, dragging him to his feet. He tore the chart out from under Carder's blouse, screaming at him.

"Whore's son of a dog! Do you think Patch didn't tell me? He was returning this to you so you would not suspect how much more we really know. Patch wanted to tell you far too many things for his own good. It matters not, Carder. You shall join Patch soon, as will those monks in the temple!"

Ontez threw his door open, "Mr. Wright!" Wright appeared out of nowhere.

"Mr. Wright, take this idiot above! Have him secured to the mainmast. We will treat the crew to some bloodlust. Mr. Irwin will flog the lieutenant, here, to his death!"

Wright entered the captain's quarters and grabbed Carder by his long blond hair. He jerked him up and extracted him from the cabin. Carder was not going to cry out for the pleasure of these sadists. Wright took Carder forward and spied Robert Turnan.

"You there, Mr. Turnan! Take this wretch forward and secure him to the mainmast. Have Mr. Brass call all hands to the foredeck to witness the prisoner's punishment."

Ontez burst out from down below.

"Hold there, Mr. Wright!"

Ontez stepped smartly past Wright, and placed his face squarely in front of Carder's.

"You didn't think I'd forget that little keepsake now, did you, Carder?"

Ontez reached into Carder's waistcoat pocket and pulled out his necklace.

"Something to remember you by, eh, old man?"

Carder sprang into action. He knew that this was his only chance to escape. He grabbed the necklace from the unsuspecting Ontez and broke loose from Robert Turnan's grip. He made it to the rail, and was over the side in an instant. His fall to the water seemed to take an eternity. The necklace floated above him in his clenched fist.

"Damn you, Carder! Damn you, damn you, damn you!"

Ontez was beside himself. He ran to the rail, ready to jump in after him when he spotted a figure moving some type of watercraft towards Carder. At the same time, he heard a great commotion behind him! His crew was scattering for cover!

Even the terrible Ontez Neuron cowered when in the semi-darkness, he saw the biggest wave he had ever encountered on any ocean, or on any planet. It was speeding toward his ship to break right on top of them.

EARTH: MEXICO

Everyone had eaten, and the surfers were finalizing their plans of support for Moore and Heart, who were only a few years older than the surfers. They decided to bring them into their circle. It would be the smartest and safest thing for everyone concerned. It also would keep too many questions from being asked. Lester was running it down.

"You will be my cousin, Mr. Moore, and we will stick to that story. Mr. Heart is your lifelong friend who wanted to come to surf the waves of California and meet some real beach bunnies. Sid here, is your boy. That means that you will call your uncle John, dad instead of uncle, right Sid?"

The only reply Sid now made to anyone was, "Bitchen."

Everybody laughed. Wally mentioned the other important considerations.

"Les, you and Sow are the best sailors. It would be the smart thing for you to sail back up with Captain Balls and Sid Bitchen. Shmee can ride back with us."

"I was thinking the same thing, Wally. Preacher could drive you guys back and I can drink rum with Captain Balls while he shows me the ropes."

"Moore and I had reached the same conclusion, Mr. Lester. We thought it best for at least one of you to sail with me because of your familiarity with navigating these waters."

"We all seem to agree with this plan. What kind of coach do you have, Mr. Lester? How many horses are there…? That's odd, where are your horses?"

Moore was thoughtful for a moment and continued.

"I haven't seen, heard, or smelled any horses."

"Lester's coach is called a woody, Captain. It runs with 90 horses."

"That's preposterous, Mr. Sow. I know you fellows like to have a good joke, but…"

"You calling me a liar, Mr. Shmee?"

"Sow is telling you the truth, Mr. Shmee. The Ford V-8 flathead has about 90 horsepower, give or take a few horses.'

"If this is true, where are the stables? In fact, where is the coach? Heart and I would like to see it."

"Yes, by all means. May we have a look at your coach, Mr. Lester?"

"Hell yes, you can see her. Hey, Preach, show these guys the coach."

Lester threw his keys to Preacher.

"Hey, Sid, you wanna come?"

Sid jumped right up to follow Preacher.

"Bitchen."

The group watched Sid and Preacher disappear over the small sandy dune. Shortly after, they heard the noise of the engine firing when Preacher started it up. Moore and Heart were startled by the sound and looked at each other in complete awe, as the front end of the woody with its shiny chrome grill appeared at the crest of the dune. Moore shouted at Heart.

"Bloody hell! By all that is holy!"

Heart shouted back at Moore.

"In the name of the king, what is that?"

"That," said Wally, "is the greatest surf vehicle of all time. It is none other

than the 48 Ford Woody. Gorgeous ain't she?"

Moore could only sit down and stare. Heart staggered towards the vehicle in utter disbelief. Yet, there behind the windshield were Preacher and Sid, standing on the seat so he could see out. Heart reached out to touch the bright, shiny, black front fender, and Preacher honked the horn. Heart almost jumped out of his skin and the surfers went into hysterics. Preacher backed the woody up, and he and Sid returned to the campsite, where they found Heart checking the inside of his trousers down around his knees. He remarked rather coldly.

"Thank you, Mr. Preacher, I believe you may have caused me to besmirch my britches."

Heart did not find this funny, which had the opposite effect on the surfers. Heart felt a sense of uncertainty for their new found acquaintances.

"Hey, Mr. Shmee, did you really drop a load in your trou?"

Heart had an already growing dislike for his moniker.

"Are you referring to my mess, Mr. Preacher? Yes, quite so, indeed!"

Preacher threw Louis a roll of toilet paper and an extra pair of baggies that he brought along.

"Bitchen, Mr. Shmee! Everything is copasetic. Use this to wipe yourself, it should help.

Throw your pants in the ocean, the salt water will clean them out."

Lester said he and Sow were going to dive for some abs for dinner, and that Preacher and Wally should get the extra blankets for everyone. Tomorrow, after surfing, they would head back up to the Pink Party Pad.

"What are abs, Mr. Preacher?"

"They are a totally bitchen shellfish, Captain Balls. Gourmet meals in the half shell."

"Sow! Did you bring the abalone bag?"

"I've got it right here, Lester. Let's go find dinner!"

Heart approached Lester.

"Would you mind going to our ship and bringing back the open keg of rum?"

"It would be my pleasure, Mr. Shmee."

No one saw Heart visibly wince at the name. He didn't like it at all. Lester and Sow jumped into the water, paddled slowly, checking the bottom as they looked about the reef. Lester dove down with the bag, while Sow stayed with the boards. Sow would dive, and then Lester. It went this way only a few times because the surfers didn't harvest more than they needed.

Sow paddled out to the ship alone. He checked the lines, making sure everything was secure and then he retrieved the small open keg of rum from the forward hold. Sow noticed the repair a member from the wave rider tribe refitted into the bulkhead. He could see some kind of design and reached out to run his hand over it. He touched the board and it made him jump. He grabbed the keg and got out of there fast. He didn't tell anyone about what happened.

By the time they got out of the water, Wally and Sid had gathered plenty of firewood and Preacher had brought down the blankets and sleeping bags. Sow cleaned the abalone and sliced up steaks for Lester to tenderize them, pounding them with a wood mallet. They always brought some butter and a frying pan in case there was the chance to prepare this meal.

The smell reminded Moore and Heart of Mr. Gnarles' cuisine. Never in their entire lives had they ever tasted anything like fresh, pan fried abalone steaks. The rum had mellowed everybody, and they were all ready to crash.

Moore proposed a toast.

"To our new family and destiny!"

The surfers hooted at the toast and finished their drinks. No more words were spoken and one by one they all drifted off to sleep. They woke early, surfed, came back in and cleared the campsite. They reviewed their plans to rendezvous at the prince of motors and said brief farewells.

"Preacher, you drive. Sow, keep them away from Hussongs, and head straight for the border."

"Bitchen, Lester. See you back at the pad."

They hugged each other and then Moore, Lester, and Sid paddled all the surfboards out to the boat. By the time they loaded the caravel, the woody had already departed and was on the road headed North. Moore would lay awake all night thinking about his niece. There would be many more sleepless nights to follow.

EARTH: THE SHALLOW TEMPLE

The sound of the drums could be heard beyond the outer reefs in front of the Shallow Temple. They were calling another enormous swell. Master Flow and Gnarles had already paddled out to the pirate ship *Red Tide*. They secured the ship's rudder into a 'fixed' position, attaching the line to the bowsprit, and beyond to Gnarles' Traveler. Their plan was to release the ship from the Traveler during transcendence. No one at the temple was sure of the outcome.

Gnarles was forward of the bowsprit and Master Flow waited aft of the stern. He would
rescue Carder when the time came. Master Flow's parting advice to Gnarles was short and to the point.

"Be careful, Gnarles, cut loose of the line while you transcend."

"Don't worry, Master Flow. I'll release the vessel somewhere in the middle of it all."

Gnarles' adrenaline started flowing. He could just make out the huge, dark wave, blotting out the horizon. Ontez wanted to jump ship after Carder, but he knew his chances of survival were better if he stayed on board. Except for Wright and Irwin, the deck was cleared. They stood faithfully beside their leader.

"We must get to my quarters, now!"

"What of the prisoner, Lord? Shall I jump in and get him?"

"Don't be a fool Ven-Ra! I know we are near the Shallow Temple, but we are our first concern. Get below!"

Master Flow watched Carder hit the water and moved quickly to grab him; he was unconscious. As Marina described, Carder was holding the necklace in his hand. It was an exact replica of the necklace Marina displayed to them earlier. He calmly removed the amulet from Carder's hand and placed it around his own neck. He pulled Carder onto his Traveler in time to paddle into the monstrous wave, the unconscious man at his feet. He dropped in and charged for the shoulder of the wave, pulled out and paddled toward the safety of the channel. He could see the monks standing at the water's edge, their torches held high guiding him to shore.

Gnarles had already positioned his Traveler into the giant wave that lifted him so quickly, he could hardly feel the tug of the ship. The Traveler worked its magic and Gnarles stood, rushing to reach the bottom of such a steep incline. The ship following him was free falling down the face of the liquid mountain. His Traveler was doing all the work, although the ship gained plenty of momentum on its own. Gnarles repeated the sacred mantra, vanishing into the portal, pulling the ship in his wake.

He released the tow line inside a barrel of a different time and place. He rode the wave as far inside as possible, wasting no time getting away from the impact zone as fast as he could manage. The conditions were extremely dangerous, caused by the extra-large surf, and it was a moonless night.

He searched for the shoreline, then returned his focus to the breaking waves outside where the silhouettes of the broken halves of the ship were being torn apart on those reefs. He felt a pang of guilt for the men who suffered such a tragic and horrible death, but there was no sorrow in his heart for Ontez Neuron, Brotus Promo or Ven-Ra.

He couldn't hear the wood breaking up or the anguished cries of those who perished. The pounding surf buried those pleas for mercy, as the *Red Tide* came apart on the jagged rocks. He paddled to shore.

Once he made it to the beach, he took off his backpack and removed a pair of rubber slippers, shorts and a warm, long sleeved shirt. He changed his trunks, put on his shirt, and slipped his pack on again. Gnarles picked up his Traveler and walked off into the night.

Later that morning, as the day began to show itself, three stragglers approached the coastal highway. They meandered across the road to wonder at a billboard with a large advertisement written in Spanish. The aliens looked up at the photo display of a family cruising along in their brand new 1962 Ford station wagon. They returned their gaze to the coastline, surveying the long, desolate, and deserted highway before them. Ontez Neuron and his two henchmen had survived.

www.ingramcontent.com/pod-product-compliance
Lightning Source LLC
LaVergne TN
LVHW011931070526
838202LV00054B/4581